THE GHOST
WHO SOUGHT REDEMPTION

Haunting Danielle

The Ghost of Marlow House
The Ghost Who Loved Diamonds
The Ghost Who Wasn't
The Ghost Who Wanted Revenge
The Ghost of Halloween Past
The Ghost Who Came for Christmas
The Ghost of Valentine Past
The Ghost from the Sea
The Ghost and the Mystery Writer
The Ghost and the Muse
The Ghost Who Stayed Home
The Ghost and the Leprechaun
The Ghost Who Lied
The Ghost and the Bride
The Ghost and Little Marie
The Ghost and the Doppelganger
The Ghost of Second Chances
The Ghost Who Dream Hopped
The Ghost of Christmas Secrets
The Ghost Who Was Say I Do
The Ghost and the Baby
The Ghost and the Halloween Haunt

The Ghost and the Christmas Spirit
The Ghost and the Silver Scream
The Ghost of a Memory
The Ghost and the Witches' Coven
The Ghost and the Mountain Man
The Ghost and the Birthday Boy
The Ghost and the Church Lady
The Ghost and the Medium
The Ghost and the New Neighbor
The Ghost and the Wedding Crasher
The Ghost and the Twins
The Ghost and the Poltergeist
The Ghost Who Sought Retribution

HAUNTING DANIELLE - BOOK 35

THE GHOST
WHO SOUGHT REDEMPTION

USA TODAY BESTSELLING AUTHOR
BOBBI HOLMES

The Ghost Who Sought Redemption
(Haunting Danielle, Book 35)
A Novel
By Bobbi Holmes
USA TODAY BESTSELLING AUTHOR
Cover Design: Elizabeth Mackey

Copyright © 2024 Bobbi Holmes
Robeth Publishing, LLC
All Rights Reserved.
Robeth.net

ROBETH PUBLISHING, LLC

This novel is a work of fiction.
Any resemblance to places or actual persons,
living or dead, is entirely coincidental.

ISBN: 978-1-949977-80-6
A

Dedicated to Mom, my first beta reader, devoted fan, dearest friend, and beloved mother. This long goodbye is killing me, but I know you are in there somewhere, waiting to be set free. Remember, you promise to visit me in a dream hop when the time comes. I love you.

ONE

"Thanks for letting me park my car in your driveway. I should be back within an hour," Rylee Archer promised her friends Grayson and River.

"Do you even have a flashlight?" River's question sounded more like an accusation.

Rylee glanced up at the full moon and then back at River and smiled. "I don't think I'll need one."

Looking at Rylee as if she were a foolish child, River plopped his right palm on his right hip and shook his head.

"What?" Rylee asked.

"You planning on stumbling around in the dark when you get inside? You seriously think Bonnie's been paying for the electricity all this time?" River asked. "And even if she had the electricity on, do you think it would be a good idea to turn the lights on and draw attention from the neighbors?"

Rylee cringed. "Oh, you're right."

River rolled his eyes before abruptly turning to the house and marching toward it while giving a little hand wave and calling back to her, saying, "I'm getting you a flashlight."

As River walked into the house, a worried Grayson asked, "Have you even thought this through?"

"You want the truth?" Rylee asked.

Grayson crossed his arms over his chest and nodded. "That would be nice."

Rylee shrugged. "No. Not really. But today when I heard she's listing the property, it dawned on me. Maybe that's where I left it."

"Can't you just ask Bonnie if you can see if it's there?"

"Are you serious?"

Grayson considered her question for a moment and then let out a sigh. "I guess you're right. But please be careful. Call us if you have a problem. I don't know why you don't let us drive you over there."

"It's only two blocks away, and this is Frederickport. What could happen?"

SINCE THEIR FATHER'S arrest and subsequent murder, their mother had been distracted and less attentive. She had taken to drinking wine more frequently and often fell asleep right after dinner, leaving the boys to fend for themselves.

Their aunt Robyn, who lived in the main house, dropped in frequently yet seemed more concerned about their mother and would often say things like *it's a lovely day, why don't you go ride your bikes so I can visit with your mom?* In the days prior to their father's arrest, their mother would have reminded them to wear their helmets or told them how far they could ride or when to be back.

Their uncle Fred no longer lived with Aunt Robyn, so she was in the big house by herself. They'd heard they were all going to be moving, but didn't know when. They blamed their uncle Fred for getting their father the job that led to his death, and they hated Chief MacDonald, who got their father arrested.

Tonight, their aunt Robyn brought over dinner, some mac and cheese she had made with little hot dogs. They preferred the mac and cheese their mother normally made, but she hadn't been

THE GHOST WHO SOUGHT REDEMPTION

cooking much lately. Robyn set the food she brought over on the counter in the small kitchen and then checked on her sister, who was in the bedroom.

About ten minutes later, Robyn returned to the living room area. "Boys, your mother is exhausted. She needs her rest. Just let her sleep."

"She's not having dinner with us?" Eric asked.

"She's already asleep." Robyn glanced at her watch and then looked back at her nephews. "I've got to get back home. There's a movie I want to watch. I set the food on the counter. After you're done eating, put the leftovers in the refrigerator, and set your dirty dishes in the sink. And whatever you do, don't wake up your mother."

Thirty minutes later, the angry and confused nine-year-old twins, Eric and Zack Bowman, climbed on their bikes and pedaled down the street under the moonlight, leaving their helmets back at the garage apartment.

The previous day, Aunt Robyn had taken them and their mother for a car ride. Robyn had insisted their mother needed to get out of the house, and when she mentioned they might stop for ice cream, the boys were more than willing to join them.

When going down one street, Robyn had pointed out a house to their mother. She had said, "Remember Cordelia Westbrook? You know, she died."

"I didn't know that." By the tone of their mother's response, the twins didn't think she cared one way or another. But their aunt continued to ramble on about the property while their mother stared blankly out the car's passenger window.

"Her niece Bonnie inherited the house. Shocked everyone; after all, Rylee took care of her. Someone told me Bonnie's getting ready to put it on the market. I can't imagine what Bonnie's going to find in that house once she starts cleaning it out to sell. Cordelia Westbrook lived in it for years, and that family had money!"

From that overheard conversation on the previous day's car ride with their mother and aunt came an idea for a new adventure. With a stolen credit card from their aunt, stuffed in Zack's pocket, the two boys pedaled furiously, en route to Cordelia Westbrook's house, where they planned to go treasure hunting. They figured if they could break into the tunnel house using the credit-card trick learned on YouTube, surely the trick would work on the Westbrook house.

Just as the boys turned down the street leading to their destination, they noticed a woman walking alone on the sidewalk with only the moon lighting the way. They slowed down, waiting to see where she was going, and to their surprise, she walked up to the house they intended to break into.

Stealthily, the twins stashed their bikes in a row of overgrown arborvitaes and crouched behind the bushes, watching the woman.

RYLEE TRIED the key on the front door, and it didn't work. She wasn't surprised Bonnie had changed the locks. Using her key to enter the house had been plan A. Now that plan A had failed, she moved to plan B. Plan B involved climbing into the living room's side window. That was the only window on the first floor with a broken lock. She didn't have a plan C, so if Bonnie had fixed the broken lock, she was screwed. Rylee tucked the key into her back pocket and headed for the side window.

MOONLIGHT POURING through the window filled the small powder room with light. Cordelia Westbrook stared into the gold-framed mirror hanging above the vanity.

"Where did you go?" Cordelia asked her nonexistent reflection, something she had asked every day since her death. She didn't expect an answer. After a few minutes, she turned from the mirror and started back to the parlor but stopped when a noise came from the side of the house.

She went to investigate and found someone had pried open the living room's side window and was now in the process of entering the house. One sneaker-clad foot entered the living room, followed

THE GHOST WHO SOUGHT REDEMPTION

by another. The intruder wore what looked like denims with a dark hoody sweatshirt, the hood pulled over her head. It was definitely a woman; the sweatshirt could not conceal her curves.

When the woman was all the way into the room, she pulled out a flashlight, turned it on, and pointed it directly in Cordelia's face. It wasn't until the woman moved in her direction did Cordelia recognize the intruder. It was Rylee.

"Finally, you've come back. It's about time," Cordelia scolded as she moved to the side, avoiding Rylee walking through her.

Flashlight in hand, Rylee walked straight to the parlor, making no detours along the way, as Cordelia trailed behind her. Once in the parlor, Rylee turned on the light out of habit, but River had been right. The electricity was off.

Rylee moved toward the file cabinet, but before she reached it, she paused at the portrait and looked up at it, using the beam from her flashlight to illuminate the painting. She let out a sigh as she looked up into the woman's face. The artist had captured Cordelia's stern expression perfectly. "I'd like to know the truth, Aunt Cordelia. Did you really leave everything to Bonnie? I mean, that's okay. It's your money. But still."

OUTSIDE, the boys watched. Finally, the woman reemerged. She carried something, but they didn't know what. She hurried down the street in the same direction from which she had come. When she was no longer in sight, they started for the house.

CORDELIA STOOD at the window where Rylee had just climbed through. But then an insistent scraping sound came from the direction of the front door. Had Rylee returned? As Cordelia reached the entrance, two young boys came barreling into the house, slamming the door behind them.

"We did it!" one boy squealed.

Cordelia stood a few feet from the intruders and shouted, "Boo!"

The boys looked in Cordelia's direction and then ran straight through her and continued into her living room

She shivered at the abrupt assault of her energy and grumbled, "What fun is being a ghost if I can't scare anyone?"

Cordelia followed the boys as they ran through her house, poking their noses in all the cupboards, cabinets and drawers while laughing.

"Where are your parents?" Cordelia asked. "Do they know you're breaking and entering?"

"Dad told me sometimes people hide money in the freezer."

"Freezer? You're not looking in my freezer, are you?" Cordelia followed the boys into the kitchen.

Once there, one boy ran to the refrigerator and opened it.

"The light's out," the boy announced.

"I bet the electricity is off." The other boy walked over to the kitchen light and tried flipping it on. "See. No electricity."

"Good thing the refrigerator is empty. Otherwise, the food would be all gross. Aunt Robyn said this house has been vacant for a long time. I bet the freezer is empty, too." The boy opened the freezer, and as he suspected, it, too, was empty.

After closing the freezer, he walked to the pantry, opened it, and then pointed the beam of the flashlight along its shelves.

"Come on, let's check out the bedrooms," his accomplice suggested. "If there's anything in there, it's just old food they didn't throw out."

The boy with the flashlight turned to the other boy. "Remember that fake soup can Joey Palmer showed us?"

"You mean the one you can hide stuff in?"

The boy nodded. "There are some soup cans in there. Maybe they aren't all real soup cans."

Cordelia shook her head. "No, no, no. Don't go in there. You stay out of there!"

The other boy rushed to the pantry, and together they started inspecting each soup can, all the while Cordelia stood behind them, trying to swat their hands away from the cans, yet with no success. Finally, one of the boys shouted, "Oh my gosh, it's one of those cans! I really found one." Both boys moved out of the pantry into a brighter area of the room, where the moonlight spilled onto the kitchen floor.

Cordelia stood behind the boys, muttering, "No, no, no," while still swatting at their hands. She stopped swatting and cringed when the one boy opened the can and dumped an assortment of gold and gem-encrusted jewelry onto the floor. "Oh, my gosh! We're rich!" one boy shouted.

"You need to put that back. That does not belong to you."

The boys paid no attention to the ghost, whom they couldn't see. Instead, they returned to the pantry and sorted through the rest of the cans, where they found one more fake soup can, this one crammed with a roll of twenty-dollar bills.

TWO

If she had a breath to take, she would draw it in deeply, filling her lungs with the cool ocean air, and then exhale slowly, as if she had all the time in the world. Her slender legs absently moved back and forth, reminiscent of the hours spent on the tire in her family's backyard. But she had no lungs to fill with crisp air, nor slender legs, only the illusion of a body, an illusion of a young woman breathing deeply, one perched on a marble headstone, not on a tire swing. One thing she had was all the time in the world.

Pamela Beckett gazed across a section of the Frederickport Cemetery, a stretch of green lawn dotted with century-old headstones and bordered in colorful hydrangea plants, their flower clusters an exhibit of vibrant pink, blue, and lavender. She wore her brown hair long and flowing, and to a stranger, they might guess her age to be no older than nineteen or twenty. Yet that too was an illusion. She had been decades older than that at the time of her death.

"Pamela, there you are!" a voice called out.

She turned toward the voice and spied Wesley Sadler sprinting in her direction. She doubted Wesley would have been able to run like that at the time of his death, considering the illusion of the body he presented. Unlike Pamela, his appearance matched the man he had been at the time of his death: a short, chubby, balding man, who looked years older than the sum total of his thirty-five years of life.

"What are you doing over here?" Wesley asked when he finally reached her.

"I like it here. I should have been buried on this side of the cemetery. The headstones are more interesting. Marble instead of boring bronze. I resent being buried under a dull flat grave marker; its only redeeming characteristic is the ease with which a lawn mower can plow over it."

"Yeah, but if you hang out over here, when someone comes to visit your grave, you're going to miss seeing them."

Pamela scoffed. "No one comes to see me. Aside from those people from Marlow House, and they aren't friends."

"Then why do you bother staying? Why don't you move on?" Wesley asked.

"And why do you stay? You've been here longer than me."

"It's complicated. You're lucky." Wesley turned his back to Pamela and buried his hands in the pockets of his jacket—both of which were nothing more than an illusion. Silently, he stared across the cemetery. There hadn't been a funeral for over a week, and it had been relatively quiet during that time.

"Lucky? How? That I squandered the life I'd been given? I lived my entire life in the house I grew up in, and most of those years, I lived alone. You're afraid to move on because you don't want to face the consequences of the life you lived, while I refuse to move on because I never really lived."

Wesley turned around to face Pamela but paused when he spied a man walking in their direction. "We're not alone." Wesley nodded toward the man.

Still sitting on the headstone, Pamela turned around and watched as the man Wesley mentioned continued down the walkway toward them. For a moment the man seemed oblivious to Pamela and Wesley's presence, but when he was about eight feet away, he halted, looking from Wesley to Pamela and back to Wesley.

The two spirits stared at him, a stocky middle-aged man with a buzz cut.

"You can see me?" the man blurted.

Pamela and Wesley laughed, and then Pamela said, "Either you're a medium or a ghost. Which is it?"

The man stared at Pamela and blinked a few times before answering, "I'm dead. So I guess I'm a ghost."

"Where are you buried?" Wesley asked. "I don't remember your funeral. I've met all the spirits at this cemetery."

The man shrugged. "I wasn't buried. I was cremated."

"Does that hurt?" Wesley asked. "I always wondered about that."

The man shook his head. "No. It didn't hurt, but it wasn't fun to watch. Not something I would recommend."

"What are you doing here?" Pamela asked. "Is your urn here? Do they have a place for urns at this cemetery?"

"No. My urn isn't here. I don't have an urn. I wasn't cremated in Frederickport. When they were done, they dumped my ashes in the ocean. As far as I know, there was no funeral."

Wesley winced. "That's harsh."

"Ahh, so your ashes drifted this way, and you followed them?" Pamela suggested.

"I have no idea where my ashes ended up, aside from watching them get dumped in the ocean. I came back to Frederickport to find my family."

"Well, unless you have a family of mediums, it's going to be a rather one-sided visit," Pamela said. "And if you're talking about the spirits of your family buried here, my bet is that they've already moved on. There are only a few spirits hanging around this cemetery. But who is your family? If they're here, Wesley and I have probably met them."

"No. They're alive. Not here."

"I don't understand," Wesley said. "Then why are you here?"

"I guess I was looking for some help. Ever since I was killed, no one has seen me. Until now. Well, except for one spirit who moved on."

"You look rather young," Pamela observed. "How did you die?"

"I was murdered."

"Murdered!" Pamela and Wesley chorused.

He nodded in reply.

"Are you here to get someone to help you find your murderer?" Wesley asked.

"No. My killer has already been caught. He was caught right away. I suppose I should clarify; I've already found my family. They live here, in Frederickport. But they can't see me. And I wondered if there were others like me, someone who knows more about this dead thing. I figured the best place to look was at a cemetery." He paused a moment and added, "When we first met, you mentioned something about mediums?"

Pamela moved from the headstone and stood next to Wesley. "Yes, a medium, someone who can communicate with our kind. I suppose you have come to the right place. Frederickport has several known mediums. They seem to cluster together, you know."

The man shook his head. "No, I didn't know."

"Oh yes, over on Beach Drive." She paused a moment and added, "Do you know where Beach Drive is?"

"Yes, yes, I do. It's the street where Marlow House is located."

Pamela nodded. "One of the first mediums I ever talked to was Danielle Marlow."

"Are you telling me Danielle Marlow is a medium?" the man asked.

Pamela's grin widened. "Yes, and so is her husband. Also, two of their neighbors. Oh, not next-door neighbors, but close neighbors. Heather Donovan and Chris Johnson. Although, I think Eva told me his real name is Chris Glandon. Also, the police chief's youngest son. I believe his name is Evan."

The man shook his head in denial. "No. I don't believe any of this. This is some sort of dream. A terrible dream." He walked to a nearby park bench and sat down. He leaned forward and stared at his feet while continuing to shake his head in denial while muttering something about how the nightmare kept getting worse.

"I'm not sure why you're so upset." Pamela frowned. "Dead is dead."

"Who murdered you? And why?" Wesley asked excitedly as he and Pamela moved toward the man, stopping a few feet from him.

After a moment, the man looked up at the two ghosts. "Why do you care?"

Wesley shrugged. "I'm just curious."

"I suppose I was murdered because I wasn't a good person."

"There are lots of people I could describe that way, but they don't get murdered," Wesley said. "You must have really pissed someone off. What did you do?"

The man sat up straight, leaned back on the bench, and looked at the two spirits. "Let's just say I made a lot of poor life choices, and they caught up with me."

Wesley sat down next to the man on the bench and said quietly, "I get what you mean. I made a lot of poor choices too. That's why I'm still here. No one killed me, but if I had stuck around, I could see it happening."

The man looked at Wesley. "Why is that the reason you're still here?"

Wesley shrugged and leaned back on the bench. "When we die, we usually move on. Unless we choose to stick around—like Pamela here and me and you. Pamela has her reasons for not moving on, and I guess I'm still here because I'm a chicken."

The man frowned. "You're afraid to move on? The spirit I saw who moved on said it was beautiful, peaceful. What are you afraid of?"

Wesley looked at the man and cocked his head slightly. "Being held accountable, of course. Once we pass over after this place, we must face the consequences of our actions from our lifetime."

"Are you telling me this isn't it? There is more beyond whatever I am right now?"

"You didn't think that once you died, you wandered around the living, not being seen or heard? For eternity?" Pamela asked. "Didn't you just tell us you witnessed a spirit move on?"

"I assumed I wasn't allowed to move on. I thought staying here, like this, was my punishment."

Both Pamela and Wesley laughed. When the laughter stopped, Pamela said, "Oh, no. I suppose you could wander among the living, like Wesley here. But eventually, you'll have to pass over and face the consequences. At least, that's what I've heard."

"When I was waiting for them to cremate my body, there was someone else being cremated. Her name was Amy. She told me she had been a homeless, living alone on the streets. She didn't have anyone. After she watched her body turn to ash, she looked over to the other side of the room and said, 'I'm ready to move on now.' It was like she was talking to someone. But no one was there. Then this light streamed down from the ceiling, and she floated up. As she ascended, she called back to me, telling me how beautiful it was, and that I was going to love it. Then she just disappeared. She seemed so happy. So peaceful. Later, after I was cremated, I spoke out and said I was ready to move on. Nothing happened. Nobody was there, but no one had been there when Amy said it. So I said it again. Nothing. It was then I assumed my hell was here, on earth, forever being among the living, who could neither see nor hear me."

"I'm not sure if there is a heaven or hell, just that when you move on, you have penance for your sins here depending on the severity of your sins," Pamela explained. "At least, that's what I understand."

The man groaned.

"Come on, it can't be that bad. What did you do?" she asked.

"There is a long list, but I suppose at the top of my list, I murdered someone."

"Is that why someone murdered you?" Wesley asked.

The man shook his head. "No, not directly. He didn't know the person I killed."

"Wow," Wesley said in a low voice. "You really must have been a bad person."

"I suppose I was."

"I don't want to scare you," Wesley said, "but you'll be eventually called to the other side, and depending on your sins, I don't think you're going to enjoy yourself."

The next moment, the man disappeared.

Pamela sat down next to Wesley, where the man had been sitting moments earlier. They said nothing. After a few minutes, Pamela said, "I wonder who he murdered."

"No clue, but he gave me an idea."

Pamela turned to Wesley. "What kind of idea?"

"Maybe the mediums can help me set things right. It's not like I murdered someone, not like that guy. I never thought to see if they could help me."

"Why don't you ask Eva about it?" she suggested.

He cringed and shook his head. "No. Eva makes me nervous. I don't like to be around her. And that friend of hers, Marie, she's too bossy. Reminds me of my wife. I don't want to talk to them about this."

"You do realize Marie and Eva are tight with the mediums? They'll find out."

"Remember, both Marie and Eva are at that summer festival. They'll be gone for a while."

THREE

Walt Marlow remembered a time when he once resented the outdoor kitchen and barbecue area Danielle had built in the side yard, not far from Marlow House's kitchen door. In those days, Walt could not step outside the house his grandfather had built in 1871, a Second Empire–style mansard that Walt lived in today. Technically, he could have stepped outside, but it might have meant he would have been forced to move on, leaving Danielle behind. Because of that, he could not join Danielle and her guests when they used the outdoor area, and he'd watched them from inside his home through the windows.

But those days were in the past, and on this late June evening he sat outside with Danielle and their friends and houseguests, Lily and Ian Bartley, while the twins napped in a nearby playpen, and young Connor Bartley threw the ball for his golden retriever, Sadie, on the nearby lawn.

Earlier that evening, Ian had grilled burgers in the outdoor kitchen while Walt used his telekinetic abilities to bring the side dishes and dinnerware outside, while Danielle and Lily each held a baby and visited.

But now the sun was setting, and the ocean breeze chilled the air while the sounds from the waves hitting the shore, across the street behind the Bartley house, gently serenaded the small group.

Gripping the arms of her patio chair for support, Lily awkwardly stood, her baby belly protruding and her back slightly arching. Danielle thought she looked uncomfortable, and sympathized, having not that long ago been pregnant.

Once standing, Lily's hands moved from the chair's arms to her back, as if they might help hold her up. That morning, Danielle had braided Lily's long red hair into a french braid, yet a few strands had since broken free and curled, framing her face.

Ian, who sat in a patio chair next to Lily and across from Walt and Danielle, asked, "You okay, babe?"

"It's getting late. Connor hasn't even had his bath yet. Do you guys realize it's almost nine?" Lily looked out to the grass area where Connor ran around with Sadie.

Danielle glanced at her watch. Lily was right. "I love the longer summer nights, but I guess it is getting kind of late for Connor. At least he doesn't have to go to school in the morning."

"It's not about Connor. I'm talking about me." Lily groaned. "I should have given him a bath before we ate."

"Lily, sit down," Ian ordered. "I'll give Connor his bath. He's okay. Let him run around until it gets dark, and maybe he'll sleep in late."

"I'm kind of over this." Lily looked down at her belly. "But I have another three weeks."

"It's going to go fast," Danielle promised. "Connor's little sister is going to get here before you know it."

"Sit down," Ian gently urged.

Lily was about to respond but let out a gasp and then looked down, staring at her flip-flop-clad feet.

"What's wrong?" Walt asked.

"My water broke!" Lily continued to stare down at her now wet feet.

Ian jumped up. "Are you sure?"

Walt also stood, but remained silent as he anxiously watched Lily.

"Well, I didn't pee my pants!" Lily grabbed hold of her belly. "I'm not supposed to do this for three weeks. It's too early!"

Danielle stood and rushed to Lily's side. "It's going to be okay. I was early with the twins, and everything worked out."

"I suppose this solves one problem." Lily looked at Ian. "Promise you won't say anything to your sister or parents until the baby is born."

CONNOR HELD Walt's hand as he stood by the side of his parents' car, with the passenger door open and Lily sitting inside while his father walked to the driver's side of the vehicle. Minutes earlier, Ian had driven his car over from their garage across the street and parked along the front sidewalk of Marlow House.

"You be a good boy for Walt and Danielle. I love you," Lily told her son as she shut the door. While Ian had gone for the car earlier, she had explained to Connor that his little sister might come early, so Daddy was taking her to the hospital to check.

A few minutes later, as Walt and Connor stood on the sidewalk, they watched the car drive away while Connor waved bye-bye to his parents.

After a few moments, Walt leaned over and swooped Connor into his arms before starting back to the house. "Someday, when you're older, I might tell you about how Uncle Walt saved the day when he picked up a tree so your parents could get to the hospital to deliver you." Walt chuckled at his own words and pushed open the back gate leading to Marlow House's side yard, where Sadie greeted them, her tail wagging.

The sun had finally set, yet lingering twilight broke the night's darkness, along with the string of patio lights draped over the outdoor kitchen, the back door light, and whatever illumination filtered out from Marlow House through the window blinds.

A few minutes later, Walt found his wife inside the kitchen with the twins. Walt and Danielle had agreed to watch Connor while Ian took Lily to the hospital. The Bartleys, who lived across the street, had moved into Marlow House several weeks earlier, to make it easier for the construction workers to complete the work on their house's remodel before their new baby arrived. But now it looked like the baby had a different idea. Walt and Danielle weren't strangers to such surprises, as their twins had shown up early, arriving during their baby shower.

Before leaving for the hospital, Lily had insisted she wasn't experiencing any contractions, not even a twinge. But with Lily's water broken, Danielle couldn't imagine the hospital would send her home if there were no contractions. From what she had read about such things, if a woman didn't go into labor within twenty-four hours after her water had broken, they would typically induce labor.

The two adults got the twins and one toddler upstairs. Walt and Danielle carried the twins into the nursery as Connor trailed behind them with Sadie.

Placing Addison in one crib, she looked at Connor and then back at Walt, who was just laying Jack in the second crib.

"I suppose it wouldn't hurt to let Connor skip his bath for one night," Danielle whispered.

Walt and Danielle glanced down at the boy, who was now lying on the floor, giggling while Sadie licked his face.

Danielle shook her head. "I take that back. The way he and Sadie have been rolling around in the grass all night, he could use a bath."

CONNOR SAT in the warm bathwater, surrounded by bubbles and what his grandma Bartley might describe as an unnecessary number of bath toys. Minutes earlier, he had fallen asleep on the bathroom floor while Walt filled the bath with water, and he initially balked when Walt made him stand up and strip off his clothes. But then a toy airplane took flight from the bath, leaving a trail of bubbles floating down from its wings while circling the bathroom.

Connor forgot his objections, now eager to remove the rest of his clothes so he could follow the plane back into the tub. Three months shy of his second birthday, the toddler didn't understand why toy planes only seemed to take flight when he played with Walt and Marie. He had often handed his grandma Bartley one of his toy planes, urging her to make it fly, but she never seemed to understand what he wanted.

But now, sitting in the bath, Connor had turned his attention from the plane, now floating amongst the bath bubbles, to the plastic clown attached to the tile wall above the tub's rim. Whenever Connor hit the clown's nose, a bubble formed from its mouth. If Connor repeatedly tapped the clown's nose, the bubble grew larger and larger until it popped or floated away.

Giggling at the growing bubble, Connor was prepared to tap the clown's nose again when he froze upon seeing a man's face in the center of the bubble, staring at him. Connor's eyes widened, and he turned to show Walt and Danielle. They stood together, leaning against the bathroom counter, arms crossed over their chests, as they quietly chatted amongst themselves.

Noticing Connor looking their way, Danielle stopped talking to Walt and asked Connor, "You ready to get out, bud?"

Instead of answering, Connor looked back at the bubble. It continued to hang precariously from the clown's mouth. The man's face, still in the bubble, smiled at Connor.

Frowning at the bubble face, Connor was about to look back at Danielle when she knelt by the tub, washcloth in hand, to complete the bath. As Danielle soaped up and then rinsed Connor's wet and nude body, Walt shook out a clean bath towel, preparing to dry Connor off when Danielle finished the job.

Passively allowing Danielle to bathe him, Connor focused his attention on the bubble face. He pointed to the bubble, saying something that sounded like clown. Danielle, who didn't bother to look at where Connor pointed, mumbled, "Yes, the clown face has bubbles," while pulling Connor to his feet and gently lifting him up to the waiting towel in Walt's hands.

Distracted by the bubble head, Connor went limply into Walt's arms as he continued to look back to the tub, his attention on the large bubble and the strange face staring at him. In the next second, the bubble broke free, floating across the room, the face inside still watching Connor, while Walt and Danielle failed to notice, until it popped, and the bubble and the face inside disappeared.

TOGETHER, Walt and Danielle tucked Connor into his bed at Marlow House. They turned off the bedroom light yet left on the nightlight. Stepping out into the hallway, Danielle left Connor's door ajar so they could hear him if he called out.

They stood in the hallway outside Connor's door, their voices a whisper. "He was certainly fascinated with that bubble-machine thing Heather bought him," Walt noted with a low chuckle.

"I wish Ian would call. I'm worried about Lily."

"I imagine Ian's a little too busy to stop and call anyone right now," Walt reminded her. "But why do you think Lily made Ian promise not to call his family until the baby was born?"

"A couple of days ago, Kelly asked Ian if she could be in the labor room with him and Lily when the baby was born."

"Really? What did Lily think about that?"

"It was a hard no. But Kelly told her to think about it for a couple of weeks and to consider changing her mind."

CONNOR SNUGGLED DOWN in the bed, his head peeking out from under the covers. The room wasn't entirely dark but cast in shadows. Light from the partially open bedroom door slipped in from the hallway, and he could hear the muffled voices of Walt and Danielle.

He was about to close his eyes when he noticed a dark shadow moving from the window to the foot of his bed, stopping there. Clutching the edge of his blankets in his hands and pulling them up to his chin, Connor's eyes widened as the shadow morphed into what appeared to be a man, his face the same face from the bubble.

Now standing at the foot of Connor's bed, the strange man looked down at the young child.

"Hello, little boy. You can see me, can't you? Want me to show you a trick?" The man moved his hands around like a magician until a bubble appeared.

FOUR

Danielle Marlow, then Danielle Boatman, had just turned thirty when she moved to Marlow House five years earlier. She had inherited the property from her great-aunt, the wife of her paternal grandfather's brother. When she moved to the small coastal town of Frederickport, Oregon, to turn the property into a bed-and-breakfast, she never realized how much her life would change in such a short time, or how many close friends she would make. Moving to Frederickport proved to be the best decision of her life.

One of the biggest changes, she was now a mother to twins and married to her soulmate, Walt Marlow, who had willed the Marlow estate to the mother of Danielle's great-aunt. Of course, if Danielle shared that information with someone outside of her close circle of confidants, people would think she was insane, because Walt looked like a man in his mid-thirties, not like someone who had been born in 1899 and who had been murdered in 1925, fifty-nine years before Danielle's birth.

The twins, Jack and Addison, were almost two months old now. Danielle had quickly lost the baby weight and weighed less than when she had first moved to Oregon. At five feet five, Danielle's greatest body change wasn't losing fifteen pounds, it was the increase in her bra cup size, which she found annoying because none of her blouses fit. She had recently stopped pulling her long dark hair into a fishtail braid and instead wove it into a french braid, which took her less time.

When helping Walt bathe Connor, Danielle had set her cellphone on a hall table outside the bathroom door, where she had forgotten it. She was still standing with Walt outside Connor's room when the phone rang.

"Maybe that's Ian!" Danielle rushed down the hallway, Walt trailing behind her. A moment later, Danielle answered the call while Walt silently listened to her side of the conversation. She was obviously talking to Ian.

When the call ended, Danielle turned off her cellphone, slipped it in her back pocket, and looked up at Walt. "Lily started having contractions on the way to the hospital. He didn't say how far apart they were; I didn't ask. But she's okay and in a labor room."

"I heard you ask him if he wanted you to call anyone."

"He said not to. I think he's afraid if his sister finds out Lily's at the hospital, she'll show up and want into the labor room. He doesn't want to deal with that."

They were still discussing Lily and standing by the hall table when Sadie and Max came upstairs, walking toward them. Walt looked at the dog and cat, who had stopped several feet away, staring in his direction. Silently, Walt conveyed the update concerning Lily and told Sadie it was alright to go into Connor's room, where the golden retriever wanted to sleep.

Max remained standing with Walt and Danielle in the hallway while Sadie walked by the pair, rubbing against each of them before continuing to Connor's room. Danielle leaned down to Max and picked him up. He began to purr. "The twins are sleeping, and we haven't heard a peep from Connor since we put him to bed. But I don't think I'm going to sleep, not thinking about Lily."

Before Walt could respond, barking came from Connor's room.

"What the heck?" Danielle muttered as she set Max back on the floor and rushed with Walt down to Connor's room. By the time they reached it, Connor was sitting up in his bed, crying, while Sadie stood facing the corner of the room, still barking.

"Sadie!" Walt snapped.

Sadie stopped barking and looked at Walt. Danielle rushed to Connor and picked him up, soothing the boy. She then heard crying coming from the nursery. Sadie had woken the twins.

"Sadie, I can't believe the barking. You never bark in the house when the babies are sleeping," Danielle scolded as she absently patted the toddler's back, trying to calm him while glancing toward the open doorway, the cries of her babies calling out to her.

Walt turned to Danielle and took Connor from her arms. "Go check on the twins, and I'll see what's up with Sadie and get Connor back in bed."

CONNOR HAD STOPPED CRYING and sat on the side of the bed with Walt while Sadie stood by Walt's side, silently telling him about the man she found in Connor's room when she first walked in, and how the man disappeared when she barked at him.

Walt looked from Sadie to Connor. "Who was the man Sadie barked at?"

Connor looked up into Walt's eyes. "Clown."

"It was a clown?" Walt frowned.

Connor shook his head. "Bubble."

DANIELLE HAD FINALLY GOTTEN both the twins back to sleep when Walt stepped into the nursery with Max.

"Where's Sadie?" Danielle whispered.

"I told her to stay with Connor."

Danielle arched her brows. "Is that a good idea?"

"Let's go to our room and talk." Walt glanced down at Max and added, "You stay with the twins."

"What's going on?" Danielle frowned from Walt to Max, back to Walt.

Walt motioned for Danielle to follow him out of the room while Max jumped up on one rocker and curled up. Reluctantly, Danielle followed Walt out of the room, down the hall, and into their bedroom.

"What's going on?" Danielle asked, her voice no longer a whisper. She took a seat on the edge of the bed and watched Walt, who was still standing.

"Sadie started barking because when she walked into the room, there was a man standing at Connor's bedside."

Danielle stood abruptly. "A man?"

Walt waved for Danielle to sit back down while he took a seat at the bench of her dressing table, his back to the dressing table as he faced her. "More accurately, a spirit, considering he vanished not long after Sadie started barking."

"You mean a ghost?"

Walt shrugged. "Apparently."

"Whose ghost?"

Walt shook his head. "I have no idea. Dogs aren't great at giving descriptions, but according to Connor, it was a clown."

"A clown?"

"Let me rephrase. When I asked Connor who the man was, all he said was clown. I assumed that meant the ghost looked like a clown, but when I asked him if the man was a clown, his answer was bubble."

Danielle frowned. "What does that mean?"

"I have no idea. And how Sadie described the ghost, it doesn't sound like someone in a clown costume. Sadie is staying in the bedroom with Connor and promises to come get us if the ghost returns, and not to bark. It's not like a ghost can hurt Connor. Plus, according to Sadie, Connor didn't seem to be afraid of the ghost. He was actually engaging with him when Sadie came into the room, and Connor only started crying after Sadie barked and the ghost disappeared. Max is staying with the twins, and he'll come get us if the ghost shows up there."

The two sat in silence for a few minutes, each thinking about the evening's events. Finally, Danielle said, "This isn't the best night for a new spirit to come calling."

"I suppose we should give Heather and Chris a call; have them be on the lookout for our new ghost."

HEATHER DONOVAN LIVED two doors south of Marlow House. Her boyfriend, Brian Henderson, had brought her home thirty minutes earlier, after the two of them returned from the movies. Since Brian had to get up early for work the next morning, he gave Heather a kiss after walking her to the front door and headed back to his car to drive home.

Heather had just finished taking a shower and was wrapped in a towel when she walked into her bedroom and heard her cellphone ringing.

"It's kind of late," Heather muttered aloud as she walked to the dresser and picked up the phone. Before answering it, she looked to see who was calling. It was Danielle.

"Hey, what's up?" Heather plopped down on her bed, the damp towel still wrapped around her body.

"Sorry to call so late. I hope I didn't wake you."

"No. Brian and I went to the movies tonight. He has to work early, so he didn't stay over. What's up?"

"Connor had a visitor tonight—a new ghost." Danielle then told Heather about the visitor.

"What is the deal with Marlow House? Is it like a ghost magnet?"

"According to Eva, mediums attract spirits, especially spirits who want to communicate with the living. And since there are four of us on Beach Drive—"

"That we're aware of," Heather interrupted.

"What's that supposed to mean?"

"Well, there are four mediums we know about on Beach Drive. But there could be more."

"True. Anyway, I wanted to give you the heads-up."

"Okay, I'll be on the lookout. Is this freaking Lily and Ian out? They figured with the poltergeist gone, Marlow House would be ghost-free except for Marie and Eva."

"They aren't here."

"Where are they?"

Danielle cringed inwardly but said, "Please don't tell anyone. And whatever you do, don't let Kelly know you knew."

"What are you talking about?"

"Lily's water broke tonight. She's at the hospital in labor."

"Oh, my gosh! She's not due for three weeks. But why don't you want Kelly to know I know Lily's in labor?"

"Because Kelly doesn't know." Danielle then explained why Kelly wasn't told.

"Why would she want to be there? That would be awkward having random people in the delivery room."

"Kind of like when I had the twins?"

"Hey, Brian and I were helping you deliver those little impatient imps!"

Danielle laughed. "Which I appreciate."

"So how is Lily doing?"

"I haven't heard. It's not like we can go down there and hang out in the waiting room. We have Connor and the twins. But we talked to Ian about thirty minutes ago. All I know, she's in the labor room, and I assume Ian is with her. Hopefully, the labor is quick, like it was with Connor."

"Well, that's exciting. Glad it's not me."

Danielle and Heather talked a few more minutes before saying goodbye. When the call ended, Heather tossed her cellphone onto the nightstand and got out of bed. She finished drying herself off, dropped the towel onto the floor, and slipped into an oversized T-shirt. Just as Heather leaned down and picked up the towel to take to the bathroom, a man appeared in her bedroom.

Clutching the damp towel in one hand, Heather stood up straight and let out a shriek before yelling out the man's name. "Clay Bowman!"

FIVE

Clay Bowman, the man who had, on several occasions, attempted to murder Heather and who had plotted to kidnap the twins and murder their parents, stood less than five feet from Heather. After her initial scream and blurting Clay's name, Heather threw the towel at him. It flew through his head before landing on the floor.

Clay flinched. "Why did you do that?"

Heather immediately resumed her calm, no longer looking like a frightened child who had just turned the crank of her first jack-in-the-box and experienced both fear and surprise after releasing its occupant. Instead, she glared at Clay with contempt. "I wanted to make sure you were dead. Although the first clue should have been you appeared out of nowhere. Plus, I was told you were dead. Of course, one can't always be sure."

"Wow, you really are a medium."

Heather rolled her eyes and then walked around Clay and picked up the towel while saying, "And you're dead." She continued to her bathroom with the towel, leaving Clay standing in her bedroom.

"Hey, wait!" Clay called out before rushing after her.

Now in the bathroom, hanging her towel on a rack, she tried to ignore Clay.

"You aren't afraid?" Clay asked from the open doorway.

Heather turned to the ghost, looking him up and down before saying, "What is there to be afraid of? You're a ghost. You can't hurt me."

"I don't want to hurt you," Clay insisted.

Heather rolled her eyes and started for the door. "Move, or else I'm walking through you, and I understand that's an unpleasant experience for a ghost."

Clay quickly moved from the doorway and then followed Heather from the room.

"So mediums aren't afraid of ghosts?" Clay trailed behind Heather.

She stopped in the hallway and turned to face him. "I can't speak for all mediums. But I understand I have nothing to fear from a ghost. Although, like you, they can be annoying. What do you want? Why are you here?"

One thing Heather had learned about ghosts—which she didn't plan to share with Clay—was that new ghosts, or ghosts who only stayed around on this plane for a short time, typically never learned to harness their energy. A ghost at Clay's stage probably didn't even realize that was a possibility. And while Eva had assured them a ghost could never physically harm a living person who wasn't evil, it didn't mean a ghost with harnessed energy couldn't torment said living person. The ghost of Presley House had proved that when he locked Danielle in his basement. But Heather didn't want to think about those possibilities. Instead, she would present a brave front and give Clay no reason to stick around.

"I came because I heard you were a medium. Why else would I be here? If you couldn't see me, what would be the point?"

"It would be a typical voyeury thing for a psychopath to do." Heather paused for a moment and then balled her hands into fists, placing them on her hips as she leaned toward Clay. "Hey, were you just at Marlow House? Scaring a little kid? That's a stupid thing for you to do. As it is, you don't need more marks against you."

Clay shook his head. "No. Why would I go to Marlow House? Yes, I know they're also mediums, but I didn't think they would help me. After all, I tried to kidnap their kids. As a parent, I wouldn't forgive someone for trying to mess with my kids."

"Are you saying you weren't over there tonight? Talking to a little boy? He's about two?"

Again, Clay shook his head. "No. I promise. I didn't go over to Marlow House. There would be no reason to."

Dropping her fists from her hips, Heather straightened her posture and looked Clay up and down. "Who told you I was a medium?"

"After I was…you know…"

Heather crossed her arms over her chest, her eyes narrowed. "Murdered."

"Yes. After I was murdered, it took me a while to realize I was dead."

"Didn't you see your body? That would be a big clue for me, seeing my bloody body just lying there, all dead like. I heard a prisoner murdered you; someone you pissed off more than me. You were great at making friends. Not."

"Wow. You're cold."

Heather laughed. "You tried to kill me. Multiple times. Heck, you tried to frame me for the murder you committed. Did you expect me to feel sorry for you? Frankly, I was relieved when I heard you were dead. It meant you couldn't come back."

"But here I am." His voice was not taunting, more matter-of-fact.

"Yes. Here you are. Okay, you were telling me who told you I was a medium."

"At first, I thought people were ignoring me. But then I eventually realized I was dead, and people couldn't see or hear me. Somehow, I found where they had taken my body. Long story short, there was another one like me there, and she moved on, I guess. She called out to me, telling me how beautiful it was. But I wasn't able to go. I tried. But couldn't. So I figured I was doomed to travel the earth for eternity, not being seen or heard as the punishment for my crimes."

Heather frowned and tapped the side of her face with a forefinger, considering his words. After a moment, she said, "I don't think that's how it works. All spirits eventually move on. Although, some choose to stick around, yet I've never heard they have to stick around."

"I don't know how any of that works. But I came back to Frederickport and stopped at the cemetery. I met several like me over there."

"Ghosts. Just say it. They're ghosts. You are a ghost."

Clay shrugged. "Ghosts. They told me about the mediums on Beach Drive."

"So, what, you just wanted a live person to talk to? You thought to stop by so we could chat? You want to be buddies now, since no one else can see or hear you?"

"I know you don't like me."

"That is an understatement." Still standing in the hallway, Heather glanced to her bedroom door and then to the staircase, as if trying to make a decision. After a moment, she looked back at Clay. "I'm hungry. I never got popcorn at the show. You can tell me what this is all about downstairs."

HEATHER SAT on a recliner in her living room with a big bowl of popcorn on her lap, and her feet propped up on the chair's footrest. She had pulled her long black hair into a messy bun atop her head, with her bangs cut straight, just above her dark eyebrows. Her black eyeliner had washed off during her shower, and only a trace of her dark burgundy lipstick remained.

Bella, Heather's calico cat, sat on one of the recliner's arms next to Heather, its tail swishing as the feline stared at Clay, who sat across the room on a sofa. Bella had been sleeping behind the sofa when Clay had first arrived upstairs. She had continued to nap when Heather came downstairs to make the popcorn, Clay trailing behind her.

It wasn't until Heather came into the living room with her popcorn that Bella woke from her nap and found her human was not alone. The cat recognized Clay, gave him a hiss, and then retreated to Heather's side, where she now hunched down, her gaze never leaving him.

Clay looked uneasily at the cat. "Is she talking to me?"

Heather took a bite of popcorn, smiled, and then glanced down to Bella before looking back at Clay. "What is she saying?"

Clay frowned. "It isn't very nice."

"Well, you did try to kill her human, and you shot her friend."

Clay looked from the cat to Heather. "What friend?"

"Hunny, Chris's dog."

"Is this normal for cats to see and talk to people like me?"

"Not sure you're a people anymore. Just say it. Embrace it. Ghost."

"Okay, is it normal for cats to see and talk to ghosts?"

Heather shrugged and took another bite of popcorn before answering, "It's been my experience that dogs and cats can see ghosts and communicate with them. Other animals too, like mountain lions. But I'm not sure if it's all animals." Heather took another bite and then said, "So why don't you tell me why you're here so you can leave? By the time I finish this popcorn, I expect you to be gone, and I'm going to bed."

"Funny, I never believed in ghosts."

"What did you think happened when you died?"

Clay shrugged. "I figured it was like going to sleep."

"You never believed in heaven or hell?"

Clay shook his head. "No. But after talking to the ghost at the cemetery, it sounds like there might be something of a hell waiting for me."

"That's my understanding. Which is why I was saying it would have been a stupid thing for you to try scaring Connor."

"Who's Connor?"

"The little boy at Marlow House I thought you talked to tonight.

You see, very young children, like dogs and cats, can often see ghosts. And if you decide to scare the kids, well, that's demerits against you when you finally move on and have to settle your tab."

"I didn't go to Marlow House tonight."

"It doesn't matter what I believe." Heather glanced upwards for a moment. "And about that ghost thing, technically, you're also a spirit. When in this realm, you're a ghost, but also a spirit. But when you move on, you're no longer a ghost. Just a spirit. Anyway, why did you want to talk to a medium?"

"I need someone who can help me communicate with other living people."

About to take another bite of popcorn, Heather paused and let the popcorn in her hand fall back into the bowl. "You want me to give someone a message for you?"

Clay nodded. "Yes."

Heather set the bowl of popcorn on the side table, reached over, and lowered her footrest and stood up while saying, "No. I'm not doing you any favors. I'm not Whoopi Goldberg, and you are definitely not Patrick Swayze."

"Please, please hear me out," Clay begged.

Begrudgingly, Heather sat back down on the chair, but didn't raise the footrest. "Okay, I'm listening."

"I never imagined I could seriously experience judgment after I died."

"A good person doesn't need to be threatened with hell to treat people right."

Clay stared at Heather. "Have you always believed in hell?"

Heather grabbed the bowl of popcorn sitting on the end table and moved it back to her lap. Bella, who had been sitting on the arm of the chair, was now curled up on the floor near the recliner. "I don't necessarily believe in hell now. At least, not some fiery brimstone sort of place. I just know that after we move on, there are consequences for crappy behavior. But did I always believe this? No. I wasn't always a medium. When I was a child, growing up, my parents were basically atheists. So hell wasn't a thing."

"When did you start believing in something more?"

Heather shrugged and took a bite of popcorn. "It's a long story. But let's just say, when I started connecting with the past—learning more about my family, sins of the past, that I began believing that I not only need to worry about my sins, but the sins from my bloodline."

Clay leaned back on the sofa. "Wow. What type of sinners did you have in your family tree?"

"A serial killer or two." Heather ate some more popcorn. Technically speaking, her grandfather and his twin weren't serial killers, yet they had silently sat by while their father—a serial killer—killed one of their friends.

Clay stared at her for a moment and then finally stammered, "Oh...Well, then maybe you'll understand."

Heather frowned. "Understand what?"

"My sons. I might have been a horrible husband and a bad cop, but I love my boys. I don't want them to end up like me. When they die, I want them to experience what Amy experienced."

"Who's Amy?"

Before Clay could answer her question, a man appeared in the middle of the living room. Clay had met him before. He was the short, chubby, balding man from the cemetery.

SIX

Clay stood up and walked to Wesley, standing several feet from him. "What are you doing here?"

Wesley grinned at Clay. "I suspect the same thing as you."

Setting the popcorn bowl back on the side table, Heather stood. "What the heck is going on? Why has my house turned into Grand Central for ghosts?"

Wesley turned to Heather and smiled. "Are you a medium or a ghost?" He then glanced at the bowl she had just set down, seeing what remained of the popcorn. "Ahh, you must be the medium. Ghosts don't eat popcorn. Although, it would be nice if we could."

"You need to leave." Clay tried giving Wesley a shove to move, but his hand moved through Wesley's chest.

"Hey, stop that!" Wesley took a step back from Clay.

"I'm talking to Heather about something important. It's private."

"I want to talk to her, too. I'm not going anywhere. After all, if we hadn't told you about the mediums on this street, you wouldn't be here."

"Fine. I'll come back later, after you go." Clay disappeared.

"Good." Wesley turned his full attention to Heather. "Hello. My name is Wesley Sadler."

"Were you over at Marlow House a little while ago?"

"Yes. I talked to the kid over there. But then this darn dog comes in, starts barking, and I hear babies crying down the hall. I didn't see the point of sticking around, thought I'd try over here."

"What kind of ghost are you? Scaring little kids like that? You should be ashamed of yourself!"

Wesley's eyes widened as he took a step back from Heather. "Why are you yelling at me?"

"Because no self-respecting ghost goes around scaring little kids!"

"I didn't scare him. He was smiling at me." Wesley took another step back from Heather, but she kept closing the distance between them. "I did a magic trick for him so he wouldn't be afraid."

"You said yourself babies were crying! You made the twins cry!"

"I didn't make anyone cry. If anyone did, it was that stupid dog!"

"Sadie isn't stupid!"

"Please don't yell at me."

"Don't tell me what to do! You barge into my living room and…" Heather would have finished her sentence, but before she got the rest of the words out, he vanished.

Heather glanced around the room. Both ghosts were gone, but for how long? Heather heard a meow. She looked at Bella, who now stood on the recliner, looking at Heather.

"I think we should sleep somewhere else tonight." Heather headed back upstairs to retrieve her cellphone. Once Heather had her phone, she called her boyfriend.

Brian answered the call with, "Heather, is everything okay?"

"Did I wake you up?" Heather sat on the side of her bed, holding the phone by her ear while Bella curled up on her lap.

"No. I was just getting into bed. What's up?"

"Clay was here. Can I come over to your house?"

"THANKS FOR LETTING ME BRING BELLA," Heather told Brian. She snuggled up with him under the blankets on his bed while Bella curled up on the foot of the mattress. Heather had just finished telling Brian what had happened at her house.

"If I can believe Clay, I figure he's going to be back tonight, and I just wanted to sleep without worrying about getting up in the middle of the night to use the bathroom and find him sitting in my bedroom."

"I have to admit, when you first said Clay was at your house, I thought…"

"You thought they were wrong, and he was still alive," Heather finished for him.

"Yeah, then I realized what you meant. But I have to say, for a moment there, it about gave me a heart attack."

"Well, I'm not so thrilled about having to deal with his ghost, but I have to say, being dead has mellowed him out. He's not as cocky. He didn't insult or threaten me once, which was very un-Clay of him."

"What does he want?"

"I got the feeling he wants me to talk to his sons. He's worried about them following in his footsteps, especially now that he knows death isn't the end of the road, and just because someone avoids consequences in this lifetime doesn't mean it won't eventually catch up with them. I don't know what he expects me to say to them. But we never discussed it because that Wesley dude showed up wanting to talk to me, and Clay got all flustered. He obviously didn't want an audience when explaining what he wanted me to do."

"Well, if he waits around to come back, he'll have to find another medium. From what I understand, his wife and sons are leaving town in a couple of weeks. Who do you think the other ghost is?"

"He's obviously the same one who showed up at Marlow House tonight. I'm pretty sure he's one of the ghosts Clay told me about from the Frederickport Cemetery. His name is Wesley Sadler. I wish Eva and Marie were here. I'd asked them what they know about this guy."

"When are they supposed to be back?"

"Marie said they would be back before Lily's baby arrived. Of course, she didn't expect Lily to go into labor for another three weeks. Maybe you could check him out, see who he is."

"I'll do that in the morning."

Heather snuggled closer to Brian. "I wonder how Lily is doing."

"Why don't you call Danielle? She's probably heard something."

"Remember, you can't tell Joe you know Lily went into labor tonight. But I can't call Danielle. It's late."

Brian chuckled. "Do you honestly think Danielle is sleeping, considering Lily is in labor, not to mention their uninvited guest? Plus, you should tell her about Clay and that you have the name of the ghost who showed up at their house."

LILY'S LABOR was longer than it had been with Connor, but by three the next morning, Connor's little sister, Emily Ann, was born, a healthy baby girl who came in at just under six pounds, and the doctor told the relieved parents that while they wanted to keep mother and child in the hospital for a couple of days, they didn't feel the baby needed to stay in the NICU after they released Lily from the hospital, which meant Emily Ann could go home with her mother.

Several hours later, just as the sun came up, Ian sat by his wife's side as she nursed their new daughter.

"She is beautiful, like her mama," Ian whispered.

Lily, not taking her eyes off her new daughter, smiled as she cradled her in her arms. "You have to bring Connor in to meet his sister today. The nurse said it would be okay."

Lily sat in a chair next to the bed while she nursed Emily Ann. Ian reached over and brushed strands of Lily's hair from her eyes. "I will. By the way, I keep getting texts from Mom and Kelly, wanting to know when they can come meet our daughter."

Lily looked up at Ian. "I need to tell my parents."

Ian smiled at Lily and absently leaned over and tucked a strand of her hair behind her right ear before stroking the back of his hand over Emily Ann's forehead. "When I texted your mom last night, telling her you were in labor, she made me promise to call her after the baby was born, no matter what time. So I've talked to her already."

"What did she say?"

"Not much; she just started crying."

"That sounds like Mom." Lily leaned over and kissed her baby's forehead. Emily Ann had just fallen asleep. "Times like this, I wish my parents lived closer."

WALT HAD SET up two portable baby swings in the kitchen of Marlow House. About five hours after Lily gave birth, Addison and Jack each sat in a baby swing, happily entertained while Connor sat in a highchair in the kitchen, eating breakfast, and Walt and Danielle sat at the nearby table, drinking coffee.

Sadie came rushing through the doggie door into the kitchen, and a moment later, the kitchen door opened, and Ian walked inside.

"Daddy!" Connor called out, reaching for his father.

"Hey, bud." Ian walked over to his son, ruffled his hair, stole a bite of his cereal, and gave the boy a quick kiss.

"Congratulations, Dad," Danielle greeted. She started to get up to get Ian some coffee, but he quickly told her to sit back down as he got himself a cup and poured some coffee. A moment later, he joined Walt and Danielle at the table.

"Lily wanted me to come home and get some sleep, and when I go back over, she wants me to bring Connor so he can meet his new sister."

"When do you think she'll be up for a visit?" Danielle asked.

"I'm sure she would love to see you this afternoon. But right now, she's sleeping. It was a long night." Ian glanced over to his son, who seemed oblivious to the discussion and more intent on arranging his pieces of dry cereal into a line on his highchair tray.

"Have your parents or sister been over to the hospital yet?" Danielle asked.

Ian shook his head. "No. I told them the same thing I told you: wait until this afternoon. Lily needs her sleep."

They discussed the labor for a few minutes, leaving out any graphic descriptions, as Connor was within earshot. Danielle and Walt didn't bring up last night's unexpected visitor, believing Ian had enough on his mind right now. Finally, Ian asked, "How was Connor last night?" He turned to his son and asked, "Were you a good boy last night for Walt and Danielle?"

"Clown," Connor announced.

"Clown?" Ian frowned.

Walt and Danielle exchanged glances.

"Bubble," Connor blurted.

"Oh, you took a bath with that clown bubble machine Heather gave you."

"He did, but I'm not sure that's what he's talking about," Danielle said.

"Or perhaps it is," Walt muttered.

The next moment, the subject of the conversation appeared in the room. Ian was the only one who couldn't see him.

Connor pointed to the ghost and shouted, "Clown!"

Sadie started barking, but Walt quickly silenced the dog. And then Walt looked at Danielle and said, "Sadie says it's the same one from last night."

"Same what? Why did Sadie start barking?" Ian asked.

Connor continued to point at the ghost and again said, "Clown."

"Someone has joined us. And for some reason, your son keeps calling him a clown, although I'm not sure why. He doesn't look like a clown," Danielle explained.

Ian frowned at his now silent dog and then looked to where Connor pointed, seeing nothing. "Are you saying there's a ghost in the kitchen with us?"

"Hello, I'm sorry to barge in like this. I never meant to cause a problem," the ghost apologized.

"Yes. He's standing right there." Danielle pointed to the ghost. "His name is Wesley Sadler. He showed up last night, and Connor keeps referring to him as clown."

"How do you know my name?" the ghost asked.

Danielle looked at the ghost. "You told Heather last night. She told me."

"I don't like her. She reminds me of my wife. Always screaming. I wanted to ask her to help me, but all she did was yell at me."

"Who is Wesley Sadler, and why is he here?" Ian asked.

"That's what we want to know." Walt turned to the ghost. "Why are you here?"

SEVEN

Before Wesley answered the question, the kitchen door opened, and Kelly Morelli, Ian's sister, popped her head into the doorway and said, "Hello." She stepped into the house and closed the door behind her.

"Hi, everyone. Excuse me for dropping in, but I saw Ian's car out front, and I figured he was back from the hospital."

"I got here a few minutes ago," Ian explained.

"Morning, Kelly," Danielle and Walt chorused, still sitting at the kitchen table.

"Kiwi," Connor called out from his highchair.

Kelly walked to her nephew and, in doing so, stepped into Wesley.

"Clown!" Connor called out, pointing to his aunt.

Wesley quickly stepped away from Kelly and gave a shiver. "That was gross."

Kelly frowned at her nephew. "Why did you call me clown?"

Connor pointed to the ghost Kelly couldn't see and babbled something she couldn't understand.

Kelly turned to her brother and shook her head, confused at her nephew's ramblings, but she quickly changed course and asked, "How is Lily? How is my niece? When can I see them?"

"Like I told you on the phone, not until this afternoon. Mama and Emily Ann are sleeping."

Walt stood up. "Kelly, can I get you some coffee?"

"That would be great." Kelly flashed Walt a smile.

"Go ahead and sit down." Walt walked to the cabinet to get another coffee cup while Kelly made her way to an empty chair at the table. In doing so, she again walked through the ghost.

"Stop doing that!" Wesley shouted. "No one is even listening to what I want to ask you. Everyone keeps walking through me."

Wesley vanished, and then Connor said, "Clown!"

"What is he talking about?" Kelly asked as she sat down and turned back to her nephew. Connor pointed to where the ghost had been, while slamming his other hand on the highchair tray.

Walt handed Kelly a cup of coffee while Ian distracted his son. By the time Walt sat back down in his chair, Connor seemed to have forgotten the ghost, and Kelly turned her attention to her brother.

"Why didn't you guys call me last night?" Kelly asked Ian.

"It was late. I didn't want to wake you up."

"How late?" Kelly asked.

Ian shrugged. "I don't know, after ten?"

Walt and Danielle exchanged glances but didn't comment. It hadn't been that late.

"I really wanted to be there," Kelly whined.

"Sorry, Kelly, but I didn't even think about it. Lily's water broke, and at the time she wasn't having contractions, so she was a little worried, especially because she wasn't due for three weeks. We just took off to the hospital."

Kelly turned her attention to Danielle. "Why didn't you call me?"

"We were kind of busy too," Danielle said. "We had two infants and a toddler to get ready for bed."

"Come on, one of you couldn't have taken a few minutes to call me?"

"It really wasn't my place. It was Ian and Lily's news."

"Oh poop. That is ridiculous," Kelly grumbled.

"Kelly, we called you as soon as the baby arrived," Ian reminded her.

"I wanted to be there during the labor."

"I told you Lily was not comfortable with it."

"But Lily said she would think about it," Kelly countered.

"No. I think you're the one who told her to think about it for a couple of weeks after she said no."

"And she said she would think about it."

"And she did. The answer was no."

"She didn't think about it for two weeks. I just asked the other day."

Ian rolled his eyes. "She really didn't have a chance to give it two weeks, considering the baby came a couple of days after you asked her."

"Which would have been plenty of time to allow me to be there. I can't believe you would do that."

"Kelly, the important thing is Lily and the baby are both healthy," Danielle interjected. "And frankly, I understand Lily not wanting anyone in the labor room with her but Ian and the medical staff."

"You had Brian and Heather with you when you had the twins," Kelly reminded her.

Danielle chuckled. "I really didn't have a choice. It was sorta a surprise, and I needed their help."

Kelly slumped back in the chair, the mug of coffee cupped between her hands. "I just am so disappointed. I really wanted to be there."

"Why?" Walt asked.

Kelly glanced up at Walt and then back down at her coffee. She didn't answer immediately. But finally, she said, "I thought it would be a good way to bond with…with Lily."

"You wanted to bond with Lily?" Danielle asked.

"I thought if I was there with her and Ian during such an important time that I'd share something with them that they didn't share with anyone else." Kelly sipped her coffee.

Ian let out a sigh and reached over, giving his sister a pat on the knee. "I love you, Kelly, but someday when you have a kid, I don't want to be in the labor room with you."

Kelly glanced at her brother and wrinkled her nose. "Ew, I wouldn't want you there."

Ian arched his brows at his sister, holding them in that position as if waiting for her response. After a moment, Kelly chuckled and reluctantly said, "I guess I understand why Lily didn't want me there."

ON SATURDAY MORNING, Joe Morelli walked into the chief's office and found Brian Henderson sitting at the desk at the computer. Brian glanced up briefly from the monitor and gave Joe a nod and a quick hello before looking back at the screen.

"What are you doing in here?" Joe strolled to the desk and then glanced down at a slip of paper sitting next to the keyboard. Sprawled across the paper in handwriting he recognized as Brian's was the name Wesley Sadler.

"Just looking up something."

Joe reached down and picked up the small piece of paper, giving it a closer look. "Wesley Sadler, that name sounds familiar. Who is it?"

"That's what I'm trying to find out."

Joe dropped the paper back on the desk. "What for?"

"Just doing a favor for a friend." Before Joe could ask another question, Brian said, "Hey, Heather told me Lily's baby came early. You're an uncle again."

"That's what I've been told. I guess her water broke last night, and they went to the hospital. The baby came early this morning. Kelly was a little upset."

"Upset, why? I heard the baby's healthy despite being early, and the mother is doing good."

"She really wanted to be in the delivery room during the birth."

"Really? Lily was okay with that?"

Joe shrugged. "She just talked to Ian about it the other day. No one knew it was going to come this early."

"The most important thing is the baby and mother are fine."

Joe was about to say something else when his name was called through the intercom to come to the front office. As soon as Joe left, Brian resumed his search.

After a few minutes, he found an obituary for a Wesley Sadler from Fredrickport, who had died in January. It included a headshot of the deceased. Brian screenshot the image, AirDropped it to his phone, and then messaged it to Heather, asking, "Is this him?"

A few minutes later, Heather called Brian.

"That looks like him. What did you find out?" Heather asked.

"I'm just starting. Before I go down the rabbit hole, I wanted to make sure I was chasing the right rabbit. I'll call you when I get more information."

"Thanks, Brian."

"Did you go back home?"

"I'm over at Chris's house. I figure if Clay follows me here, at least I'll have another medium to help me deal with him."

BRIAN HENDERSON TOLD Joe he was going to Heather's house for lunch when he left the police department that afternoon. He didn't bother telling Joe he was actually going over to Chris Johnson's house, where Heather was spending the afternoon.

Early in his relationship with Heather, he'd occasionally felt pangs of jealousy over Heather's relationship with Chris Johnson, aka Chris Glandon. But who could blame him? Chris, who was Heather's friend, boss, and fellow medium, was also ridiculously rich and had a face and body that drew the attention of women and gay men.

Heather was also much younger than Brian. Theirs was an age gap that often drew criticism. From the outside, people often saw nothing more than a man in a midlife crisis dating a woman young enough to be his daughter, with some wondering if he intended to start a family at his age, or if Heather understood he'd be more like a grandfather to their hypothetical children than a father.

Brian had no desire to remarry, and had already had a vasectomy, while Heather had no desire to marry or have children. Brian, a no-nonsense seasoned cop, found an unexpected comfort in the quirky company of an offbeat medium, who, unlike other younger women he had dated, never tried to impress him or anyone else, and despite looking like a member of a witches' coven, she held a rigid code of ethics he respected.

When he arrived at Chris's house, he found Heather and Chris sitting on the back porch, eating pizza and watching the ocean while Hunny, Chris's pit bull, and Bella napped nearby.

Chris offered Brian a beer but was reminded Brian had to go back to work. Instead of a beer, Chris brought Brian a glass of iced tea and offered him some pizza, which he accepted.

They chatted briefly about the newest resident on Beach Drive, Emily Ann Bartley, and then turned their attention to the information Brian had learned about the ghost.

"He was an insurance agent, lived in Frederickport, but died in California this past January. He was at some work seminar when he had a heart attack. Married, no kids. They brought the body back to Frederickport, and he's buried in the local cemetery. That's about all I could find on him."

"Why hasn't he moved on?" Chris wondered.

"And why did he go to Marlow House?" Heather asked.

"If this guy has been hanging out at the cemetery, wouldn't Eva and Marie know him?" Brian asked.

"Yeah, but we can't ask them until they get back," Heather explained.

"Well, at least you know who he is," Brian said.

"I'll tell Danielle about him when Chris and I go over to Marlow House in a little bit. We're going to watch the twins while they go over to the hospital to see Lily and the new baby. When they get back, Chris and I are going to the hospital to see them. Want to meet us over there?"

"I'd love to, but Joe's planning to go over there with Kelly, and I promised to be back at the station. The chief's not working this weekend."

"I bet you're glad the chief is back to work," Chris said.

"Clay, as a replacement, made us appreciate the chief more," Brian said with a snort.

"I don't even want to think about Clay," Heather groaned.

Chris looked at Heather. "You're going to have to face Clay sooner or later. I know what it's like being stalked by a ghost. He's not going to give up until he tells you what he wants."

"Isn't stalk the same as haunt?" Brian asked.

"I guess it is." Chris turned his attention back to Heather. "But my point being, let's find out what he wants from you. After we come back from the hospital, let's go over to your house, and I'll stay with you. Maybe he'll show up."

EIGHT

After Brian left for work on Saturday afternoon, Heather and Chris gathered up the used paper plates, napkins, empty cans, glasses, and the pizza box, taking them inside. Once in the kitchen, Heather set the dirty glasses in the sink while Chris put the trash in the kitchen can.

"Let's walk up to Marlow House?" Heather suggested. "I could use the exercise since I didn't get to run this morning. We can leave my car here and drive it home when I'm ready to deal with Clay."

Heather stood at the kitchen sink, handwashing the glasses they had used, while Chris awkwardly folded the pizza box so he could shove it in the trash can atop the debris he had already put in the can.

"No problem."

Heather turned off the water and looked at Chris, watching him give the folded pizza box a second shove. "Wouldn't it be easier to take that out to the trash bin instead of putting it in there?"

"Why?" Chris gave the box a final shove, pushing it all the way into the trash can. With a smile, he put the lid back on the can.

Heather rolled her eyes and silently grabbed a dishtowel to dry off the now clean glasses before putting them back in the cupboard.

"Can we go next door first? Adam dropped the keys off last night, and I haven't checked out the house."

"What, you didn't get a final walkthrough?"

"I told him not to bother. But I'm curious what it looks like."

"Sure. I'm kinda curious to check out the house, too. Did they finally come get the rest of their stuff?"

"Mia said she took everything she wanted, and a couple of days before the close of escrow, some guy Austin hired showed up to pick up what Austin wanted."

A few minutes later, Chris and Heather left Chris's house, locking the door behind them while leaving Bella and Hunny behind. They headed to the house next door, which had been owned by the Crawfords and now belonged to Chris.

"What are you going to do with two houses next door to each other?" Heather asked as she stood on what had been the front porch of the Crawford house, waiting for Chris to unlock the door.

"I'm not sure, but Walt and I are trying to figure out what to do about the tunnel. Me owning this house, and Walt and Danielle, Marlow House, will make it a little easier to figure things out. It was never an ideal situation, having the Crawfords owning one exit to the tunnel. Austin promised to keep his side secure, which he obviously didn't do." With the door now unlocked, Chris pushed it open and motioned for Heather to enter first.

Heather didn't budge and shook her head. "No way. You go in first. This is your creepy tunnel house."

Chris chuckled and entered the house while saying, "It's not a creepy house."

WHEN HEATHER and Chris reached Marlow House, after checking out the property Chris had recently purchased, Ian was just driving away with Connor, heading to the hospital to see Lily and the new baby. Danielle greeted Chris and Heather right after they walked into the entry hall from the front door.

"I was just going to call you," Danielle told them.

THE GHOST WHO SOUGHT REDEMPTION

"We were checking out Chris's new house," Heather announced.

"I heard escrow closed. How's the house?"

Heather shrugged. "It's a house. I expected it to be creepier."

Danielle chuckled.

"Why were you going to call us?" Chris asked.

"You guys don't need to babysit now. If you want, you can go to the hospital with us. Afterwards, Walt and I are going to stop at Pier Café for an early dinner. You're both welcome to join us."

"What about the twins? Is Marie back?" Heather asked. She stood in Marlow House's entry hall with Chris and Danielle.

"No, she's not back. But Joanne offered to stay with them. She comes on Mondays to clean, and when she heard Lily had her baby, she offered to watch the twins when she's here."

"Do we trust her?" Heather asked, her question serious.

Danielle grinned at Heather. "Yes. She's watched them a few times already, and she's really pretty good with them. In fact, the first couple of times she watched them, Marie was here, observing."

"Wow, a ghost is better than a baby cam." Heather snickered.

"Yep. Marie gave her approval," Danielle said.

"Okay. If it's good enough for Marie."

Chris rolled his eyes at the banter between the two women, and when they seemed to be finished, he told Danielle, "Brian found out a little bit about your ghost."

HEATHER AND CHRIS joined Walt and Danielle in the parlor while they waited for Joanne to arrive. Danielle sat in a recliner, nursing the twins, while Heather filled them in on what Brian had learned about Wesley.

"An insurance agent?" Danielle repeated after hearing about his occupation. "Was there anything suspicious about his death?"

"Not according to Brian," Heather said. "Just some poor schmuck who died too young, probably from eating too much junk food."

"Why do you say that?" Chris asked.

"He didn't look healthy," Heather said.

"He's dead. Of course he doesn't look healthy," Chris countered.

"You know what I mean. If that's how he looked when he died, he certainly didn't look like a healthy thirty-five-year-old man. Heck, Brian looks younger than him, and more fit."

"Of course Brian's more fit. He's alive." Chris snickered.

"I wonder why he hasn't moved on and why he wants to talk to a medium," Danielle muttered.

"It could be something about his wife." Walt looked at Heather. "You said he was married, right?"

"Oh, that reminds me," Danielle interrupted. "Something the ghost said about his wife."

"What was that?" Chris asked.

"He didn't seem to like Heather because she reminded him of his wife. Claimed she screamed a lot, just like Heather."

Chris snickered at Danielle's words.

"I do not scream!"

They all looked at Heather.

"THIS IS RIDICULOUS," June Bartley grumbled. She sat with her husband and daughter in the visitors' lounge in the maternity section of the hospital, waiting for permission to see Lily and their new granddaughter.

"Ian and Lily want Connor to be the first one to meet the baby," Kelly reminded her mother.

"Oh pooh. Connor is practically a baby himself. He doesn't care if he gets to see her first. I doubt he even understands what's going on."

"It's what Ian and Lily want," John told his wife. "We'll get to see her soon enough. I'm just glad everything is okay."

Kelly slumped back in the chair. "If I'd been allowed to be in the labor room, I would have already met her."

June looked at her daughter. "I don't understand why you wanted to be in the labor room. There was a time the father didn't even go in the labor room."

"Dad was with you when you had me and Ian."

"True. But that's different." June took a moment to consider what Kelly had just said and then chuckled before saying, "Now that I think about it, my mother was a little shocked at the whole natural childbirthing thing. She claimed we were going backwards, that it sounded like something her grandmother did. But we took Lamaze classes. Your father was my coach. I gave birth to both you and your brother without an epidural. It all went very smoothly."

"You cursed at me and slapped me twice," John said under his breath.

June looked at her husband and frowned. "What did you say?"

"Nothing," John muttered.

June turned her attention back to her daughter. "But some of my friends took the whole thing a little too far."

"What do you mean?" Kelly asked.

"One of my friends had her sister come into labor with her and—"

"That's sort of what I wanted to do," Kelly interrupted.

"The sister took a home movie of the entire thing. I'm sorry, but I don't think any woman giving birth needs to have her lady bits filmed."

Kelly giggled.

"Can we change the subject?" Not waiting for an answer, John looked at Kelly and asked, "When is Joe getting here?"

Kelly briefly glanced at her watch. "He should have been here by now."

"Yes, we probably shouldn't be talking about lady bits when Joe gets here," June said.

John looked at his wife. "Please stop saying that."

June frowned. "Saying what?"

John shrugged. "You know."

"Oh, you mean lady bits?" June asked.

Kelly giggled again.

"Oh, look who's here!" June said brightly. They all turned to see Joe, Ian, and Connor had just walked into the waiting room.

IAN WALKED into Lily's hospital room carrying a package. He had left Connor out in the waiting room with his family, wanting to make sure his wife was ready for guests. He found Lily sitting in the glider rocker next to the hospital bed, holding their daughter.

Lily looked up at Ian and smiled. "I just fed her, and she fell asleep. Where's Connor? I thought you were bringing him."

"He's in the waiting room with the whole damn family." Ian chuckled and then added, "I wanted to make sure you were up to a visit." He walked closer and gave her a quick kiss and then dropped one on his sleeping daughter's brow.

"I'm eager to see Connor, not so sure about the whole damn family." Lily chuckled and then asked, "What's the package?"

Ian looked at the package. "Oh, this?" He looked back at Lily. "Your mom sent it. Told me you'd know what to do with it."

"Open it, please."

Ian quickly opened the package and was surprised to find a baby doll—an extremely realistic baby doll. Now holding the doll, he looked back to Lily and asked with a frown, "Don't you think Emily Ann is a little young for this right now?"

Lily chuckled. "That's not for Emily Ann. It's for Connor."

Ian looked at the doll again and frowned. He looked back at Lily. "Connor?"

"Yep, Mom told me she planned to get Connor a baby doll."

"You didn't happen to tell her what happened to the last baby doll you bought him?"

"You mean the only one I ever bought him? But yes, I did. Mom said this will be different because she was getting him a realistic doll that looks like a real baby. Claimed it would help him adjust if we both had a baby to take care of."

Ian chuckled. "That's rather hippy-dippy of her." He tossed the doll on the bed and then gathered up the trash from the package and shoved it in the nearby trash can.

"That's Mom."

IAN LIFTED Connor into his arms and carried him into the hospital room to see Lily and the new baby. Lily smiled at her husband and son as they entered the room. Upon seeing his mother, Connor held out his arms to her.

"Hi, Connor. Want to meet your new sister?" Lily asked.

"Baby!" Connor cried out excitedly.

Ian set Connor on the floor. The toddler ran to his mother and new sister. After spending time with the Marlow twins, Connor had already learned how to be gentle, so he brushed his hand over the swaddled infant's body and leaned forward, placing a light kiss on her forehead. He stared at the baby for a few minutes when Lily asked, "You want to see what your grandma Miller got you?"

Connor looked up at his mother, who then looked at Ian. "Why don't you show him?"

Ian picked the doll up from the bed and handed it to his son as Lily said, "See, Grandma got you your own baby to take care of."

Connor took the doll from his father, holding it by one foot. He looked at it for a moment and then tossed it over his shoulder. It landed on the floor, and he turned his attention back to his mother and sister.

AFTER IAN BROUGHT Connor back to the waiting room, Ian's parents went in to meet the new baby. When the grandparents finished their visit, the rest visited the mother and infant in shifts, with Kelly and Joe going next, followed by Walt and Danielle, and then Heather and Chris. While Lily was happy to see everyone, she was exhausted by the time the last ones said goodbye.

The group stood in the waiting room, preparing to leave, as Ian gave his wife a final goodnight before leaving. June looked at Danielle and Walt and asked, "Who is watching the twins?"

"Joanne." Danielle smiled.

"Oh, that's your housekeeper?" June asked.

"Yes, and a friend. She's also good with the babies."

"It's wonderful you have so much help, especially since there are no grandparents," June said. "We're going to celebrate at Pearl Cove. Ian and Connor will be coming with us, and you're all invited to join us."

"Thanks for the invite. But I think Walt and I are going to grab a quick bite at Pier Café and then head home."

"Ahh, yes. You're nursing like Lily. Can't really be away that long at this stage." June smiled at Danielle and then looked at Heather and Chris. "But you're both invited."

"Thanks for the invite. But I'm afraid Heather and I have work we need to finish up tonight," Chris told her.

June arched her brows. "You have to work on a Saturday?"

"Unfortunately, something unexpected came up last night that we have to deal with. And I am afraid I need Heather to help me." Chris flashed June his most charming smile.

NINE

It was fairly busy at Pier Café when Danielle and her group stepped into the diner late Saturday afternoon for an early dinner. They didn't have to wait long for a booth, as one busser was clearing a table. After he finished and walked away from the booth, Danielle's group claimed it. She sat next to Walt, while Heather and Chris sat on the opposite side of the table, facing them.

They had just picked up their menus when Carla showed up with a pitcher of water and questions. Carla looked at Heather and asked, "Are we waiting for Brian before you order?"

Heather smiled over her menu at Carla. "No, he's working."

"When I saw you guys walking in, I was hoping the twins were with you. I still haven't seen them."

"They're two months now, so you'll probably see them in here next week," Danielle said.

"I hope so!" Carla began filling the empty water glasses on the table. "Wish you would have brought them with you today."

"They're home with Joanne because we just came back from the hospital. Lily had her baby last night," Danielle announced.

Carla stopped pouring the water and slammed the pitcher on the table. "No! I thought she wasn't due for another three weeks."

"One thing I've learned, babies come when they want," Heather said with a snort.

"Is everything okay? She was having a girl. Right?" Carla asked.

"Emily Ann," Chris answered. "Mother and baby are doing well."

Carla glanced around the table. "Did you guys take any pictures?"

They all pulled out their cellphones and took turns showing Carla the pictures they had taken at the hospital. After Carla finished commenting on the photos, she handed back the last phone and asked, "Aren't they still staying at Marlow House?"

"Yes. The plan was to move back before the baby was born. They hoped their addition would be finished and the new nursery set up before then, but what do they say about the best-laid plans?" Walt chuckled.

"But we're going to be okay," Danielle said. "Fortunately, we have a lot of help."

"You do have Joanne. I wish I had a Joanne." Carla finished filling the water glasses and then took their drink orders and left their table.

"You also have a Marie." Heather snickered after Carla was out of earshot. "And an Eva, but she's useless when it comes to changing diapers." Heather glanced at Chris and added, "Sort of like Chris."

"Hey, I've changed a few diapers," Chris argued. He then turned to Danielle and Walt and asked, "I wonder if Eva and Marie are going to come back early now that Lily had her baby."

"They don't know," Heather said.

Chris shrugged. "Sometimes Eva knows things."

"True," Danielle agreed. "But if they don't come back right away, we may need to deal with this Wesley if he returns. I have no idea what he wants."

"And I have to deal with Clay," Heather groaned.

"Hey, I'll be with you," Chris promised.

"I wish we knew a little more about Wesley. When someone says they need something from us, I'd rather find out as much about them as possible," Danielle said.

"You might want to ask Carla if she knows the guy," Chris suggested.

"Not a bad idea," Walt agreed. "She seems to have met everyone in town, and she has a knack for remembering names."

When Carla returned to the table with the drinks and to take their order, Danielle asked, "Carla, did you ever know an insurance agent named Wesley Sadler?"

Carla, who had just set the last drink on the table and was about to get out her order pad and pen, paused a moment and looked at Danielle. "Wesley Sadler? Yeah, he died not long after Christmas. Heart attack. Can't say I was surprised considering how that guy liked his junk food, and from what I heard, his idea of exercise was sitting in front of the television and watching football."

Heather elbowed Chris. He looked at her with a frown while she whispered, "See, I was right."

"Why do you ask?" Carla asked.

"One of my friends from California called me recently to congratulate me on the twins. When we were talking, she mentioned someone who lived in Frederickport and wanted to know if I knew him. She said he sold insurance."

"You're going to have to tell your friend her friend died," Carla said.

"Not sure they were friends exactly. She's also in the insurance business." Danielle smiled sweetly.

"So what happened to this guy?" Heather asked.

"I was told he went on a business trip to California and had a heart attack."

"Poor wife. My friend mentioned he was married," Danielle said.

"Yeah, he was. Wesley was a frequent customer. Once in a while, he would bring his wife, but not often. Usually because he would come during the week, for breakfast or lunch when he was working. His wife never came alone or with friends, not until after he died."

"She comes in now?" Heather asked.

"Not as much as she did right after he died. Now she comes in once in a while, but back then she was coming in at least once a day. She'd talk about her husband and how much she missed him and how her home was so lonely. She regretted never having kids, saying if she had kids, then she wouldn't be alone now."

"That's sad," Heather said.

Carla shrugged. "I guess. But I confess, I wanted to tell her she was wasting her tears. He wasn't worth it."

"Why do you say that?" Walt asked.

"Because when Wesley used to come in here alone, he was always hitting on me, trying to get me to go out with him. Not that I would, even if he weren't married. The guy didn't exactly have sex appeal. But apparently his wife thought he did. His death turned her into a basket case, but she was also annoying."

"What do you mean, annoying?" Walt asked.

"It's not that I didn't feel sorry for her, but sheesh, enough is enough. And when she wasn't telling me about her beloved dead husband—like every freaking time I waited on her—she was annoying other customers who sat down at the table next to her."

"I wonder if we ever saw her in here," Danielle said.

"I wouldn't doubt it. You just didn't have the misfortune to sit next to her. You probably saw Wesley in here, too, but he was sort of a forgettable-looking guy, someone you don't really notice. Although, the same can be said for the widow," Carla said.

"But she's not a regular anymore?" Chris asked.

"No. She comes in once in a while. Ever since she started dating her brother-in-law about three months ago, she's perked back up." Carla chuckled.

"Wow, for being so heartbroken, she didn't wait long to start dating," Heather said.

"When you say brother-in-law, are you talking about Wesley's brother?" Chris asked.

"Yep. Apparently, he was looking after his brother's grieving widow, and while she was busy crying on his shoulder, I guess they hooked up. Supposedly, they're getting married. Not sure when."

"After dating only three months? Wow. Do the brothers look

alike?" Heather asked. "Did the grieving widow fall for the brother-in-law because he reminds her of her husband?"

Carla laughed. "Hardly. They look nothing alike, and that's because they're not blood brothers. One of my friends used to date the brother, and when I mentioned how he looked nothing like Wesley, she said that's because they were both adopted. She also said he was a dog, but he's not bad to look at. I have to admit, not sure what he sees in the once grieving widow. She and Wesley were sort of a matching pair."

After Carla took their order, she left their table.

"I told you," Chris said after Carla was out of earshot.

"Told us what?" Heather asked.

Chris flashed Heather a grin. "Carla has dirt on everyone." He looked at Danielle and added, "And you never disappoint."

Danielle looked at Chris with a frown. "What is that supposed to mean?"

Walt chuckled. "I think Chris is referring to how quickly you conjured up an imaginary friend who mentioned Wesley."

Chris nodded and turned to Walt. "Does it ever bother you how quickly and convincingly your wife can lie?"

Walt shrugged. "It can be unsettling at times."

Later, after Carla brought their food order and left their table, Walt asked, "At the hospital, you told June you were working tonight. Is Clay the work?"

"Yes. I'll try to be with her when Clay comes back. Two mediums are better than one when dealing with an unwanted ghost. But there is no guarantee that will be possible." Chris picked up his burger and took a bite.

Heather groaned. "I hope when he sees my car in my driveway, he'll come back and tell me what he wants, and then he can move on. While I understand he can't hurt me, it is nerve-racking having a spirit like that just popping into my space whenever he wants. Hopefully, seeing Chris there won't scare him off." Heather stabbed her salad with her fork.

"Are you leaving Bella and Hunny over at Chris's house?" Danielle asked.

About to take a bite of her salad, Heather paused and looked at Danielle. "Yeah. We don't need Hunny seeing Clay again, considering what that jerk put her through."

"One good thing came out of Clay attacking Hunny," Chris said.

They all looked at Chris. "What possible good came out of that?" Heather demanded.

"There was a time I wouldn't leave your cat alone in my house with Hunny. But now, instead of tormenting Hunny, Bella insists on grooming her. It's like your cat has adopted my pit bull."

AFTER DINNER, Walt and Danielle dropped Heather and Chris back at his house so Heather could pick up her car, which Heather and Chris planned to drive back down the street to Heather's house.

"Good luck. I hope Clay shows up and you two can convince him to move on," Danielle told Heather and Chris as they stood on the sidewalk next to the Ford Flex, its windows down and Walt and Danielle inside the vehicle.

"I doubt Clay is going to be eager to move on," Chris said. "But we'll have to see."

They said their goodbyes, with Heather and Chris waving goodbye to the Flex as it drove away.

"Let's go check on Hunny and Bella first," Chris suggested.

Ten minutes later, Heather and Chris were in Heather's car after checking on their dog and cat, heading the short distance to her house.

"Thanks for helping me, Chris."

"No problem. I'm actually curious to find out what Clay wants. You said he didn't have the same chip-on-the-shoulder attitude as the last time we saw him?"

"No. Not at all."

Chris shrugged. "Some people improve with death."

Instead of driving down the street and parking in front of Heather's house, they drove in the same direction Walt had gone minutes earlier, driving up the street before turning right and then making another right into the alleyway that ran behind Marlow House and Heather's house.

Minutes later, they pulled into Heather's driveway behind her house, where she parked her car and turned off the ignition. She didn't get out of the car immediately, but took a deep breath, gathering her courage.

Chris, still sitting in the passenger seat, unlatched his seatbelt and reached over and patted Heather's shoulder while humming a familiar tune from one of his favorite movies. "Come on, Heather, sing it with me."

Heather laughed, and then she and Chris sang the chorus from the *Ghostbusters* theme song.

TEN

It was about five p.m., so the sun was still up when Chris and Heather arrived at her house on Saturday. It would be another four hours before sunset. Afraid that if Clay saw Chris, he might wait until he believed Heather was alone before returning, Chris took a seat in the rocking chair tucked into a dark corner of the living room, while Heather sat in the recliner, brightly lit from the sunlight coming through the front window. Heather turned on the television, and together she and Chris silently watched a movie on cable.

They had been watching the movie for about an hour when Chris glanced at his watch. He was about to say something to Heather when the sound went off on the television and the picture turned to static. The next moment, Clay appeared in the living room, standing between Heather and the television. The ghost faced Heather.

Heather picked up her TV remote and turned off the television. "I suppose I can thank you for interrupting my movie?"

Clay glanced at the television and back at Heather. "I'm not really sure how I did that. But I was trying to find a way to turn it off."

"Not bad for a new ghost." Heather tossed the remote back on the side table. She leaned back in her chair and lifted the footrest with her bare feet on it and leaned back. "I thought you might show up."

"I wanted to talk to you while you were alone." Clay clearly had not yet noticed Chris sitting in the dark corner, watching him.

"Why? Most people can't see you. What would it matter?"

"True. But we can't have a conversation with other people around. It would be awkward for you to participate."

"I suppose they would assume I was talking to myself."

"Something like that." Clay paused a moment, as if remembering something, and then asked, "When you were in the jail cell after I arrested you for Camilla's murder, you weren't alone, were you? You were talking to someone, weren't you?"

Heather smiled. "That's right. I was talking to a couple of ghost friends."

Clay nodded, as if it all made sense now.

"Why didn't you want to talk to me in front of Wesley? He's one of you."

Clay shrugged. "Because this isn't any of his business. I just met the guy. I don't need to share my personal life with other ghosts."

"It might be insensitive of me to point out, but you don't have a life anymore."

"No. No, I don't."

"I'm going to tell you something. And if you leave immediately, when you return, I'll ignore you. I'll pretend you're not there. So if there is some favor you want from me, you won't get it. Trust me, I'm stubborn, and if I choose to ignore you, you will be dead to me."

Clay frowned. "Umm, I'm already dead. But what could you possibly say that would make me leave?"

"Hold that thought. And remember, if you leave now, it will be your last goodbye." Heather motioned over to the far corner of the living room. "Clay, do you remember my boss, Chris Johnson? Or as his friends know him, Chris Glandon."

Clay quickly turned around, looking at where Heather motioned.

Chris stood up and stepped out into the light. "Hello, Clay. How's death treating you?"

Clay didn't budge from his spot. "They told me you were also a medium."

"What exactly do you want from the mediums?" Chris asked as he walked toward Heather, who remained reclined in her chair.

Clay glanced nervously from Chris to Heather. "I guess karma is real."

Chris walked to the empty recliner next to Heather and sat down. "Why do you say that?"

Clay shrugged and walked over to the sofa. He sat down and faced Chris and Heather. "Considering how I treated you when I was alive. And now that I'm dead, and apparently facing some sort of judgment, and I need a favor from you." Clay let out a snort and shook his head before continuing, "There is some irony here. I need help from a medium, and it turns out the closest mediums include a couple I intended to kill, a woman I tried killing, and a man I harassed, and even the youngest medium no doubt has issues with me, since I tried taking his father's job. Yeah, karma is real." Clay gave a bitter laugh and leaned back on the sofa.

"What's this favor? You think we can help lessen your ultimate punishment in some way?" Chris asked.

Clay shook his head. "I don't care about me. It's funny, when you move to the other side, things feel different. I can't seem to remember why it was so important to become police chief. Why was power so important to me? The entire concept now feels empty somehow. It has no value."

"You can't figure it out?" Heather asked.

"In an abstract way, I suppose." Clay considered how better to answer Heather's question a moment before saying, "It's like seeing a picture of a house you really want, and you end up buying it sight unseen, and spend more than you can afford. But when you actually see the house, in person, it's not as wonderful as you thought, and you realize you paid far too much for it."

"So when you died, you were able to see how much you had been willing to pay for your job as police chief?" Heather asked.

Clay shrugged. "I suppose. I was willing to pay far too much. In doing so, I undervalued my marriage and didn't see what I was doing to my sons."

"When did you realize this?" Heather asked.

"I don't know, not exactly." Clay then told them about his death and then his cremation and how he had witnessed another soul move on, experiencing euphoria, while he remained on this plane.

"Coming to those realizations will probably help you when it comes to your penance—or punishment—however it works. Not sure what you need from us," Chris said.

"I need help reaching my boys. I don't want them to make the type of choices I did and end up like me. As their father, it was my job to teach them how to live their lives. I failed miserably as a father."

Heather crossed her arms over her chest and studied Clay. "I wonder why you're still here. Why hasn't someone come and gotten you and taken you over to the other side?"

"Is that how it usually works?" Clay asked.

Heather shrugged. "I remember one time, Danielle telling me about two miserable souls getting dragged off rather unceremoniously in the afterlife."

Chris looked at Heather. "Who was that?"

"Remember the one who jumped in the body of the guy married to Lily's cousin? When Lily and Ian got married," Heather reminded him.

"Jumped in the body?" Clay frowned.

Heather turned to Clay. "Don't even go there. You think it's bad now?" Heather shivered at the thought.

"Go where?" Clay muttered.

"Don't forget what Walt and Danielle told us about Stoddard Gusarov. He hung around Marlow House for a while, being annoying," Chris reminded her.

Heather nodded. "True. And then don't forget about his wife. Or even Walt's first wife. Both were basically responsible for their husbands' deaths, and both stuck around for a while. They weren't allowed to move on." She looked at Clay. "Maybe that's what's happening with you."

Clay frowned in confusion. "I have no idea what either of you are talking about."

"I think what Heather and I are getting to—each soul has its own journey. And the Universe obviously handles each soul on a case-by-case basis. It's possible the reason no one has come to get you, or you can't move on by yourself, is that the Universe wants you to stick around until you do something."

"That something could be my sons," Clay suggested.

"That would be my guess, because you obviously have a strong feeling about it," Chris said.

Heather grinned at Chris. "Look at you, being all Eva-like."

Chris frowned at Heather. "What do you mean?"

"That just sounds like something Eva would say."

"Then perhaps I'm right," Chris countered.

They both looked at Clay. "What exactly did you think Heather could do for you?" Chris asked.

"I would like her to talk to my boys. Tell them she has a message from their father."

Heather let out a snort. "Seriously?"

"Yes. You can do that. I'll tell you something that only they'll know. A secret I shared with only them."

Chris shook his head. "I agree with Heather. That's a bad idea."

"She didn't say it was a bad idea," Clay argued.

Chris pointed to Heather. "Look at her expression. That's her *don't be such a dumbass* face."

Heather flashed Chris a smile. "You really know me well."

Chris shrugged. "You've given me that look enough."

Heather turned to Clay. "I can't go up to your boys and start telling them weird stuff about their dad. If your wife catches me, she'll probably have me arrested."

"She has a point. Would you want someone who looks like Heather to walk up to your sons and try to get all friendly?" Chris asked.

THE GHOST WHO SOUGHT REDEMPTION

Heather flashed Chris a glare. "Oh, shut up. I'm a freaking delight. Kids love me."

"Then what am I supposed to do?" Clay asked.

"Is this basically all you wanted from Heather? To convince your sons not to take your path? To let them know you regret the choices you made and not to make the same mistakes?"

Clay nodded. "Yes."

The sound of a door slamming shut came from the kitchen. Clay vanished for a moment and then returned. He looked at Chris. "You'd better hide; Brian is here."

Chris frowned at Clay, and Heather chuckled. She remained sitting in the recliner. The next moment, Brian walked into the living room. He stopped walking when he saw Chris. He looked from Chris to Heather and asked, "Clay?"

"Can Brian see me too? Is Brian a medium? They didn't tell me Brian was a medium."

"Clay is standing right there." Heather pointed to the ghost Brian couldn't see. "Chris and I found out what he wants."

"So he can't see me?" Clay asked.

Brian glanced from Chris to Heather. "Do you need me to leave so you can finish?"

"No." Chris turned his attention to Clay. "We'll discuss your request with the other mediums and see if anyone has any ideas about how best to help you."

"You're going to help him?" Brian grumbled. "I thought you were going to get him to move on."

"Trust us, Brian," Heather said. "You'll understand when we explain."

"Clay, in the meantime, we'd like you to go. Don't pop in on Heather again when she's alone. It's creepy. When we have something to tell you, we'll leave you a sign," Chris said.

"Sign? What kind of sign?" Clay asked.

Heather frowned at Chris. "Yeah, what kind of sign?"

"I don't know." Chris shrugged. He considered the question a moment and then said, "She can hang something on the front door. That would work."

"I know; I have a wreath. If I hang it on the front door, it means we have something to tell you," Heather said. "And unless a wreath is hanging on my front door, don't come in my house."

ELEVEN

When his mother announced she wanted to take him out to dinner to celebrate the new baby, Ian wasn't opposed to going to Pearl Cove, because it was still late afternoon, before the Saturday dinner rush, so he wasn't concerned about dining with a toddler. But when Kelly called the restaurant, she discovered they couldn't get in until five thirty because they had been hit with a large party.

Kelly made the reservation, and June insisted they all come over to her house for cocktails and appetizers before dinner. Reluctantly, Ian agreed, and it wasn't long after they arrived that Connor fell asleep on the floor of the living room.

"You need to wake up Connor and get him ready. We're going to be leaving in about fifteen minutes," June told Ian.

Ian glanced across the living room to his sleeping son. "I should just carry him out to my car and take him back to Marlow House."

"Don't be ridiculous. We have a reservation, plus you're the guest of honor for this dinner. You and Connor have to eat, anyway," June argued.

WESLEY FOUND the pair sitting in Adrian's Mustang in Bonnie's driveway. At first, he wasn't sure if they were coming or going, but when he heard Adrian start up the engine, he figured they were going somewhere. He jumped into the back seat of the Mustang as Adrian drove out of the driveway into the street.

"Come on, tell me where we're going." To his ears—if Wesley still had ears—Bonnie's question sounded flirty and annoyingly cloying.

"It's a surprise," Adrian told her. "I hope you're hungry."

Wesley peered over the back of the seat, looking to see how his wife—or more accurately, widow—was dressed. He was surprised to find her wearing what looked like a summer dress. He couldn't remember the last time he saw Bonnie wearing anything but polyester pants with elastic waistbands (no zipper), paired with unflattering blouses. She must have had a dozen pair of those pants in various colors.

It made him wonder what the occasion was and where Adrian was taking her for dinner. A few minutes later, they pulled up to Pearl Cove and parked. Bonnie squealed in delight when she realized where they had stopped. Wesley knew it was Bonnie's favorite restaurant, but one they rarely frequented.

"Wesley never wanted to come here," Bonnie said as she unhooked her seatbelt.

"The prices are too damn high," Wesley grumbled from the back seat.

"I don't know why; they have great food." Adrian unhooked his seatbelt.

"He always complained about the price."

Adrian opened his car door. "For a restaurant with this ocean view, the price is reasonable."

"Wesley used to say if I wanted an ocean view, I should pack a picnic, and we could eat at the beach."

Adrian let out a snort and, before stepping out of the car, said, "That sounds like Wesley."

"I thought picnics on the beach were supposed to be romantic," Wesley muttered.

He trailed along behind Adrian and Bonnie as they made their way to the restaurant's front entrance. Once inside, the hostess put their name on the waiting list, and they went on to the bar. Still following the pair, Wesley glanced around at the patrons. He wondered if any of them could see him. Were there any mediums in the restaurant?

Wesley stopped for a moment, looking around at the patrons while he considered his question. On impulse, he let out a scream and started jumping up and down, waving his arms. Not a single person flinched or looked at him. With a sigh, Wesley resumed his composure and continued on his way, following Bonnie and Adrian. But once they reached the bar, Wesley grew restless and decided to check out the dining room.

A few moments later, Wesley stepped from the lounge area to the dining room. It ran along a west-facing wall of windows overlooking the ocean. He noticed the hostess leading a party of six to a large table with a highchair. He recognized the youngest member of the group. It was the child from Marlow House. Wesley watched as the group stopped by the large table, and a man placed the boy in the highchair.

JUNE SAT across the table from her son, while her grandson sat next to both of them at the end of the table. The hostess had placed a piece of paper and three crayons on the highchair tray to amuse Connor. Yet Connor wasn't interested in coloring; instead he smiled at something to his right.

Connor kept looking toward the center of the dining room while giggling. June watched her grandson and followed his line of vision, trying to figure out what had captured his attention. Ian, who was talking to his sister, hadn't noticed his son's behavior. It wasn't until the server returned to the table to take their order and left the table that his mother said, "Connor, what are you looking at?"

Ian heard his mother's question. He turned toward Connor in time to catch his son say, "Clown!"

"There's no clown," June told her grandson.

Everyone at the table turned to look at Connor.

"Bubble! See!" Connor said, still pointing to his right.

Kelly leaned forward to get a better view of her nephew. "What is Connor doing? Who is he talking to?"

"It looks like he's having a conversation with his imaginary friend. They're discussing clowns and bubbles," John said with a chuckle.

"Just like his mom," Kelly muttered under her breath.

June leaned toward Connor and grabbed hold of his wrist, pulling him in her direction, away from whatever had caught his attention.

"No!" Connor tried jerking his arm away from his grandmother, but she held tight, pulling him toward her.

Connor's face puckered up, as if he might cry.

"Mom, let go of Connor," Ian snapped.

Reluctantly, June released hold of her grandson. She looked at Ian. "I just wanted to show him how to color."

"Mom, he knows how to color."

Connor hugged his wrist to his chest, away from his grandmother's grasp, and turned to his right. His frown turned into a smile, and he giggled.

"What is he doing?" June reached for Connor again, but Ian quickly pushed her hand away.

"Leave him alone. He's amusing himself. Just leave him be. He's not hurting anything."

DANIELLE AND WALT sat in the living room at Marlow House, trying to decide what they wanted to watch on television. They had put the twins down to sleep minutes earlier, and Danielle had turned on the nearby baby monitor.

Walt dominated the television remote, flipping from station to station. Danielle watched her husband and shook her head while letting out a little sigh.

Turning to Danielle, Walt frowned. "What is it?"

"It's funny, four years ago you had never used a remote. And there you are, acting like you grew up with television. What's with guys and channel surfing? It must be in the male chromosome."

The next moment, they heard the front door open and shut. Sadie perked up, and Walt reminded her not to bark. She ran out from the living room to the entry hall, and a moment later Ian walked into the living room, carrying a sleeping Connor. Trailing behind him was not just Sadie, but the ghost they had seen earlier.

Once in the living room, Ian stopped and stood in front of the television, facing Walt and Danielle. Walt turned off the TV and tossed the remote on the end table while both he and Danielle looked from Ian to the man behind him.

"Okay, tell me. Is there a ghost behind me?" Ian asked. He sounded tired.

"How did you know?" Danielle asked.

"It's not Marie, is it?" Ian asked.

Walt and Danielle shook their heads and then looked at the ghost, who flashed them a sheepish smile and gave them a little wave.

"Is this the same ghost that was in Connor's room?" Ian asked.

"Yes," Walt said. "How did you know?"

"Well, my first clue was the fact something kept Connor entertained throughout dinner. And Connor kept saying something about a clown. Does he look like a clown?"

"I don't look like a clown, and I was trying to help," Wesley said. "So you could enjoy your dinner."

"No, he doesn't look like a clown. But you're right, Connor was talking about a clown after this ghost first visited him," Walt said.

"And then on the way home, the way Connor kept giggling and waving to the empty seat next to his car seat, I figured the ghost was coming home with us."

"I thought it might be a good time to talk to the Marlows," Wesley explained.

"I'm going to take Connor upstairs and put him to bed. Would you please tell the ghost to stay down here and stay out of my son's room tonight?"

"I can hear you. I'm not deaf," Wesley grumbled.

"Okay, Ian. You've had a long day," Danielle said. "He'll stay downstairs."

"I will?" Wesley frowned.

"You will if you want something from the mediums," Walt snapped.

"I'm not even going to ask what that was about," Ian muttered before turning back to the doorway leading to the entrance hall.

Wesley watched them leave. He turned back to Walt and Danielle. "That's a cute kid. He liked when I played charades with him in the restaurant."

Walt pointed to an empty seat. With a shrug, Wesley walked to the seat and sat down.

"My name is Wesley Sadler…"

"You were an insurance agent. In January, you died from a heart attack when you were in California on a business trip. You left behind a widow and no kids," Danielle finished for him.

Wesley arched his brows at Danielle. "How do you know about that?"

"Asked around."

"Do you know about my wife and brother?" Wesley asked.

"You mean the fact they're seeing each other and plan to get married?"

"Yeah." Wesley leaned back in the seat, crossing his arms over his chest.

"You're obviously upset about your brother and your wife," Danielle said.

"Her name is Bonnie. Technically, she's my widow."

"If it makes you feel any better, Carla told us your wife was devastated over your death. She grieved for months," Walt said.

"You mean three months," Wesley grumbled.

Walt shrugged. "It's still months, plural, and Carla did say she grieved hard right after you died."

"Ahh, Carla. She looks like a wild one. Always doing her hair all crazy. Hot pink one week, bright green the next. I bet she never wore pull-up polyester slacks."

Danielle frowned. "Pull-up polyester slacks?"

"So what do you want from us?" Walt asked.

"You need to stop Bonnie from marrying my brother."

"Don't you want your widow to be happy?" Danielle asked. "It's time for you to move on. You should be glad your wife found happiness again."

"I can't move on. Especially if Bonnie marries Adrian."

"I assume Adrian is your brother?" Walt asked.

"Yes."

"Why can't you move on if Adrian marries Bonnie?" Danielle asked.

"Because after Adrian marries Bonnie, he intends to kill her."

TWELVE

"Why do you think your brother plans to murder her?" Walt asked.

"It's only if she marries him. There would be no reason to otherwise. You need to help me break up their engagement." Wesley looked at Danielle. "I understand you're a good cook. Bonnie likes to cook, and she takes a class at the community center. You could join the class. Make friends with her. Start hanging out with her. Perhaps you could introduce her to some single guys. Convince her Adrian isn't for her. She also belongs to a book club at the library. Do you like to read?"

"Are you sure you aren't just jealous and don't want to see her happy?" Danielle asked.

"No. He'll kill her if they get married. And we must hurry. Adrian told her he doesn't want to wait. He wants to get married right away. He almost has her talked into it."

"None of that explains why you're convinced Adrian plans to kill her. What is his motive?" Walt asked.

"The oldest motive in the world. Money." Wesley slumped back in the chair. "My wife—widow—is a very rich woman."

"That's interesting. When Carla told us about you, she never mentioned your wife was wealthy. Carla rarely leaves out those details," Walt said.

"Carla wouldn't know. About nine months before my death, my wife inherited the estate of her aunt Cordelia. Cordelia lives in Frederickport, but she was a bit of a recluse. She didn't really have any friends. The estate was finally settled a couple of weeks before Christmas, which was about a month before my last trip to California. And then there was the life insurance."

"What life insurance?" Danielle asked.

"I sold insurance. I had a million-dollar policy on myself, and one on Bonnie. So when I died, she was the beneficiary of my life insurance."

"How much did she inherit from her aunt?" Walt asked.

"It was a couple of million, plus the property. She hasn't sold the house yet."

"None of that means your brother wants Bonnie for her money," Danielle said.

"Bonnie's not his type. But more than that, ever since he wormed his way into her life, he's been bringing up the will. He likes to remind her that if she was to die in an accident, her cousin would inherit everything. When we first had our wills drawn, Bonnie left everything to me. But if I predeceased her, she wanted everything to go to Rylee, who is not only her cousin, but her only remaining relative. But since we had that will drawn, Bonnie and Rylee had a falling-out, and Adrian is right about one thing, Bonnie would no longer want Rylee to inherit anything. I'm actually a little surprised Bonnie hasn't changed her will already."

"What was their falling-out about?" Danielle asked.

Wesley shrugged. "Bonnie wouldn't tell me."

"That is all very interesting, but I still don't understand why you're convinced Adrian has nefarious intentions," Walt said.

Wesley stood up. "Not sure what else I can say. Trust me, in my gut Adrian isn't talking to Bonnie about her will because he knows she'd hate Rylee to get anything. He wants to make sure he's the beneficiary. Of course, if she doesn't update her will, and Adrian marries her, I imagine he'll inherit her estate anyway because they'll be married then. I'm not a lawyer, so I could be wrong. But I can't move on until I fix this."

Wesley disappeared.

Danielle glanced around. "Did he leave?"

Walt shrugged. "It appears that way."

Ian walked into the living room and then paused. He glanced around. "Is he still here?"

"He just left," Walt explained.

Ian walked over to the sofa where Wesley had been sitting moments earlier and sat down. "Connor is asleep. I took a shower after I put him down and then looked in on him. He was out cold."

"Good. Are you going back over to the hospital?" Danielle asked.

"I wanted to, but Lily wants me to stay here with Connor." Ian leaned back on the sofa, crossing one leg over the opposing knee. "Now, what's the story on your new ghost?"

"He wants us to prevent a murder," Danielle began before recounting what had been said between her, Walt, and Wesley.

"Are you going to do anything?" Ian asked.

"I'm not sure what we can do," Danielle said. "I'm not even convinced Wesley's feelings have any basis in fact. He could just be angry his wife is moving on with his brother. And he certainly didn't talk about his wife as if she was his great love."

"Remember what Carla said about him," Walt reminded him.

"What did Carla say?" Ian asked.

"Carla told us that when he used to come into the diner, he'd hit on her."

"What I don't understand. If you're married and want to fool around, why would you hit on someone like Carla, who's not known for her discretion?" Ian asked.

"Oh, who would you hit on?" Danielle teased.

Ian's eyes widened dramatically. He pointed to his own chest and asked, "Me?"

Danielle nodded; her mouth turned into a mischievous grin.

"No one, of course."

"Ahh, so sweet," Danielle cooed.

Ian shrugged. "I just mean there is no one I could hit on discreetly. I would never know if Marie, Eva, or some other ghost was hanging around, and they would inevitably snitch to you, and you'd tell Lily."

With a laugh, Danielle picked up a throw pillow and tossed it across the room, hitting Ian.

CHRIS WANTED TO GO HOME, and Heather needed to pick up Bella from Chris's house. Because they had been using Heather's car that evening, she drove Chris home while Brian stayed behind and used her shower, since he hadn't gone home after work.

As they drove by Marlow House, Heather noticed the lights on downstairs. "It looks like they're still up."

"I'm not really tired. Wonder how much longer they're going to be up. I might go over there and tell them about Clay's visit."

"I thought that's why you wanted to go home; you were tired?"

"I need to go home and take Hunny out."

Heather pulled her car in front of Chris's house and parked. Hands still on the steering wheel, she turned to look at Chris, who was unbuckling his seatbelt.

"And I didn't want to be a third wheel all night," Chris added.

"I want to talk to Walt and Danielle, too, about Clay."

"So what do you want to do?" Chris asked.

Heather grabbed her cellphone from the dashboard and sent a text message to Danielle. She and Chris sat quietly for a few minutes while Heather stared at her phone's screen.

Still staring at the phone, Heather suddenly smiled and looked up at Chris. "They said to come on over. You take Hunny out while I go grab Bella. We can drop her off when we pick up Brian and then go to Marlow House."

BY THE TIME CHRIS, Heather, and Brian arrived at Marlow House, Danielle was upstairs, nursing the twins. When she came back downstairs, she found Walt had already filled Heather, Chris, and Brian in on their encounter with Wesley.

"Why do you think this Wesley dude is so sure his widow is in danger?" Heather asked Danielle when she walked into the living room.

"Oh, they already told you about him." Danielle walked to an empty chair. "At first I wondered if he just doesn't want her to get remarried." She sat down.

"I suspect there's more to it than what he's telling you," Chris suggested. "This Wesley is leaving part of the story out."

Walt looked at Chris and smiled. "I was wondering that myself."

"If there is, then he'd better tell us, or I don't see how we can help him." Danielle looked at Heather. "Did you guys already discuss Clay's visit?"

Heather sat up a little straighter on the sofa. Chris sat to her right, and Brian to her left. "No, we wanted to wait until you got down here. No reason to repeat everything twice." Heather then recounted their conversation with Clay.

When she was done, Ian gave a dry chuckle before saying, "It seems the spirits have some high expectations. The mediums need to make sure the Bowman twins stay on the right side of the law, and that Mrs. Sadler doesn't become the new Mrs. Sadler."

"At least Clay's motive seems clearer cut," Danielle said. "I imagine it can be quite a jolt to pass over and come to the realization you wasted your entire life and, in doing so, may have destroyed the one positive thing you created."

AFTER LEAVING MARLOW HOUSE, Clay had taken a walk on the beach before ending up in the tunnel under Beach Drive, between Marlow House and what had been the Crawfords' home. Standing in the dark tunnel, he remembered his first time entering

THE GHOST WHO SOUGHT REDEMPTION

the passageway, after following his sons inside. At the time, he had been so proud of the boys; they were both smart and cunning.

Yet now, he realized his folly, and he worried Heather and Chris wouldn't help him. They'd both told him to stay away from Heather and wait for them to reach out to him. Yet he knew his wife would be leaving Frederickport in a few weeks, and if he failed to reach his sons before that time, he would need to follow them and find another medium to help. He stayed in the tunnel for about twenty minutes before traveling back to the street level.

He stood just outside Marlow House, looking through the living room window. Gathered there were the mediums of Beach Drive. He wondered, were they discussing his request? But then he remembered, they weren't the only mediums in Frederickport. From what the ghosts in the cemetery said, there was another medium, one closer to his sons' age.

Clay wasn't sure how he managed it, but moments later, he stood in front of Chief MacDonald's house. There were lights on inside. Silently, Clay moved from the street to the house and into the living room. There were no lights on in the living room, but he saw light coming from the hallway. He moved to the light and found himself in the kitchen. MacDonald stood at the sink, washing dishes. The chief, like his wife, had two boys to raise on his own.

Clay left the kitchen and moved down the hallway to the first open doorway. There he found a teenage boy sitting on the bed, playing a video game, the monitor hanging on a wall across from the bed. Clay walked between the boy and monitor, and the boy continued playing. He was obviously not a medium.

Again in the hallway, Clay moved to another open doorway. He looked into the room and saw a younger boy standing in the room, his back to him. Clay moved into the room. The boy turned around and then stopped abruptly upon seeing him, his eyes wide.

"You're Clay Bowman," the boy announced.

Surprised at both the boy's words and calm, he asked, "You know who I am?"

"Yeah. And I know you're dead. How come you're sticking

around?" The boy backed up slightly and plopped down on his bed, sitting on the edge of the mattress facing Clay.

"You're not afraid of me?"

The boy's grin widened. "If you were alive, sure. I'd be afraid. But you're dead."

"How can you be so sure?" Clay asked.

The boy pointed to Clay's right foot. "Because you're standing on the Lego castle I built, and it's coming through your foot."

THIRTEEN

Clay glanced down at his feet. He hadn't noticed the Lego castle when first entering the bedroom; he had been focused on the room's occupant.

Clay studied the young boy. He remembered hearing he was a little older than his sons. Ten, perhaps? He could be eleven, considering his height. The unruly mop of brown hair atop the boy's head could use some trimming in the front, and his long eyelashes belonged on a girl.

Stepping over the Lego castle, Clay asked, "So you really aren't afraid of me? What's your name?"

"Evan. And no, I'm not afraid of you. There is really no reason to be. Eva says I'm an innocent, and spirits can't hurt innocents."

"Who is Eva?"

Evan grinned. "Eva Thorndike. You haven't met her yet?"

"Are you talking about Eva Thorndike, the silent screen star? Her portrait is at the local museum?"

Evan nodded. "Yeah. That's Eva. So, you've met her?"

Clay shook his head. "No. So you're telling me Eva Thorndike is a ghost? A ghost in Frederickport?"

"Yeah. Eva knows a lot of stuff. How things work."

"So what do you mean when you said you're an innocent?"

"I guess it means I'm not a bad person." Evan shrugged.

"So does that mean, if you were a bad person, I could hurt you?"

"Can you move stuff?"

Clay frowned. "What do you mean, move stuff?"

Evan pointed to the castle on the floor. "Can you pick up the castle?"

Clay turned to the castle, leaned over, and tried picking it up. It went through his hands as it had his feet.

"I doubt you could hurt a bad person, either."

"Are you saying some ghosts can move things?"

Evan studied Clay for a moment, cocking his head for a bit. Finally, he said, "I heard about when you were arrested at Marlow House. Heather wrapped you up with duct tape. But did you think she did it by herself?"

"What are you saying?"

"Marie helped her. Marie can move things. Now Eva, she can do stuff, like make it snow, but she can't move things."

"Who is Marie?"

"Marie's another ghost. She hangs around with Eva and is over at Marlow House a lot. You don't want to mess with Marie. She's kinda tough."

"Can this Marie, the one who can move stuff, could she hurt an innocent?"

Evan shook his head. "Nope. Eva says the Universe wouldn't allow it. It's against the rules."

"Interesting."

"So what are you doing sticking around? Most ghosts usually move on. Is it because you're afraid?"

"What should I be afraid of?"

"I heard you killed someone. And you tried to hurt Heather. The Universe doesn't like that. And, well, from what Eva tells me, eventually you gotta move on and deal with your punishment."

"To be honest, I'm not sticking around because I'm afraid for myself. I'm afraid for my sons."

IN THE NEXT BEDROOM, Eddy Junior removed his headphones and tossed them on the mattress. He glanced at the time on his watch. If it weren't summer vacation, his dad would come in about now, telling him to turn in for the night.

Eddy got off the bed and started for the door on the way to the bathroom. When in the hallway, he passed his brother's bedroom, its door open. He stopped when he heard Evan's voice. He looked into the room and saw his younger brother chattering away.

"Who are you talking to, you weirdo?" Eddy called out.

Evan stopped talking and looked at the open doorway. He climbed off the bed and walked toward his brother. When he reached the doorway, he said, "None of your business," before shutting the door.

Eddy stood alone in the hallway, looking at his brother's now closed door. He shook his head in disgust and continued to the bathroom. When he finished in the bathroom, he didn't go back to his room. Instead, he left to find his father.

Chief MacDonald was no longer washing dishes in the kitchen, but now sat in the living room, watching television. When Eddy walked into the room, he said, "Dad, can I talk to you? It's important."

MacDonald looked up at his eldest son. He reached over to the remote, muted the television, and looked back at his son. "What's up?"

"I'm worried about Evan. That kid keeps getting weirder and weirder."

"What did he do?"

Eddy walked all the way into the living room and sat on a chair facing his father's recliner while saying, "I was going to the bathroom and walked by his room. The kid is sitting there on his bed, having this long conversation with himself. Just talking and talking. No one was there but him. Just talking away."

"He might have been on the phone," MacDonald suggested.

Eddy shook his head. "He wasn't on the phone. He was talking to himself. You should seriously get that kid some help. I've been worried about him for a while now."

MacDonald took a deep breath, tossed the remote to the side table, and leaned back in the recliner. He studied his eldest son, and he had to admit the concern on Eddy's face looked sincere.

"What do you mean, you've been worried about him?"

Eddy shrugged. "I don't want to freak you, but this isn't the first time I've caught him talking to himself. He does it a lot. It's weird. Not normal."

"Have you discussed this with anyone else? A friend, your grandparents, Aunt Sissy?"

"Oh, no! I've said nothing to anyone. You're the first one I mentioned it to, except for Evan. When I've caught him doing it, I let him know it's weird. I figured that would stop him from doing it, but it seems he does it more and more these days."

MacDonald stood up. "Good. Do me a favor, don't mention this to anyone. I'll deal with it. Let's keep this in the family. I'll go talk to Evan now."

MACDONALD STOOD in the hallway outside Evan's room. He leaned toward the closed door and pressed his ear against it. He heard Evan's voice. Eddy was right. Evan was chattering away, talking to someone. Without knocking, MacDonald opened the door and stepped inside the room. Evan stopped talking and looked at his father.

MacDonald closed the door behind him. "Is Marie or Eva here with you? Your brother heard you talking."

"No." Evan shook his head. "It's Clay Bowman."

MacDonald stood up straighter. "Excuse me? Who?"

"You know the guy who was police chief when you had your operation?"

MacDonald looked around the room. "Are you saying he is here right now?"

Evan nodded and pointed to where the ghost stood. MacDonald looked that way, yet he couldn't see Clay.

"Why is the ghost of Clay Bowman in my son's room?"

"He wants my help, Dad."

"Does he now? Help doing what? Robbing the bank? Kidnapping someone new?"

"No. He's worried about his sons. He's afraid they're going to turn out like him."

"He should be worried." MacDonald glanced around the room. "Clay, I would appreciate it if you would leave my son alone. Go haunt someone your own age."

"Dad, he's dead and a ghost. I'm supposed to help him."

MacDonald turned to his son. "What are you talking about?"

"Eva says when someone has a gift like mine, it's our job to help spirits find their way to the light. It's why we have the gift."

"You think he's going to the light?" MacDonald asked. "With what he's done?"

Evan shrugged. "Well, I still have to help him move on. And he says he can't do that until he makes sure his sons know he was wrong. He said he wants them to make better choices."

MacDonald frowned at his son. "And he thinks you can convince them of that?"

Evan glanced over to where Clay had been standing moments ago. "He's gone, Dad. He just left."

MacDonald let out a sigh. He walked to Evan's bed and together the two sat on the side of the mattress.

"I think we need to talk to Eva about all this. I don't feel comfortable with you being alone with a murderer's ghost." MacDonald chuckled and shook his head.

"What's so funny, Dad?"

"What I just said. It sounded ridiculous."

"I know, because a ghost can't hurt me."

MacDonald chuckled again and wrapped his arm around Evan's shoulders. "That's not what I meant. It's not about if a ghost can hurt you or not, it's the fact we're actually having a conversation about you spending time with a ghost."

"Oh."

"Which reminds me, Eddy came to me tonight. He's worried about you."

"Yeah, he caught me talking to Clay. I'm sorry, I should have been more careful. I should have shut my door right away."

"You know, we've tried to keep all this from Eddy, figuring it was a little too much for him to deal with. But I'm wondering if we're wrong. After all, you're dealing with it, and you're younger than your brother."

"What do you mean?"

"I think it's about time we sit down and tell Eddy everything. About you being a medium. About Eva and Marie."

"About Walt?"

MacDonald shrugged. "I'm not sure. We should talk to Walt and Danielle before we say anything. Figure out how to handle it. How much to tell him? And I suppose we'll need to convince Eddy; otherwise he might call his aunt Sissy and get her to help commit us both."

Evan giggled.

"So what do you think? How do you feel about your brother knowing about your gift? We don't have to do it; I think it should be your call. But if we don't tell him what's been going on, you're going to have to be more careful, and I'll need Danielle to help me come up with some story to give Eddy that might convince him his little brother isn't crazy."

Evan considered his father's words for a few minutes. Finally, he said, "I think I would like to tell him. Sometimes I would like someone to talk to about it, and not an adult. I would like that someone to be my brother. So yeah, I want to tell him. But how do we do it?"

"I suspect this is a question for the other mediums. Let's see what they say."

"What about Clay? Can I help him?"

MacDonald groaned. "Let me think about Clay. We should also talk to the mediums about that too. I'll call them in the morning. It's too late right now."

"Thanks, Dad." Evan turned to his father, wrapped his arms around him, and gave him a hug. "I love you."

MacDonald returned the hug. "I love you too, Evan."

FOURTEEN

Danielle and Walt sat at the kitchen table, sipping their coffee while watching the twins, who each sat in a swing, their young bodies rocking back and forth as tiny stocking-clad feet kicked, and little hands grabbed handfuls of air. The pair made joyful cooing and gurgling sounds.

"I love how they smile now, and not just from gas." Danielle set her mug on the table, leaving her hand resting on the tabletop.

"They seem happy. They love those swings." Never taking his eyes off the babies, Walt reached over to Danielle, placing one hand over hers. He gently squeezed.

"Good morning." Ian walked into the kitchen, carrying Connor, Sadie trailing behind them.

Both Walt and Danielle looked up and said, "Good morning."

"You going to the hospital after breakfast?" Danielle watched Ian put his son into the highchair.

"Yes. I'm taking Connor over to see his mom, and then my mother is going to pick Connor up at the hospital while I stay with Lily and Emily Ann." Ian walked over to the pantry to grab a box of cereal while Connor playfully slapped the highchair's tray while kicking his feet. "What are your plans?"

"The chief texted me this morning. It looks like we're having a meeting of the mediums," Danielle said.

"I assume about Clay and Wesley?"

"That's part of it," Danielle said. "Apparently, Clay showed up last night in Evan's bedroom."

"That must have scared the crap out of poor Evan." Ian returned to his son and poured dry cereal on the highchair tray and then filled a sippy cup with milk.

Walt chuckled. "No. Apparently, Clay asked Evan to help him, like he asked Heather. Evan wasn't afraid; he wanted to help. Not sure what he planned to do."

Just as Ian turned away from the highchair to return the milk carton to the refrigerator, Connor tossed a handful of cereal to the floor, which Sadie quickly gobbled up. Ian scolded Connor and then added more cereal to the tray. "So is everyone coming over here?" Ian returned the milk carton to the refrigerator.

"No. We're meeting at Pier Café," Danielle said.

"Is Joanne coming over to watch the twins?" Ian asked.

"Nope. This will be their introduction to the world." Danielle grinned. "We're taking them with us."

Ian walked to the counter and poured himself a cup of coffee before taking it to the kitchen table and sitting down with Walt and Danielle. "Well, I hope Carla's working this morning. Every time I go in there, she's asking when you're bringing the twins to the diner."

BEFORE IAN and Connor arrived at the hospital, Lily had taken a shower and changed into a clean pair of new pajamas Danielle had brought for her as a gift the day before. She had just finished feeding Emily Ann and had returned her to the bassinet when her son and husband walked into the hospital room.

Connor seemed less excited to see his new sister and just gave her a cursory look before climbing up in the bed with his mother and demanding a hug.

"I don't think he finds infants such a novelty anymore," Ian said with a laugh before leaning over his wife and giving her a kiss.

Lily smiled down at her son and playfully ruffled his red curls with one hand. She pointed to the end of the bed where she had set a pile of colorful baby rattlers and several musical stuffed animals that had been given to the baby since her birth. "Why don't you go check out some of your sister's new stuff?"

Connor abandoned his mother and scrambled to the end of the bed, ready to check out the loot.

Lily looked up at her husband and whispered, "I thought that might keep him occupied for a while so we can visit." She scooted over to the center of the mattress, making room for Ian to lie on the bed with her. Together, they leaned against the pile of pillows stacked at the head of the hospital bed, while Connor amused himself with the toys. After Lily told Ian how the baby was doing and what the doctor said about their possible release date, she asked Ian how things were going at Marlow House. He told her about the new ghosts.

"Is it always going to be like this for Marlow House?" Lily wondered aloud.

"I was thinking about that myself. But then I remember you and Rupert."

Lily looked at Ian. "How so?"

"Let's say we settled in California, near your parents. And let's pretend Danielle never told you about her gift. I have no doubt Rupert would still have met Connor—maybe sooner. And how would we have dealt with Connor's reactions? We wouldn't know what was going on. Rupert might not have been as willing to leave Connor's side as he was with you, and if that was the case, it's possible Connor would continue to see and hear something that none of us can. How would we deal with that?"

"We might worry Connor has mental problems," Lily muttered.

"Exactly. Yet, according to what I've read, kids tend to grow out of the imaginary-friend stage. Eva is always saying a spirit can't hurt an innocent. If true, then perhaps the reason children typically grow out of the imaginary-friend stage—if said friend is really a spirit—maybe that spirit knows it must move on for the child's sake. If that's the case, then the question boils down to, ignorance is bliss."

"Not following you, Ian."

"Some say ignorance is bliss. Would you rather live in ignorance? Would that be more blissful? Or would you rather our medium friends tell us what our children are really seeing?"

"Plus, we'd miss all that great babysitting."

Ian laughed.

Lily glanced down at her son still amused with the baby toys, and then she looked over to the bassinet, where her daughter slept. "I don't imagine Marie is back. If she was, I'd expect her to come down here to see the baby, and since Connor said nothing about Grandma Marie, I have to assume she's not back. Unless she stopped by and left before you guys got here."

Ian shook his head. "No. They haven't seen Eva or Marie. But I imagine they wish they would return so they could join them at Pier Café."

"Oh, how was Connor at dinner last night? You didn't have Marie to keep him amused."

Ian groaned. "Perhaps not Marie, but one of those ghosts showed up at the restaurant and entertained our son while we dined." He then told her about Connor's behavior because of the ghost, and how his mother had reacted.

CHRIS ARRIVED at Pier Café first. He wanted to make sure they got the largest booth, which would provide privacy. Plus, it had a superb view of the ocean and pier, and enough space for the double stroller. While the diner often discouraged anyone from sitting down at that booth unless most of the party had already arrived, Carla wasn't about to tell Chris Glandon he couldn't have the booth. While she only called him Chris Johnson, she knew who he was. Carla might be known for lacking discretion, but there was one secret she proudly kept.

"There will be seven of us, plus the double stroller," Chris told Carla when she walked up to his booth with a pitcher of coffee.

"Double stroller? Walt and Danielle are bringing the twins?"

"Yes. Danielle says it's their public debut. Sort of like a debutante breakfast instead of a ball. And for infants. Yet I don't think the twins will be ordering any breakfast. At least not directly." Chris chuckled.

Carla filled up Chris's mug with coffee. "Who else is coming?"

"Heather and Brian, and the chief and Evan."

DANIELLE ENDED up questioning their wisdom of meeting at Pier Café, especially during Carla's shift. While she was flattered at how Carla gushed over the twins, telling Walt and Danielle they were the most adorable babies, and practically swooned when Jack gave her a bubbly smile, it didn't provide the privacy necessary to conduct their conversation.

Danielle was beginning to wonder if after breakfast they would need to go back to Marlow House so they could discuss their concerns without curious ears. Fortunately, Carla couldn't ignore her duties indefinitely, and by the time their food was delivered, Carla was forced to attend to her other customers.

Each of the mediums shared with the others what they had experienced during the last few weeks. After everyone shared what they knew, it was agreed they would first discuss Wesley.

"Chris thinks he's not telling us everything," Danielle told the others.

"Any thoughts on what that might be?" the chief asked.

"I don't have any idea," Chris admitted.

"If he wants us to help him, why wouldn't he tell us everything?" Heather asked Chris.

Chris shrugged. "Not sure. But it's a gut feeling I have."

"If Chris's gut feeling is right," the chief began, "then we need to take this seriously, like we would any tip someone called into the station. We need to find out if Adrian is planning to kill this woman." He looked at Brian.

Brian let out a sigh and gave the chief a nod. "Okay, I'll start looking in on this Adrian dude. See what I can find."

"And we'll try to get Wesley to open up on what he's not telling us," Danielle said.

Heather chuckled, and they all looked at her.

"What?" Brian asked.

"I rather like this teamwork between the mediums and our local police department. Preventing murders and setting delinquents on the right track." Heather grinned.

"Setting the delinquents on the right track might be the more challenging of the two," the chief said. "For one thing, it's my understanding Clay's widow and sons are leaving Frederickport in a couple of weeks."

Brian looked at Walt and Danielle. "What do you think is going to happen to Clay after that? Do you think he's stuck here as some sort of punishment, like Darlene was?"

"I hope not," Heather groaned. "While he doesn't seem to have that chip on his shoulder anymore, I'd rather he not hang around."

"I believe there's often a reason for things—especially those things the Universe—or God—or whatever you want to call it—decides to directly control, like when our spirits move on," Danielle said.

"If that's true, then you're saying the Universe let Stoddard stick around and haunt you. What would be the reason?" Heather asked. While Heather had moved to Frederickport after Stoddard haunted Danielle, she had heard about the incident.

Danielle looked at Heather and smiled. "Stoddard was annoying." She then looked at Brian. "Someone else was a major pain back then, too. But after we dealt with Stoddard, that seemed to be the catalyst in making that pain a little less annoying."

Brian chuckled and picked up his iced tea. Before taking a drink, he said, "You can't really blame me. I thought you were crazy and homicidal."

They all laughed and then turned the discussion back to the twins.

"I would talk to the boys, but they're not going to believe me," Evan said. "I've met them, and they're kind of mean."

"Like their father," Brian grumbled.

"I wish Marie and Eva were here. They might know how best to deal with all this," Danielle said.

"There is something else we need to discuss," the chief said.

"There's more?" Danielle asked.

"Evan and I want to tell Eddy about everything," the chief said.

Before anyone could respond, snow fell from the ceiling. Only the mediums could see it. They all looked up.

"Eva? Marie? Are you back?" Heather asked.

The next moment, the image of an elderly woman wearing a sundress and straw hat appeared floating above the booth.

"Did Lily have her baby?" Marie asked the mediums.

FIFTEEN

Carla had just finished taking an order when she glanced across the diner and noticed most of the people at Chris's table staring up at the ceiling. Wrinkling her nose, she tried to figure out what they were all looking at. Instead of putting her order in, she walked over to their booth, but once she got there, everyone stopped talking and just looked at her.

"Is everything okay?" Carla glanced up at the ceiling but saw nothing unusual. She looked back at Chris and the other members of his party.

"Everything's great." Danielle grinned at Carla before picking up a slice of bacon from her plate and taking a bite.

"You guys were all looking up at the ceiling. Was something wrong?"

"It was a spider," Heather blurted.

"Are you calling Eva and me a spider?" Marie snickered.

Carla glanced back up at the ceiling. "Where?"

"Oh, it crawled in one of the cracks," Heather explained. "For a minute there, we thought the little bugger was going to drop down and land on one of our plates. It was just hanging there, holding onto its web."

Evan giggled and quickly took a bite of his toast.

Carla looked back down at the table. "Well, that doesn't sound good."

"And it was a big one. It's surprising how those suckers can squeeze in between cracks."

"I guess I should tell someone. I don't want a spider falling into someone's food."

Chris flashed Heather a frown and then turned to Carla. "She's exaggerating. Heather insisted she saw a spider, but none of us did. I think it was a knothole in the wood. I've been telling her she needs glasses."

With a look of relief, Carla let out a sigh. "I hope you're right. The thought of a spider falling in someone's food or in my hair…" Carla shivered.

"Do you need to put that order in?" the chief pointed to the order pad in Carla's hand.

"Oh! I was just getting ready to do that." Carla flashed them an awkward smile, turned, and rushed away.

"How did you know she had an order to put in?" Danielle asked.

"When you were all looking up at what I assume were snowflakes or glitter—"

"Snowflakes," Evan blurted.

The chief gave his son a wink and said, "When the rest of you, except Brian, were distracted by snowflakes, I noticed Carla standing across the room, taking an order. She suddenly looked this way and started staring, and then she headed over here. When I glanced back at that table a few seconds ago, I noticed the people at the table glaring at us. They didn't look happy. I assume they wondered why their server hadn't put their order in yet."

"Poor Carla," Danielle said with a chuckle.

Chris looked at Heather. "That was kind of mean."

Heather shrugged. "I had to tell her something. I couldn't tell her we were looking at snowflakes and ghosts."

"You didn't need to be so specific," Chris said.

Heather shrugged. "People say lying is a sin. I figure if I'm going to sin, I should go all out."

Brian and Walt chuckled while Chris muttered something like, "See, this is what I have to put up with at work."

"Enough of all this talking about spiders! I was asking about Lily," Marie said.

"Yes, Marie, Lily went into labor Friday night. She had the baby early Saturday morning. Baby and mom are doing well, and according to a text I got from her, it looks like they'll both be coming home on Tuesday. Or more accurately, coming back to Marlow House," Danielle explained.

"How did you find out about the baby coming early?" Heather asked.

"I'm curious about that too," Chris said.

"I felt a shift in the universe at the same time Marie had this sudden urge to return to Frederickport," Eva explained. "We discussed it before we left, and we both wondered if it had anything to do with Lily and the baby. But now, now I'm not so sure." Eva, the onetime silent screen star and childhood friend of Walt during his first life, bore an uncanny resemblance to Charles Dana Gibson's drawing, the Gibson Girl. She stood next to Marie by the booth, her expression pensive as she absently tapped the side of her chin with her right index finger.

Marie turned to her fellow ghost. "What is it, dear?"

"There is something else. Something else going on." Eva looked at her friends gathered at the table. "Has something else happened since we've been gone that we need to know?"

"Now that you mention it," Walt began. Brian and the chief, the only ones at the table who could not see or hear the spirits, sat quietly and listened to one side of the conversation.

After they filled the ghosts in on what had been going on the past few days, Eva said, "I've met Wesley." No longer standing, Eva and Marie sat in imaginary chairs and floated gently next to the booth.

"I'm not exactly sure why, but he can't move on. Something

between him and the Universe, I suspect. Something he's been asked to correct," Eva explained.

Danielle arched her brows at Eva. "I don't ever remember it working quite like that."

Eva laughed, the sound light and airy. "You should know by now the rules of the universe adapt to the situation. We're all different; we have different goals."

"He claims this has nothing to do with something he's done in his lifetime. Yet from how you say it, then it sounds like it does, which makes me think I'm right, and there is something he's not telling us," Chris said.

Eva smiled at Chris and gave him a nod.

"How do you know all this?" Danielle asked. "This something he has with the Universe, is this your hunch, something he told you, or maybe something conveyed to you by the Universe?"

"Aw, Danielle, always seeking the answers—questioning the secrets of the Universe. I suspect what you need to do is ask yourself if it's your responsibility to help him, and if so, how can you find some way to prevent his brother from killing his widow, if what he is telling you is true?" Eva said.

"Eva, dear, why must you always be so cryptic? Just admit you don't know why Wesley hasn't moved on."

Eva shrugged. "I said it was a hunch."

Marie rolled her eyes. "Indirectly."

"I suppose we don't really have to help him. But we don't need him sticking around," Danielle said. "Connor seems to think the guy is hilarious and calls him clown. With Connor picking up more and more words these days, I don't think we need him chattering on about clowns with his grandmother. She might accept one imaginary friend, but two?"

"I didn't quite understand why Wesley believes his brother intends to murder his wife. While I agree, she's not really Adrian's type," Marie said.

"Did you know them when you were alive?" Heather asked. "Or are you just speaking from what you've learned since he's passed over and has been hanging around at the cemetery?"

THE GHOST WHO SOUGHT REDEMPTION

Marie shrugged. "I don't really hang around at the cemetery much myself. I will stop by from time to time." Marie glanced at Eva and back to Heather while saying, "And it wasn't until Angela moved on did Eva start visiting the cemetery. Like me, she doesn't spend a great deal of time there."

"I don't think either of us has interacted much with Wesley since he arrived," Eva said. "He seems a little intimidated by our presence."

"Since Pamela arrived, I've heard he tends to stick around her," Marie said.

"Pamela Beckett, she hasn't moved on yet? I thought she had," Danielle asked.

"No. She's still there. At least she was before we left last week," Marie said. "As for Wesley, he was my insurance man. Well, he was until he gave me some ridiculous advice that could have cost me had one of my properties burned down. I told him what I thought of his incompetence before I changed insurance companies. Which could be a reason he seems to avoid me when I'm at the cemetery."

"Did you ever meet his brother or wife?" Danielle asked.

"Both of them. His brother works at the auto part store. I find it hard to believe he's plotting to marry and then murder his sister-in-law. It's not like Wesley and his wife were rich. Like I said, he wasn't that good of an insurance man. I imagine he had a life insurance policy that Bonnie got after he died, but is that worth risking going to prison for?"

Police Chief MacDonald had quietly finished his breakfast while listening to one side of the conversation. He glanced over at his son, wondering if he was getting bored. But then he saw his son attentively hanging on to every word, making him a little jealous for not being able to hear the entire conversation.

"It's not just the insurance money," Danielle said. "Bonnie got an inheritance from her aunt. Which apparently was substantial."

Marie frowned at Danielle. "What aunt? She's Cordelia Westbrook's niece, but Cordelia is still alive."

"Actually, she passed away last year," Danielle said.

"Really?" Marie frowned.

"You didn't know?" Heather asked.

"It's not like we were friends. And considering her age, I imagine there wasn't a funeral. Most of her family was gone, and I suspect all of her friends," Marie said. "Cordelia was probably cremated. I imagine Rylee and Bonnie are sitting pretty right now. Rylee is her other niece."

"Wesley claims she left her entire estate to Bonnie. Apparently, there was some sort of lawsuit with Rylee contesting the will."

"I can imagine," Marie muttered. "If Cordelia left her estate to Bonnie, I would be surprised if Rylee didn't contest the will."

"And Bonnie won. She got everything," Danielle said.

"Now that, I can't imagine," Marie muttered.

"Interesting," Eva said. "So Wesley has told you what he wants, yet you aren't sure he's being transparent about everything. Now what about Clay? You say he wants to set his sons on the right path before he moves on. Does his desire come from sincere fatherly concern and love, or does he see it as a bargaining chip, paying down his penance?"

Heather shrugged. "He keeps saying he doesn't care about himself; he only cares about his sons."

Eva smiled. "Well, it really doesn't matter. The Universe sees what's in his heart, and if there is a way to nudge his sons down the right road, their souls will be the better for it regardless of how it may or may not benefit their father's soul."

"I would like to go see Lily and the new baby," Marie said. "Then afterwards, perhaps we can meet back at Marlow House and see how best to handle the requests of these new ghosts."

"There is something else we need to discuss." Walt spoke up. He looked at Evan. "Edward and Evan think it's time to tell Eddy about Evan's gift."

"It's just getting more and more difficult keeping something like this hidden from Eddy. And frankly, I no longer feel right about it. If something happened in the future, when both Eddy and Evan are adults, and Eddy learned about all this, I don't want him to look back on his childhood and think it was all a lie. That Evan and I had kept this monumental secret from him."

SIXTEEN

A rustling sound came from the bassinet. Ian got up from the bed, and when Lily started to get up too, he told her to stay put; he would check on the baby. Connor followed his father off the bed, and together they stood over the now squirming infant, her face slightly flushed.

Connor wrinkled his nose. "Stinky."

Ian chuckled. He glanced at Lily. "I think our little angel just filled her diaper. Where are they?"

"I can change it." Once again, Lily started to get out of bed.

"Don't be silly. Stay put. You need your rest. It's not like I don't know how to change a diaper." He glanced at Connor, who had not yet started potty training, and then looked to Lily, who pointed to the diapers sitting across the room on a shelf.

Just as Ian grabbed a diaper, a nurse walked into the room.

"How are we doing in here?" the nurse asked brightly.

"Doing wonderful," Lily called out from the bed. "Dad there is preparing to change his daughter's diaper for the first time."

The nurse looked at Ian. "First time?"

Ian motioned to his son. "I have almost two years of practice."

The nurse snatched the diaper from his hand. "In that case, I

BOBBI HOLMES

am going to give you a quick lesson on changing a girl, which is slightly different from changing a boy. Especially if she just did what I suspect." The nurse wrinkled her nose and then led Ian back to the bassinet after grabbing a package of wipes.

"My name is Rylee." The nurse introduced herself before starting with her diapering lesson. When Rylee finished her lesson, she washed her hands and checked on Lily.

Ian washed his hands after Rylee and walked to the bassinet and carefully picked up his daughter after re-swaddling her. Gingerly holding her in his arms, Ian walked to the rocker and sat down, his son by his side. "She's so small. Much smaller than Connor was." Several times, the toddler reached out to touch Emily Ann, but Ian gently pushed his hand away. "You always need to wash your hands first before touching the baby."

Finished with Lily, Rylee turned to the rocker. "Hey, Connor, why don't you let me help you wash your hands?"

Connor let Rylee lead him to the room's sink. After she washed and dried his small hands, Connor raced back to his father.

"Can I get you anything?" Rylee asked the parents.

Ian glanced at the wall clock. "I don't think so. But thanks for asking. My parents are supposed to be here any time now. They're picking up Connor, and he'll be spending the rest of the day with my mom. I plan to stay here with Lily and Emily Ann."

The hospital door opened, and in walked Ian's parents, June and John Bartley.

"There they are now," Ian said without getting up.

"Oh, let me see that baby!" June gushed just as she rushed over to Ian's side, but he quickly stopped her.

"Wash your hands first," Ian reminded her.

June rolled her eyes, and her husband chuckled. Together, the grandparents washed their hands while Rylee walked to the bassinet and started changing the sheets.

By the time the grandparents reached the rocker, Ian had stood up, still holding the baby. June first went to Lily, who was still in bed, sitting up and leaning against the pile of pillows against the headboard. June asked how her daughter-in-law was and then quickly sat on the rocker, waiting for Ian to place her granddaughter in her lap.

"When are your parents coming?" John asked.

Lily let out a sigh and leaned back on the pillows. "They were planning to come after the baby was born, but we thought that would be after we were back in our house. So I'm not sure what the plan is. We haven't had a chance to talk about it."

As they visited amongst themselves and Rylee quietly attended to her business, an unexpected visitor entered the room. He didn't come through an open doorway. He walked through a wall, and only one person in the hospital room could see him.

"Clown!" Connor called out as he toddled away from the rocker toward the ghost.

"Hey, little buddy. I thought you might be here. I was getting lonely. No one to talk to. Want to see another trick?"

All the adults in the room, except Rylee, who was preoccupied, turned to Connor. Ian and Lily exchanged quick glances and looked back at their son.

"He's doing it again," June said, looking up from the bundle in her arms.

"The boy has a good imagination," John suggested.

"What's with this new obsession with clowns?" June asked. "And invisible clowns, at that."

"I'm kind of curious; why do you keep calling me clown?" Wesley asked.

"Bubble clown. Bubble clown!" Connor reached out to Wesley.

"Bubble clown?" Lily muttered. She looked at Ian. "Do you think this has something to do with that clown bubble dispenser Heather gave Connor for his bath?"

"Oh, Heather, that explains it," June scoffed.

"What are you talking about, Mom?" Ian asked.

"Obviously, Heather taught Connor to do whatever he's doing. But it's embarrassing, especially in public, like at restaurants. I never understood why you let her babysit."

Rylee, who had been standing by an open closet, taking a quick inventory to see what she needed to replenish, heard June's words and was curious about what they were all talking about. She stepped out of the closet and turned around.

"Rylee?" Wesley called out. "You're working here now?"

Unable to see or hear Wesley, Rylee glanced around the room and then returned to the closet. Wesley followed her, and behind Wesley came Connor.

"I wondered if you were still in Frederickport," Wesley asked Rylee, yet only Connor heard his words. "Really sucks about what Bonnie did to you. I admit, I was looking forward to spending all that money with Bonnie. But hey, maybe getting that heart attack was my karma for not speaking up when you guys were fighting this out in court. But you know how stubborn Bonnie can be."

Connor stood behind Wesley, facing his back. Wesley stood behind Rylee, her back to him as she finished up in the closet. Connor reached out for the ghost and called out, "Clown trick!"

"What is that child doing?" June asked.

Rylee turned around, looking through Wesley at Connor. "What do you need, buddy?"

Ian walked to Connor and picked him up. The boy squirmed in his arms.

"Oh, he's not bothering me," Rylee told Ian.

The next moment, Connor reached out in another direction and called out, "Gamma Marie!"

THE TWINS SLEPT in the portable cribs, shoved against a wall in Marlow House's living room. Danielle had insisted the chief sit in the recliner so he could raise his leg because of his knee surgery. The others, Walt, Brian, Chris, and Heather, along with Danielle, sat in random seats in the room, with only Evan sitting on the fireplace hearth. The boy sat petting Sadie and Max, with the golden retriever sitting to Evan's right, and the black cat with the white-tipped ears curled up on Evan's lap.

Brian had just asked Heather if Marie and Eva had returned when Ian came walking unexpectedly through the living room door,

THE GHOST WHO SOUGHT REDEMPTION

carrying Connor. Once he entered the room, he placed the boy on the floor, feet first. The toddler scrambled toward Evan and the basket of toys sitting next to the fireplace.

"I thought Connor was staying with his grandmother today," Danielle asked.

"He was going to. But I think we had a visit from a ghost." Ian walked to the nearest empty seat and sat down.

"You mean Eva and Marie? Not sure how that changed things," Danielle asked.

"They were there too. But I'm pretty sure Connor's clown ghost showed up." Ian then recounted what had happened at the hospital. He ended by saying, "Lily didn't want Connor going home with my mother, not knowing if this new ghost would be following him there. And while I suspect Marie would have stayed with Connor to make sure he was okay, there was no way we were going to get Connor to stop chattering on about the clown and then reaching out to Marie. Like we keep saying, one imaginary friend isn't that unusual, but two?"

"I wonder why he keeps calling him clown," Heather asked.

Ian looked at Heather. "Lily wonders if it has something to do with that clown bubble dispenser you got Connor."

"You know, it might." Danielle spoke up. "Connor was playing with it in the bath the night Wesley showed up. Connor was rambling on about a clown when I took him out of the tub. Although, I can't figure out what the connection might be between him and the clown toy."

"Are you suggesting Connor saw Wesley when he was in the bath? If that's the case, why wouldn't you have seen him?" Chris asked.

Danielle shrugged. "It probably has nothing to do with it."

They all stopped talking when snow fell from the ceiling.

"They're back," Heather told Brian. The next moment, Marie and Eva stood in the middle of the living room.

Connor, who had since dumped over the basket of toys, waved at Eva and Marie and then continued playing with the toys.

"I imagine Ian told you what happened at the hospital," Marie said.

"He thought Wesley might have been there," Danielle said.

Marie nodded. "That silly ghost. He was surprised when we showed up. At first, he didn't notice us; he was so busy badgering Rylee."

"Badgering Rylee?" Danielle asked.

"Yes, Bonnie's cousin. She's a nurse at the hospital. I was surprised to see her. So was Wesley, from what I gathered. I asked him what he was doing there. He said he was bored, and Connor was the only one he could talk to—except for you, of course." Marie gave a little wave around the room, showing she meant all the mediums when she said *you*. "But I suspect he didn't feel you would appreciate him barging in for an idle chat, not if he wanted you to help him."

"He wanted to chat with a toddler?" Heather frowned.

"Apparently, he did a few sleight-of-hand tricks, which Connor found amusing. I suspect Wesley enjoyed playing to a willing audience."

"He really is a clown," Heather said with a snort.

"Perhaps we should get to work," Eva suggested.

SEVENTEEN

While Evan was with his father on Sunday, his older brother, Eddy, had spent the day at a friend's house. Edward had sent Eddy a text earlier that afternoon, telling him to be home by five because he planned to order a pizza for dinner, and he wanted to have a family meeting. Eddy, who had ridden his bike to his friend's house, made it home on time. He parked the bike in the garage and went on into the house, finding his brother and father in the living room, watching television and waiting for the pizza to arrive.

He noticed someone had pulled the coffee table away from the couch and had set up two TV trays where the coffee table had been, with a third TV tray in front of his father's recliner. A stack of napkins and paper plates had been placed on the coffee table. They were obviously eating in the living room. His father greeted him and suggested he get something to drink and wash his hands because the pizza would be arriving soon.

Eddy never asked his father what the meeting was about. He assumed it was probably about his little brother's strange behavior. He wondered if his dad was planning on getting Evan in counseling.

When Eddy returned to the living room after going to the

kitchen to wash his hands and get a soda, he found the television off and his dad at the front door, taking the pizza from the delivery guy. After his father closed the door and carried the pizza to the coffee table, Eddy asked, "Can't we watch TV while we eat?"

"No. Like I said, we're having a family meeting." Edward set the pizza box on the coffee table and opened the lid. "Boys, go ahead and get some pizza."

Five minutes later, both Eddy and Evan sat on the sofa, each in front of a TV tray, eating pizza, while their father sat on the recliner. Eddy thought the whole thing felt a little weird because they had never had a family meeting pizza dinner in the living room before. They silently ate for several minutes before Edward said, "Eddy, I imagine you're wondering what this meeting is about."

Eddy glanced from his father to his brother, back to his father. "Does Evan know?"

"Yes, he does. The meeting is about Evan. We want to tell you something."

Eddy looked at his brother and said, "Evan, you are my little brother. I'll always be here for you. I can be a butt sometimes, but that's kinda what brothers do. But I do love you. And it's okay to ask for help."

Evan smiled at his brother, but withheld comment.

Edward looked at Eddy and said, "That's nice of you to say. And I'm sure Evan will appreciate your support. Part of supporting your brother is for you to promise not to ever discuss with anyone what we tell you tonight. Not your friends, Aunt Sissy, or your grandparents. Not anyone unless you check with me first. This is a private family matter. When we explain things to you, I want you to know I'm the reason Evan never talked to you about this before. I told him not to discuss it with anyone, not even you."

Eddy frowned. "Is that such a good idea?" He glanced briefly at his brother. "You kinda make it sound like there's something to be ashamed of. Evan shouldn't be ashamed to get help. He shouldn't hold it in like some bad secret. If he wants to talk about it, he should be able to."

"Eddy, you've been Googling, haven't you?"

Eddy shrugged. "What do you mean, Dad?"

"After you came to me the other day. What did you Google, mental health?"

"Daaaad…Evan can hear."

"It's okay, Eddy. And I'm proud of you. I know you care about your brother. And that's important. Family is important. But you can put away your concern because Evan doesn't need a therapist or a psychologist. But there is something going on in your brother's life that I've been aware of for about five years. Something that we've been keeping from you."

"What do you mean?" Eddy frowned.

"It's something we've been dealing with. I wasn't sure how to bring it up with you, and I realize that was wrong. You're a part of this family. Plus, your brother wants me to tell you."

"Oh my god, is Evan dying?"

Edward smiled at his son. "No. It's nothing like that. In fact, it's nothing bad. Just very unusual. Well, at least I used to think it was unusual."

"What is it?"

"First, promise that whatever we discuss in this room tonight does not go farther than the three of us."

"I promise."

Edward wiped his hands off on a napkin, pushed the TV tray to one side, and leaned back in the chair. "Do you understand what a medium is?"

"You mean those guys who speak to dead people?"

"I suppose. But I think they usually call them spirits."

"There's this guy I started watching on YouTube. He said he was a medium. In his videos he did these readings. I was at Aunt Sissy's once, watching one of the videos. She asked me what I was watching. I showed her. He was doing a reading for a lady who wanted to talk to her dad. The medium seemed to know all this stuff about her father, which only the daughter knew. But Aunt Sissy said it was all fake. She said you can find all sorts of things online about people, and that's probably how he found all that stuff. Like from Facebook. She said no one can talk to the dead."

"Well, your aunt Sissy is wrong."

"What do you mean?"

"Grandma Kat could speak to spirits," Edward said.

"Grandma Kat? Does Aunt Sissy know?" Eddy remembered his father's grandma Kathy, who had been affectionately called Grandma Kat because that was what his father had called her when he was little. Eddy had been around eight when she died.

Edward shook his head. "No. No, she doesn't."

"I want you to tell me more about Grandma Kat being able to talk to dead people. Sounds really cool. But what does this have to do with Evan?"

"Apparently that gift—the ability to see spirits and—"

"What do you mean, see spirits?" Eddy interrupted. "Are you saying Grandma Kat could see ghosts?"

Edward nodded. "Yes. She could see, hear, talk with them."

"Wow, that's cool."

"Here's the thing, Eddy, sometimes the ability to see spirits is passed down in the family."

"Are you saying I could one day see spirits?" Eddy asked.

"No. Although, maybe it's possible that you could one day."

"So what are you saying, Dad?"

"I'm saying your brother has the same gift my grandmother had. He can see and communicate with spirits—or what you might call ghosts."

Eddy stared at his father, his face void of expression. He then looked at his brother, who flashed him a sheepish smile. After a moment, Eddy said, "No way. Are you for real right now?"

"I'm quite serious."

"I don't believe it."

"It's true. And Evan isn't the only medium in Frederickport."

"Who else?" Eddy asked.

"I can't say right now. And this isn't something I can talk about publicly. This is why you can't say anything to anyone. It could cost me my job."

"Why would it cost you your job?" Eddy asked.

"For one thing, people would think I'm crazy."

Eddy stood up and picked up his paper plate and partially eaten piece of pizza. He held his plate in one hand and with his other hand picked up his napkin, wadded it up, and then tossed it on his plate. He picked up his soda. "Is there anything else?"

"You don't want to talk about this?" Edward asked.

"What's to talk about?" Eddy walked to the kitchen.

"He didn't believe you," Evan said when Eddy was out of earshot.

"No. I don't think he does."

"What do you think he's thinking?"

"I suspect he's processing what I just told him. Let's give him some time. At the moment, he seems to think we're trying to pull some trick on him, and he doesn't know why, and I think his feelings are hurt."

EDDY FINISHED his pizza in the kitchen alone. When he was done, he threw his trash in the kitchen can and headed to the bathroom to take an early shower. After his shower, he closed his door and climbed into bed. When his father peeked into his bedroom thirty minutes later, he found Eddy sitting in bed, playing video games.

"You already take your shower?" Edward asked from the doorway.

"Yeah." Eddy refused to look his father's way.

"You want to talk?"

"No."

"Okay. But when you're ready to talk, I'll be here. I'm not trying to play some joke on you."

"Whatever."

"I love you, Eddy."

EDDY OPENED his eyes and found himself sitting on his grandmother's porch swing. It gently swayed back and forth. He turned his head to the right and found he wasn't alone. There, sitting next to him, was his beautiful mother.

"Mom?" Eddy asked in surprise. His mother was dead, but there she was, smiling at him. *Is this a dream? It has to be a dream.*

"You're mad at your dad. You shouldn't be mad at him; he loves you so much. And he's done such a good job with you and Evan. I'm so proud of all of you."

"Why did you have to die, Mom?"

Cindy shrugged. "It was my time. I didn't want to go, but I've been here all along, watching over you. And I could see you were hurt tonight. You thought your father was lying to you."

"He said Evan could talk to dead people. That's not possible. Why did Dad lie to me?"

"You're talking to me," Cindy said with a laugh. "I'm dead."

"That's different. This is a dream. You're not really here."

"Are you sure? Does this feel like a regular dream?"

"No, but…"

"Hi, Mom," came a new voice.

"Hi, Evan."

Eddy turned to his left, and there, sitting next to him, was his brother. "What are you doing here? Why am I dreaming about you?"

"I don't think you have anything to do with it," Evan said.

Eddy frowned. "What are you talking about?"

Evan leaned forward, looking past his brother to his mother. "You arranged this dream hop, didn't you?"

"Yes, dear. I figured it was the easiest way for him to believe."

Eddy frowned. "Dream hop?"

Cindy turned to her eldest son, reached out, and cupped his face in her hands. She looked into his eyes—eyes so much like his father's. He didn't blink.

"I want you to listen very carefully to what I have to say."

Eddy stared into her eyes, unable to move.

"When you get up in the morning, ask your brother what you

did last night. He'll say the two of you went on a dream hop. That will prove everything your father told you was true. I love you, Eddy."

EDDY WOKE up on Monday morning with the early sunshine streaming in his bedroom window. Sitting up in bed, he rubbed his eyes and grumbled, "That was the weirdest dream." He stumbled out of bed and headed for the bathroom.

After using the bathroom, Eddy went to the kitchen, where he found his brother and father sitting at the kitchen table, with his father drinking a cup of coffee and his brother eating a cinnamon roll.

"Good morning," his father greeted.

Reluctantly Eddy said, "Good morning." He glanced at the breakfast bar and saw an Old Salts Bakery sack sitting on the kitchen counter. He walked over to the counter and helped himself to a cinnamon roll from the sack. "What's the occasion?" Edward understood what his son meant. He was asking why Edward had bought cinnamon rolls, as they were considered a special treat in their house.

"Aren't you supposed to ask me something?" Evan asked.

Standing at the breakfast bar, cinnamon roll in hand, Eddy turned to face his brother and father at the kitchen table. "What do you mean?"

"You are supposed to ask me what we did last night. And then I tell you we were on a dream hop with Mom."

The cinnamon roll slipped from Eddy's hand, falling to the floor as he stood frozen in the kitchen, his mouth agape.

EIGHTEEN

Those who had met the chief's late wife, Cindy MacDonald, often remarked how much Evan favored his mother, while her older son, Eddy, looked like the chief's mini-me. On Monday morning, Eddy and Evan were sitting on their front porch when their father stepped out the door, on his way to work, and stopped to talk before leaving.

"You boys are spending the day together? Right?" MacDonald adjusted his shirt's collar.

"Oh yeah," Eddy said with a nod. Evan had given him the abbreviated version of his medium experiences, but Eddy wanted more details.

"I called Danielle, and she said if you boys wanted to go over there today, maybe to help with any of the questions Eddy has, you are more than welcome. But before you leave, have something to eat. All you boys had for breakfast was a cinnamon roll. Make yourself a sandwich or something."

"Okay," Eddy and Evan chimed.

Edward looked at his eldest. "And remember, don't discuss this with anyone else beyond the circle of people we mentioned. Not your best friend or your aunt or grandparents."

"Don't worry, Dad. They would think I'm nuts," Eddy scoffed.
Edward laughed. "Yes, yes, they would."

EDDY SUGGESTED they walk to Marlow House instead of riding their bikes. The main reason, he wanted to talk to his brother on their way over. There were many questions he wanted to ask before they arrived at Marlow House. Neither boy remembered their father's instructions to eat something before heading out.

"I can't believe you were actually talking to the ghost of Clay Bowman the other day. He was really standing right there in your bedroom?"

"Yeah. And Dad wasn't too happy about it."

"I can imagine. Wow. Weren't you afraid?"

"Nahh. He's a ghost. Nothing he can do to me."

"So a ghost is just sort of there, like air? I've always heard ghosts can slam doors and fool with electricity."

Evan stopped walking and looked at his brother. "I thought you didn't believe in ghosts before?"

Eddy shrugged. "I didn't say that." Evan started walking again. "I just didn't know if people could really communicate with the dead."

"We call them spirits, not really the dead. That sounds kinda creepy. Spirits that stick around are called ghosts. But some ghosts like to be called spirits."

"How do you know all this?"

Evan shrugged. "I've just learned it, I guess. Some of the other mediums have told me. Some things the ghosts tell me."

"That's fire! So a ghost can't slam doors and stuff? Because if a ghost could slam doors, they should be able to move other stuff that could hit you."

"Some ghosts can move stuff. Danielle calls it harnessing energy."

"Then why do you say ghosts can't hurt you?"

"Eva says the Universe won't let a ghost hurt an innocent."

"Who is Eva?"

"Eva Thorndike. Her painting is in the museum."

Eddy stopped walking and looked at his brother. "No way. Are you saying you've talked to Eva Thorndike's ghost?"

"Yeah. She's real nice."

"And you never told me before?"

Evan shrugged. "And you would have believed me?"

"No. But wow. That's sick. Wow."

They continued to talk when something was mentioned about Heather. Eddy said, "I can see Heather being a medium. She looks like someone who could talk to dead people."

"I told you, it's spirits or ghosts."

"I meant nothing bad about it. After all, Heather is fire."

"What do you mean?"

"Look at her. She's like the girl all the guys want to date, but they're all afraid to ask her out. I can't believe she's dating Brian. He could be her grandpa."

"Brian's pretty cool."

"I suppose. Can't believe he's known about all this, too. It's like there was an alternate universe going on, and I didn't know anything about it. I wish I could tell someone."

"But you can't."

"I know."

CHIEF MACDONALD SAT in his office with Brian on Monday morning. He had just finished telling him how Eddy had received the information about his brother.

Brian, who sat in a chair facing the chief, shook his head and let out a sigh. "It's a lot to take in for someone Eddy's age. Hell, it's a lot to take in at my age. So he didn't believe you at first?"

"He reacted a little like Ian, now that I think about it. Thought we were trying to pull some joke on him, and he didn't appreciate it. But his mother, she came through."

"That must be weird for you."

"What do you mean?"

"Knowing that someone you love, someone who is the mother of your children, whom you planned to spend your life with, is no longer here. But then she is. It's like she's watching over you. Not in an abstract way I used to hear people say before I was taken up on that mountain with Heather and Walt. It was always something people would say to make you feel better. But no one really knew for sure. But now, well, it's more…"

Brian paused while searching for the right word, but the chief beat him to it when he said, "Tangible?"

Brian nodded. "Yeah."

"When people said it before, it comforted me in an abstract way. But it's different now, and when I think about it, weird might be an apt description." The chief chuckled and then got serious again. "But at the same time, it's confusing. If it's possible for Cindy to visit the boys in a dream hop, why doesn't she do it more often? She visited us a couple of Christmases ago. Why can't I visit her every night? Or at least every Christmas?"

"At one time, I would have asked that same question. But something I've learned from Heather is that we have our lives to live here, and for whatever reason, those who pass on have things they must do on the other side."

"What about Eva and Marie?"

"According to Heather, Eva says the Universe has its reasons for doing things, and we just need to trust it and continue living our lives as best we can."

A perfunctory knock came at the open doorway, followed by, "Am I disturbing something?"

Brian turned to face the doorway and saw Joe standing there.

"Come on in." The chief waved Joe into the office.

Joe walked to one of the office chairs and sat down. "I just thought you might be interested in something I just learned. It involves Carpenter's arrest this morning."

"You're talking about what happened over at the hobby shop?" the chief asked.

Joe nodded. "Yes."

"What happened at the hobby shop?" Brian asked.

"Two boys broke into the back of the store early this morning before it was open. The owner came in to work and found them filling up a large box with items that the store owner assumes they were planning to take with them. Considering their age, they were released back to the custody of their mother," Joe explained.

"I was aware of most of that," the chief said.

"But did anyone tell you the identities of the boys?" Joe asked.

The chief shook his head. "No, Colleen mentioned it this morning. She didn't say who the boys were. I don't think she had their names at the time. Why? Do we know them?"

"We all worked with their father, Clay Bowman."

The chief leaned back in his office chair. "Really?"

Joe nodded. "What do they say about the apple not falling far from the tree?"

"Someone needs to talk to those boys, straighten them out," Brian said as he and the chief exchanged glances.

"YOU WANT to get an ice cream before we go to Marlow House?" Eddy asked his brother. They had just reached where Beach Drive intersected with the road leading into the pier parking lot.

"I don't have any money," Evan said.

"I've got plenty of money. I mowed four yards last week, and Aunt Sissy finally paid me for cleaning out her garage."

"Yeah, but I don't wanna spend all your money."

"Don't be silly." Eddy gave Evan a little nudge, pushing him toward the pier.

As the boys continued to the pier, Eddy said, "Maybe we should wait until after lunch before we get ice cream. I didn't have much for breakfast. Just that cinnamon roll."

Evan stopped in his tracks and groaned. "We were supposed to eat before we left."

"I didn't want a sandwich; I want a burger."

"Where are we going to get a burger?" Evan asked.

THE GHOST WHO SOUGHT REDEMPTION

"Where do you think?" Eddy gave his brother another nudge, and they continued to Pier Café.

EVAN FELT important sitting with his high-school-age brother at Pier Café. Eddy had even said he was going to buy Evan lunch. The last couple of years, ever since Eddy became a teenager, he didn't want to hang out with Evan and seemed annoyed when he had to watch Evan on the days their dad worked, and he couldn't stay at Aunt Sissy's or with a friend.

Last night when they had gone to bed, Evan worried his brother was mad at him. He wasn't sure how to convince Eddy they weren't making it all up. He might have asked Marie to move something, but Eddy had been led to believe Walt Marlow was an amateur magician, and Eddy would just assume Walt was in on the gag.

When their order arrived, Evan wasn't sure how he was going to finish his entire hamburger, and he didn't want to waste any because Eddy had spent his own money buying their lunch. But then Eddy said, "Hey, if you can't eat all your burger, I'll eat it." Evan grinned and quickly cut the burger in half and gave one half to Eddy.

Keeping his voice low so other diners wouldn't hear their conversation, Eddy asked Evan more questions about ghosts while they ate their lunch. Suddenly, Evan stopped eating, setting what remained of his burger back on his plate as he stared past his brother.

"What's wrong?" Eddy glanced behind him and saw nothing but an empty booth. He looked back to his brother.

"There is one behind you. In the booth."

"One what?" Eddy asked.

"A ghost."

Eddy frowned and turned around again. He saw nothing out of the ordinary. He looked back at his brother and smiled. "You almost got me."

"What are you talking about?"

"Telling me there is a ghost in the booth behind us. There's nothing there."

"Obviously you can't see it."

Eddy rolled his eyes. "You told me yourself that when you first see a ghost, you don't know it's a ghost because it looks like a regular person. So if there was a ghost sitting in the booth behind me, you wouldn't know it was behind me." Eddy smiled confidently.

"Well, I would if the person who I thought was a ghost just walked through Carla before he sat down."

Eddy abruptly turned in his seat, again looking at the empty booth behind theirs. Unbeknownst to him, the ghost in question had overheard their conversation and was now turned in their direction, the ghost's elbows propped up on the back of the booth, chin resting on a balled fist, his face just inches from Eddy's face.

"Hello," the ghost greeted.

NINETEEN

Eddy paid for their lunch, and the two boys left Pier Café and headed to the nearby ice-cream shop.

"Is he still with us?" Eddy whispered as they walked up to the ice-cream counter.

Evan glanced back at the ghost and gave his brother a nod.

"I used to enjoy coming down here." Standing behind the boys, Wesley glanced over the menu posted on the wall behind the counter. "I always ordered chocolate peanut butter. My wife liked pistachio. I can't stand pistachio. That woman always had a weird taste in food."

"What's he doing?" Eddy whispered.

"Talking about how pistachio ice cream sucks."

Eddy shrugged. "Well, he's not wrong."

The boys took their ice-cream cones and started on down the pier toward the street, with Wesley following along beside them.

"Are you guys friends, or is he your brother?" Wesley asked.

Evan glanced over at the ghost. Before taking a lick of his ice cream, he said, "We're brothers."

"So you must both be Chief MacDonald's boys."

"How do you know who our father is?"

"What is he saying?" Eddy asked.

"It's common knowledge around the cemetery that one of the police chief's sons is a medium."

"What is he saying?" Eddy repeated.

"I guess I'm sorta famous at the cemetery," Evan told his brother, not sounding impressed. He took another lick of his ice cream.

Eddy frowned. "What do you mean?"

Evan stopped walking and turned to the ghost. "Why are you following me? What do you want?"

Eddy also stopped and turned to watch his brother.

Wesley shrugged. "I'm bored. I've asked some of the other mediums to help me with something so I can move on, but they don't seem to be taking me seriously."

"Chris thinks you're keeping something from them. Maybe if you tell them everything, they might help you."

Eddy glanced around nervously, hoping no one was watching them, but then stepped in front of his brother, making it look as if Evan was talking to him. But when he did so, Wesley let out a squeal and jumped out of the way. Evan laughed.

"Ew…why did he do that?" Wesley frantically rubbed his hands over his clothes—both of which were nothing but an illusion created by his energy—as if attempting to wipe off equally imaginary dirt.

"Why did you laugh?" Eddy asked.

"You just walked through him. Ghosts hate that."

Eddy and Evan left Wesley behind, still standing in the middle of the sidewalk, waving his hands around his body. They were about to Heather's house when the annoying ghost finally stopped with his dramatics and caught up to them.

"Tell your brother that wasn't a nice thing to do," Wesley demanded.

"Stop following us." Evan chomped down on the last bit of his sugary cone, its tip filled with ice cream.

"He's still there?" Eddy asked.

Evan, his mouth full, nodded to his brother.

When they arrived at Marlow House a few minutes later, Wesley

THE GHOST WHO SOUGHT REDEMPTION

stopped at the sidewalk and didn't follow them up to the front door. Evan rang the doorbell while telling Eddy the ghost was standing down by the street.

"Evan, Eddy, your dad said you might stop by," Danielle greeted after opening the front door.

"A ghost followed us here," Eddy said excitedly.

Danielle arched her brows in response while Evan pointed down to the sidewalk. Stepping outside the house, Danielle looked toward the street and saw Wesley.

"How long has he been there?" Danielle asked.

Evan told Danielle how they had run into the ghost at Pier Café, and how he had then followed them to Marlow House.

Danielle motioned to the still open front door. "Why don't you boys go on inside? You'll find Walt in the living room. I'll go have a word with our ghost."

"I can't believe this," Eddy muttered under his breath while he followed Evan into the house.

"HELLO, Wesley. Why are you following children around?" Danielle asked.

"I did nothing wrong. I just wanted someone to talk to."

"Aren't there others like you that you can talk to?"

"Not really. Most of them are just passing through and aren't here that long. And when they are here, they just want to talk about how they died. It's boring."

"So you'd rather talk to children?"

"It has nothing to do with age. They are alive. You're alive. You have no idea how lucky you are. To be able to eat ice cream again. Dying sucks."

"I'm sorry. I'm sorry you had a heart attack."

"Yeah, me too. Stupid doctor. He told me I'd be fine if I just took my medicine. But here I am. Dead."

"You could move on. From what I understand, dying isn't the end. It's simply closing one door and opening another."

Wesley rolled his eyes. "Oh please. I've heard that cliche before. But I can't move on. Not until I know my wife is safe from Adrian."

"Are you telling me you can't move on—or you won't?"

"Why does it matter?"

"If you can't move on, there is more to this than you're telling us. And if that's the case, there is nothing we can do to help you until you are completely honest with us."

KELLY and her mother turned down Beach Drive. They planned to drop off lunch for her father, who was working at her brother's house with a small crew. After bringing him some food and checking on the workers' progress, they intended to head over to the hospital to see Lily and the baby.

Just as Kelly pulled into her brother's driveway, June looked across the street at Marlow House and said, "What is Danielle doing? It looks like she's standing in the middle of the sidewalk talking to herself."

"She's probably on her cellphone." Kelly pulled all the way into the driveway and put her car in park.

June, who was now turned around in the passenger seat, still looking across the street, said, "I don't see a phone in her hand."

Kelly turned the ignition off. "She's probably wearing earbuds."

DANIELLE GLANCED across the street and noticed Kelly's car parked in Lily's driveway and someone getting out of the vehicle. She wondered if they had seen her talking with Wesley or, from their perspective, talking to herself.

"Just stop bothering children." Danielle turned back to her house. "It's creepy."

"What do you mean, creepy? That's insulting," Wesley called after Danielle.

THE GHOST WHO SOUGHT REDEMPTION

Danielle continued toward her house, and when she was halfway down the walkway, she looked back toward the street. Wesley was gone. She pulled her cellphone from her back pocket and dialed the chief. She wanted to tell him the boys had arrived safely at Marlow House.

ONCE JUNE and Kelly entered Ian and Lily's house, June set John's lunch in the kitchen and then headed upstairs to tell her husband she brought lunch. When she returned to the kitchen, she asked Kelly, "Doesn't your brother have binoculars around here somewhere?" June started opening drawers. They could hear the workers up on the second floor.

"Well, I don't think they keep them in the kitchen," Kelly said before walking to the living room. "What do you want them for?"

June followed her daughter. "Just help me find them."

They opened the end table drawers and then started opening the cabinets under the bookshelves.

"Here's a pair," Kelly called out, holding a pair of binoculars in her right hand.

June snatched the binoculars from Kelly and rushed to the front window. Kelly followed her mother. "What are you doing?"

June held the binoculars to her eyes, frantically focusing them while looking out the window toward Marlow House. "I want to see what Danielle is doing. She's standing on the walkway now. Looks like she's still talking to herself. Do you think she has postpartum depression? Women do strange things when they have postpartum depression."

Kelly rolled her eyes at her mother's inability to get the binoculars focused. Shaking her head, she snatched them back from June and looked out the window.

"I told you," Kelly said with disgust. She turned back to her mother and handed her the binoculars. "She's talking on the phone. Now I feel like a peeping tom."

"I certainly didn't see a phone when she was on the sidewalk."

"YOU REALLY SHOULDN'T STAND out on the sidewalk and talk to ghosts," Walt teased Danielle when she entered the living room a few minutes later.

"I know. It was dumb of me."

In the living room with Walt and Danielle were Eddy and Evan, along with Eva and Marie, while the twins napped in their portable cribs along one wall. Evan talked to Eva and Marie while Eddy stood silently, listening.

Danielle walked over to the boys and asked Eddy, "How are you doing with all this, Eddy?"

Eddy looked at Danielle and shrugged. "It feels sort of unreal. It's not like I can see or hear anything different. I have to take everyone's word for it. That feels kind of weird."

"I understand. You know Ian Bartley, right?" Danielle asked.

Eddy nodded. "Sure."

"His wife, Lily, is like you. She's known for a while. But Ian didn't know at first. And before they were married, she felt she needed to tell him. But he didn't believe her. It took a while for him to come around. I understand."

"Dad said you've always been able to see ghosts."

"The first time I remember seeing a ghost was my grandmother right after she died. But I suspect I always could. I just didn't realize it. Like Connor, Lily's little boy. He could always see ghosts, which is natural for many children. It's when they get older, they lose the gift. But sometimes, like with me and your brother, we don't lose it."

"It's not that I don't believe what you're saying, but I'll admit, part of me keeps waiting for you to tell me this was some big joke. It just doesn't seem real."

"I understand you saw your mother last night?"

"Yeah, but that was a dream."

"A dream I was in too," Evan reminded him.

"True, but it's possible I was talking in my sleep last night and you overheard me," Eddy suggested.

Danielle glanced over at Marie and then looked back at Eddy. "I have an idea. Something we can show you that might help get rid of that feeling that we're all trying to punk you."

"What?"

"Did Evan explain how some ghosts can harness their energy?" Danielle asked.

Eddy nodded. "He told me about Mrs. Nichols using her energy to save Heather."

"Tell Eddy he can call me Marie."

"Marie says it's okay to call her by her first name."

Eddy shrugged and muttered, "It really doesn't feel real."

"How would you like to sample a little of Marie's energy? Maybe fly around the living room?"

Eddy's eyes widened. "No way."

"Is it okay?" Danielle asked.

"It would be cool but—" Before Eddy could finish his sentence, his body lifted off the floor. He looked down at his sneakers now dangling several inches above the large throw rug.

AFTER KELLY HANDED her mother the binoculars, June had set them on the coffee table and gone back upstairs to tell her husband they would be leaving to go see Lily and the baby, and not to forget his lunch was sitting on the kitchen counter.

When she came back downstairs, Kelly went to use the bathroom and on the way there reminded her mother to put the binoculars back in the cabinet under the bookshelf. While Kelly was in the bathroom, June retrieved the binoculars. But before she put them away, she gave them one more try.

Standing by the living room window, she looked through the binoculars toward Marlow House. After a few strategic turns, she could bring Marlow House and its large living room picture window into focus.

Her hands clasping the binoculars, June stood frozen at the window, watching what looked like a boy flying around Marlow House's living room, his feet not touching the floor.

TWENTY

"You ready to get out of here?" Ian asked Lily. He sat on the edge of the hospital bed while she sat in the nearby glider rocker, nursing Emily Ann. Next to Ian on the bed, Connor played with the toys Ian had bought Connor that morning before coming to the hospital.

"I just wish we were going home. Don't tell Dani I said that. I appreciate they're letting us stay there. It's much better than living in a construction zone with a toddler and newborn. But still." Lily let out a sigh.

"I understand. If it makes you feel any better, Dad's over there today with his crew, working to finish it up so we can move back home."

"It's going to be wonderful when it's done. I can't wait."

"I want you to know I already set up the portable crib we used for Connor in the bedroom we're in, so Emily Ann can sleep in the room with us. Danielle put together a list of what she calls infant necessities, so we can set up our makeshift nursery. We plan to put it together tonight. I was going to get the box of infant clothes Connor used and get them washed, but Danielle pointed out they would be too large. So before Connor and I came over here this morning, we stopped and bought Emily Ann her first wardrobe."

"Oh, you did that?" Lily grinned.

"It was actually kind of fun. Heather helped me, but don't tell Kelly. She would probably be hurt that I didn't call her to go shopping with me."

"I imagine the baby shower Heather was going to give us is now cancelled. Most of our friends have probably already given us what they had planned to give for the shower," Lily noted. "How did Heather happen to go with you?"

"This morning, before I left Marlow House, she called to ask if there was anything you needed. I told her I was going to stop at the new baby store in town and get some stuff, and she asked when I was going to be there and if I needed any help. For a woman who insists she doesn't want kids, she seems to know what an infant needs."

Lily laughed. "Heather once told me kids and babies were like books."

"Books?" Ian frowned.

"Yes. She said some people love books, but they prefer to check them out of the library and return them."

Ian laughed. "She'd rather borrow our kids and then return them?"

"Something like that."

"How are you doing?" a voice called out from the now open doorway. Both Lily and Ian looked to the doorway to see a nurse walking into the room. It was Rylee.

Lily glanced down at the nursing infant in her arms. "She just fell asleep."

"Are you ready to go home?" Rylee asked when she came farther into the room. "From what I understand, you will both be discharged tomorrow."

"I'm ready to get out of the hospital," Lily said.

They chatted with Rylee as she tended to her tasks, checking both Lily and the baby. They discussed when Lily would probably be discharged in the morning and what to expect. Rylee was just wrapping up with Lily when Ian asked, "How long have you been working at the hospital?"

Rylee smiled at Ian. "About five months now."

"So you're not from Frederickport?" Ian asked.

"I grew up in Damascus."

"I assume you don't mean Damascus, Syria?" Ian teased.

Rylee laughed. "No, Damascus, Oregon. It's about twenty minutes from Portland. But I had an aunt who lived in Frederickport. I used to visit her a couple of weeks every summer."

"Does she no longer live in Frederickport?" Lily asked.

Rylee shook her head. "No, she passed away last year. I used to be a traveling nurse, and then, about two years before my aunt passed away, she asked me to be her caretaker. She wanted to stay in her home, but she realized she could no longer take care of herself. She was in her nineties. I became her caretaker. After she passed away, I took a break from nursing and eventually came back to Frederickport and got a job at the hospital. And here I am."

"That's nice that your aunt had someone from her family to take care of her," Lily said.

"She didn't have much of a family left. She never had any kids, and her husband died years ago. There was only me and my cousin."

"Does your cousin live in Oregon?" Ian asked.

"She actually lives in Frederickport. But we're not close." Rylee then changed the topic.

"That was kind of abrupt," Lily told Ian after Rylee left the room.

Ian chuckled. "I about got whiplash she changed the subject so fast."

"She didn't want to talk about her cousin."

Ian nodded. "It appears that way."

Lily narrowed her eyes and studied Ian for a few moments before asking, "You seemed a little too interested in her history. What's up?"

Ian was about to tell Lily about Rylee's connection to the ghost who had visited Connor, something he hadn't had a chance to tell her, when his mother and sister barreled into the room.

Connor immediately climbed off the bed upon seeing his grandmother and aunt, but June seemed more interested in telling Ian something than picking up her grandson. She absently gave Connor a hug and shoved him over to Kelly before saying, "Something strange is going on over at Marlow House."

"Strange is sort of normal for Marlow House," Lily said under her breath.

Kelly picked up Connor and gave him a hug while telling Ian, "Our mother tells me someone was flying around in Marlow House's living room. I didn't see it myself. But considering some things I've seen over on your street, flying kids is not beyond the realm of possibility." Kelly didn't sound concerned. She set Connor back on his feet and walked over to the bed, where he climbed up to show her his new toys.

"Kids? What kids?" Lily asked.

"There was only one. It looked like a boy. He was flying around. I tried to show Kelly, but by the time she looked, he wasn't flying anymore. What is going on over there?"

"It's possible Walt and Danielle are considering hosting a haunted house this year," Lily suggested.

"It is a little soon for Halloween, and I can't imagine they would want strangers traipsing through their house when they have newborns. And what does that have to do with flying children?"

"I was thinking about Walt's magic tricks. He pulled out some good ones when they did the haunted house," Lily said.

"Oh, I know what it is," Ian said. "When Connor and I left Marlow House this morning, Danielle mentioned Edward MacDonald's two boys might be coming over. It was probably one of the boys. Knowing Walt, he was entertaining the boys with his tricks."

"Exactly how does Walt make children fly?" June asked.

"Walt doesn't share his magic secrets," Lily said sweetly. "That would spoil the magic."

"Oh, Mom, he probably uses ropes and pulleys," Kelly said. "The boys aren't actually flying."

"Is that safe?" June asked. "I wouldn't want Connor flying around the house."

"Me fly!" Connor yelled as he stood up on the bed. He raised his hands up over his head. "Fly!"

OVER AT THE POLICE DEPARTMENT, Chief MacDonald sat in his office, facing Clay Bowman's two young sons. A little younger than Evan, the twins stubbornly crossed their arms over their chests in an obvious attempt to close themselves off from whatever the police chief had to say. Their mother had left them alone with the chief before stepping out into the hallway and closing the door behind her.

What none of them knew, the chief was not completely alone with the boys. Clay Bowman's spirit had arrived with his family, and now he stood quietly in the corner, observing.

MacDonald leaned back in the chair and studied the boys for a moment. "I understand you two got yourself into a bit of trouble. You're lucky you were released to your mother's custody and not sent to a juvenile detention center."

"Is that a jail?" Zack asked.

"Sort of," the chief said.

"Shouldn't our mom be in here with us?" Eric asked. "Dad always told us kids should never talk to cops without a parent present."

"Your mother wanted me to talk to you. I have her permission to talk to you without her here."

The boys slumped down in their chairs, glaring at the chief.

"I knew your father," the chief began.

"He took your job, and you didn't like that. It's because of you he got arrested and sent away. If that hadn't happened, then he would still be alive," Zack said.

"Is that what you think?" the chief asked.

The boys nodded.

"What does your mom say?" the chief said.

"She doesn't like to talk about it," Eric said.

"Boys, I'm sorry about your father. But he made some bad choices, and those choices put him in a dangerous situation. It has nothing to do with me or your mother, you, or anyone but your father. As for what happened to him, that was wrong. But unfortunately, bad things sometimes happen in those places. That's why you need to stop doing things that might put you in danger."

"We're okay." Zack shrugged.

"You boys broke into a store. That is breaking and entering. It is against the law. People get put in jail for that."

"We're kids. Nothing is going to happen to us," Zack said.

"You will face the consequences of your actions. And taking this *I don't care, I am too cool* attitude won't help you when you face the judge."

"Can we go now?" Eric hit the heels of his sneakers against the floor.

"One reason I'm talking to you boys, I'll be making a recommendation to the judge about what your punishment should be."

"You talk like we're guilty. We haven't gone to trial yet. We might be found innocent." Eric grinned at the chief.

"Perhaps, but if you aren't found innocent, then what I recommend to the judge will have weight. Not only because I am the police chief, but because I knew your father. He used to work for me, and I know your situation."

"What do you mean, he used to work for you?" Zack asked. "That's a lie. Our dad never worked for you. We moved to Frederickport so Dad could take your job because he was a better police chief."

The chief let out a sigh and sat up in his chair. He leaned forward, placing his elbows on his desk as he looked seriously at Clay's sons. "Your father worked in the Frederickport police department before you boys were born. He was a police officer; I was the police chief. His boss. Your uncle recommended hiring him to replace me temporarily while I recovered from surgery. It was never a permanent position, yet your father and uncle hoped the temporary position would lead to a full-time job in the department after I returned. You can ask your mother; she'll tell you."

Zack shook his head. "No. You got my dad arrested so he wouldn't take your job."

"That's not what happened, Zack."

"I'm Eric, not Zack," Zack spat, his expression defiant.

"No, you're not. You're Zack."

Zack shook his head. "You don't know that. We're identical twins. There is no way you know which one I am."

MacDonald leaned back in his desk chair and smiled. "About a year before you moved here, you fell off your bike. You had to have stitches." MacDonald pointed to his own right cheek. "Right about there. You still have a scar. It's barely noticeable, but it's there."

"How do you know that?" Zack asked.

"Your uncle Fred told me after you moved here. He said that's how he could tell you apart."

"I hate Uncle Fred." Zack slumped back in his chair and crossed his arms over his chest.

TWENTY-ONE

Rooftops provide a unique vantage point of a neighborhood. A perfect place for a weary soul to take refuge, Wesley thought. The ghost straddled the rooftop's ridge, with the Pacific Ocean to the west, and Marlow House to the east. Yet his peace only lasted about fifteen minutes before the hammering started. Unbeknownst to Wesley, he had chosen to take refuge while the workers inside the house ate their lunch, but they had returned to work. Wondering about the noise, Wesley moved his head through the shingles and plywood, looking down at the newly built second floor. Had any of the workers been mediums, he or she would have likely let out a startled scream at the sight of a head dangling down from the ceiling, as it turned from side to side, taking in the view. Yet there was not even a gasp from below.

Wesley pulled his head from the house and looked across the street in time to see a police car pull up in front of Marlow House and park. When the driver got out of the vehicle, Wesley recognized the officer: Police Chief MacDonald. He remembered MacDonald's sons were inside and assumed he was stopping by to pick them up. It was at that moment he had an idea.

"I am an idiot!" Wesley said aloud. The next moment, he

stood in one of the hydrangea plants bordering the front of Marlow House. The plants had already started to bloom, displaying clusters of pink, purple, and blue flowers. But Wesley was not paying attention to the colorful blossoms, but to the living room window as he inched closer to it. He wanted to peek inside the house, but he assumed there were mediums inside who might see him.

Wesley understood—in a broad sense—ghosts could harness energy. Marie Nichols used her energy in such a way. From what Pamela had told him, ghosts unconsciously used their energy when creating the illusion of their physical body. She said that one of the first ways a ghost consciously uses that energy is by changing their appearance—or making it disappear. Wesley's time on this side had been relatively short, although not as short as Pamela's, yet unlike her, he had other things on his mind, and altering his appearance seemed a waste of time, considering the only entities he came in contact with capable of seeing him were other ghosts, and those were rare. But now, he wished he understood how to stop that energy from creating the illusion of his physical being, because it would make it much easier to look in on mediums without being seen.

Since he didn't have that ability, he took a chance and peeked in a corner of the window. When he did, he saw not only mediums but two ghosts, Eva Thorndike and Marie Nichols. Fortunately, none faced the window.

Wesley was about to leave, since he had no desire to confront the mediums with Eva and Marie present. He hadn't liked Marie when she had been alive, and Eva scared him. But before he moved, both ghosts vanished.

"DAD, IT WAS SO COOL," Eddy told his father. "I was really flying."

"Sounds like you had an interesting day." The chief chuckled. He sat in a recliner while Walt and Danielle sat on the sofa together, each holding a baby, while Eddy sat on the fireplace hearth with his brother.

"It was all fun and games until Lily called," Danielle said with a snort. "We should have shut the front blinds. I saw June and Kelly were across the street. But I didn't imagine they could see inside the living room window from over there. Of course, I didn't consider June would find Ian's binoculars and become a peeping tom."

"What did they say?" the chief asked.

"They didn't say anything to us. But when they stopped by the hospital after leaving here, they told Lily and Ian about it. Lily convinced them it was one of Walt's magic tricks."

"And Danielle told me that if anyone asked how he did it," Eddy chimed in, "I'm to say I can't give away a magician's secrets."

"Which really isn't lying," Danielle said. "Walt's secret was using Marie's energy." Danielle didn't mention Walt's energy because the mediums and the chief had agreed not to say anything about Walt's background or gifts to Eddy. They worried that might be too much for the teenager to absorb all at once.

"While you were over here doing magic tricks, I was having a conversation with the Bowman twins," the chief told Walt and Danielle.

Before Walt or Danielle could respond, Wesley appeared in the middle of the living room.

"What are you doing here?" Danielle asked.

The chief arched his brows. "I assume you're not talking to me?"

"It's that ghost who followed Eddy and me back from the pier," Evan told his father.

"He's here?" Eddy asked in a loud whisper.

Evan pointed to where the ghost stood.

"Please hear me out," Wesley urged. "I obviously chose the wrong medium."

"What are you talking about?" Danielle asked.

"I should have gone to him first." Wesley pointed to Evan. "His father is the police chief. That's who can help me. It's his job to stop a murder."

"The chief already knows about your request," Danielle said.

Wesley frowned. "He does?"

"Yes. And like us, he needs more information. Let's pretend you were still alive and go directly to the chief, telling him Adrian planned to marry Bonnie for her money before killing her. He can't do anything unless you tell him everything you can to support your claim."

"That's a poor analogy," Wesley snapped. "For one thing, I already told you why, for the money. And two, if I were alive, I would still be married to Bonnie, so Adrian couldn't marry her, anyway." Wesley disappeared.

"He's gone," Evan announced.

"What was that all about?" the chief asked.

"Same thing. He wants to stop his brother from marrying his widow." Danielle looked at Evan. "If he comes back later and asks you to get your father to do something, remind him your father already knows everything, and unless he has additional information, there's nothing any of us can do."

Evan nodded.

"We have two ghosts making demands," Walt muttered. He glanced down at his daughter, swaddled and sleeping peacefully in his arms, gave her a soft smile, and looked back to the chief. "Did you have any progress with the twins? Any luck setting them back on the right path?"

"I doubt they've ever been on the right path," the chief grumbled. "One thing I learned today, I'm not the one to talk to the boys."

"Why not?" Walt asked.

"They obviously blame me for their father's death. Sadly, the only one who could reach them is their father, because despite everything, those boys have their father on some pedestal. They're convinced Clay was hired to replace me, and because of that, I framed him. They won't even listen to their mother."

"Have their father talk to them," Evan suggested.

"Their father is dead," Eddy reminded him with a twinge of big-brother snark.

"He can still talk to them," Evan said.

"You mean a dream hop?" Danielle asked.

"What's a dream hop?" Eddy asked.

Evan looked at his older brother and, with equal snark, asked, "Seriously?"

Frowning in confusion, Eddy stared at his brother for a moment before everything clicked into place. "Oh, the dream with Mom?"

Evan nodded.

"Will they understand it's not a regular dream? That Clay was really there?" the chief asked.

"Dream hops have a distinct quality," Danielle reminded him. "And when they wake up, I would be surprised if they didn't tell the other one about the dream. Once they do that…"

"If they both have the same dream, it will convince them their father was really there," the chief finished for her.

"I guess we need to tell Clay he's the only one who can help his sons. We can't do it," Danielle said. "And we'll need Eva and Marie's help to guide Clay in his first dream hop."

"How are you going to get ahold of him?" the chief asked.

Danielle flashed the chief a smile and set the sleeping baby she held on the sofa between her and Walt. She picked up her cellphone and called Heather. When Heather answered the call, she said, "Hang up the wreath when you get home."

ERIC OPENED his eyes and found himself sitting on a picnic table in the middle of the forest. He wasn't alone. Across from him sat his brother, Zack.

Confused, Zack looked around. "Where are we? This almost looks like the place Dad took us camping last year."

Eric stood up. "How did we get here? This is weird." Tucking the tips of his fingers in the back pockets of his denim pants, he looked around.

Zack remained seated and nervously cracked his knuckles. "Last

BOBBI HOLMES

thing I remember is going to bed. Who brought us here? How did we not wake up? Did someone drug us?"

Eric moved to Zack's side of the table and sat down nervously. "I don't know, but this is creeping me out."

A crow flew over to the table and landed several inches from the boys. They looked down at the bird in confusion. Eric reached out and waved his hand at the bird. "Go away!"

The next moment, the bird vanished, and a voice said, "Zack, Eric…"

The boys twirled around in their seats and looked at their father.

"Dad!" they cried out.

"I've missed you." Clay smiled at his sons.

Zack began shaking his head. "No. You're dead. You can't be here." He looked at where the crow had been seconds earlier. "No, crows don't disappear. This is a dream. I'm dreaming."

"This isn't a regular dream," Eric said.

Zack looked at his brother. "You aren't really here. This is all a dream."

"No. While Eric is right, this isn't a regular dream, you're right too. I'm dead, but I'm really here, with both of you. I need to talk to you." Clay moved around the table and sat down, facing his sons.

"Okay," Zack said, stubbornly crossing his arms across his chest. "I might as well enjoy this dream."

Clay smiled at his son. "Good. But I need you to pay attention."

"If you're really here, can I ask you some questions?" Eric asked.

Clay nodded. "Go ahead."

"The police chief said you weren't hired to take over his job. You were just replacing him while he was recovering from surgery."

Clay nodded again. "True."

Zack shook his head. "See. You aren't here. Because that's a lie. You told us you were replacing him."

"I exaggerated," Clay said. "I love you both. But I did some bad things during my life. Things I regret. But what I regret most is setting a poor example. Encouraging you to do things I knew were wrong, like not being upset when you broke into the house and entered the tunnel."

Zack shook his head. "No. Our dad said we were clever. He was proud of us. I'm only having this dream because Mom made us talk to that stupid police chief."

"Listen to me, boys. Someday you'll die. All of us do. And when that time comes, the bad things you do catch up to you. The next place you break into, you might not get caught. The next time you steal something, you could get away with it. I was right, you are clever boys. If you tried, the two of you could do whatever you want. But I'd rather that be something that doesn't involve breaking the law or hurting people. Someday you'll die, and you'll have to be accountable for all the wrongs you committed in this life. And trust me, living the life I lived is not worth it."

"Are you being punished for what you did?" Eric asked.

"I haven't yet. That's why I'm here. I was given this opportunity to reach out to you boys before I move on and face my consequences. I don't want you to ever be where I am now. Please listen to Police Chief MacDonald. He's a good man."

"No, this is a stupid dream!" Zack shouted. It woke him and Eric.

"OH DANG, I had the wildest dream!" Eric said.

"Me too! It was weird. You and Dad were in it."

Eric looked at his brother. "Tell me about your dream."

TWENTY-TWO

Clay stood at the foot of the sofa bed, where his sons sat in a pile of blankets and pillows. After waking up, Eric had turned on the lamp next to the couch. Zack shared his dream first while his brother, wide eyed, quietly listened. When Zack finished, Eric said, "I had the exact same dream."

"No way."

"I did." Eric then added details his brother had failed to include.

"Holy crud! That was in my dream too. What does this mean?"

"It's obvious what it means," Clay told deaf ears. "I visited you. And now you need to take my words seriously."

"It's obvious what it means," Eric said. "Twin dreams are real!"

"That has to be it! Wow, we had a twin dream! That's so cool! But why did we have that dream? No way would Dad say that stuff."

"Boys! This wasn't a twin dream. It was me!"

"Because Mom made us talk to Chief MacDonald. And seriously, can you see Dad telling us to listen to that dude, and even telling us he's a good man?"

They both laughed.

"No!" Clay cried. "It was really me! You must listen to me! It's for your own good!"

THE GHOST WHO SOUGHT REDEMPTION

Their mother opened her bedroom door. She stepped out into the living room, wearing her pink terrycloth robe while rubbing her eyes. "What are you guys doing up? It's three in the morning." She walked toward the sofa, yawned, and paused a moment to tighten the terrycloth belt around her waist.

"Did we wake you up?" Eric asked.

"Yes, you woke me," she snapped, now standing akimbo at the foot of the sofa bed, the ghost of her husband by her side.

"We had a dream," Eric said. "Zack yelled in the dream and woke us both up."

"But now you need to go back to sleep. Like I said, it's three in the morning."

"Didn't you hear what I said, Mom?" Eric asked. "We were both dreaming."

"Yes, and Zack yelled in his sleep and woke you both. So?"

"We had the same dream!"

"What do you mean, the same dream?"

"A twin dream, Mom. Remember when you told us about twin dreams? That article you read us. They're real!"

"No!" Clay yelled. But no one could hear him.

HEATHER HAD BEEN DREAMING of jogging along the beach when she rolled over and sleepily opened her eyes. She wanted to go back to sleep, but she had to pee. Annoyed, she tossed her sheets and blankets aside and stumbled out of bed. Her bedroom was dark save for a nightlight along the wall under the window.

Groggy, she stumbled to the bathroom and flipped on the light. Even though she was alone in the house except for her cat, she shut the bathroom door anyway, out of habit. When she finished, she washed her hands and flung open the door, intending to turn off the bathroom light.

Instead, she let out a scream, for there, standing in her doorway, stood the ghost of Clay Bowman. After registering who was in her house, and now fully awake, she glared at the ghost and shouted,

"What the hell, Clay? It's the middle of the night. What are you doing?"

"There was a wreath hanging on your door. I assumed it would be okay."

"Of course there's a wreath on my front door. You know I put it there last night." Heather motioned for Clay to move away from the open doorway. She flipped off her bathroom light, and he barely moved out of the way in time to avoid her walking through him. "We've already spoken since I hung that wreath," Heather reminded him, her tone snarky and annoyed. "I didn't think I needed to take it right down. I didn't realize you'd be so dense as to see it as an invitation to drop in whenever you want! Like in the freaking middle of the night when I'm going to the bathroom?"

Clay trailed after Heather as she stomped back to her bedroom. "But it didn't work."

"What didn't work?" Heather entered her bedroom and flipped on the light. She walked to her end table and picked up her cellphone, checking to see the time. It was 4:23 a.m.

"They didn't see it as anything but a dream," Clay explained. The previous evening, Clay had visited Heather after seeing the wreath hanging on her house. During their visit, she had suggested his sons probably would not listen to a stranger, as they had refused to listen to the chief. But they might listen to him. Heather had explained dream hops and told him to go to the cemetery where Eva and Marie would be waiting, prepared to help guide him through his first dream hop.

The light had woken Heather's calico cat, Bella, who now stood on the bed, the hair on her back standing on end as the cat hissed at Clay. Heather walked over to the cat and swooped her up, hugging her to her chest. "Don't worry, Bella, that mean ghost can't hurt us." Still holding Bella, Heather walked to the rocking chair in the corner of her room and sat down, placing the cat on her lap. She stroked the feline while shifting her attention to Clay.

Clay frowned at the petite feline. "That cat hates me."

"What is she saying to you?" Heather asked while still stroking

Bella. No longer hissing, Bella curled up quietly on Heather's lap, her eyes locked on the ghost while her tail swished back and forth.

"She's imagining I'm a mouse. The visual she's giving is disgusting."

Heather shrugged. "What can I say? She's a cat, and you tried to kill her human."

"She's rather morbid." Clay shivered.

"Did I ever tell you I met Camilla's ghost after you killed her?"

Clay's gaze shifted from the cat to Heather. "Seriously?"

"You know what was so pitiful?"

Clay shook his head. "No."

"Camilla had no idea who killed her. It didn't take her long to realize it wasn't me. Someone like me isn't about to screw with that type of karma. She also didn't think you killed her. In fact, she thought you were going after me so hard because you believed I was the killer. When you tried to push me down the stairs, she begged you to stop. Telling you not to kill me because I hadn't murdered her. In some ways, it redeemed you in her mind for the briefest of moments."

"What do you mean? How did that redeem me?"

"I suppose you broke her heart. You two have an affair, and she assumes you have a life together. She blows up her marriage, and you leave town with your wife. She is betrayed, but years later she sees you again, and you end up revenging her death, or so she thinks. But then she hears you confess her murder to me."

"How did she take that? She must hate me."

Heather let out a snort. "Like I said, it was kind of pitiful when she realized you weren't trying to avenge her. You had actually killed her. And yeah, she hates you. You helped ruin her life, and years later, you ended it. Although, I can't say she still hates you. From what I understand, when we move over to the next place, our perspectives change. But don't get too full of yourself. It's not like she was still in love with you when you killed her. I'm sure she still had feelings for Brian."

"Brian, that's one thing I don't understand."

"What, that Camilla still had feelings for the husband she cheated on?"

Clay shook his head. "No. That you and Brian are a couple."

Heather rolled her eyes. "Get in line. No one understands that."

Clay studied Heather for a moment. "He's not here tonight."

"He does have his own apartment."

"From what I understand, he can't have kids."

"That works out good. I don't want kids either. What's your point?"

Clay shrugged. "The age difference might be an issue when you decide you want to start a family."

"Wow, now you're concerned about my happiness and my relationship with Brian?" Heather snarked.

"I know what it's like to make poor choices that change the course of your life."

"Well, I already have my family. I don't need to start anything. We should get back to why you're here. What did you mean they thought it was a dream?"

Clay told Heather about the dream and the boys' reaction. When he was done, she asked, "What is a twin dream?"

"My wife once read an article that suggested the possibility of shared dreams between two people who have a close emotional connection. It said twins were more susceptible to shared dreams. She read that part of the article to our boys. They are convinced that the dream last night was nothing more than a twin-shared dream brought on by their meeting with MacDonald and what he said about me."

"Well, crud. That sucks. In the morning I'll call the mediums and see if they have any ideas. But do me a favor and go down to the cemetery. You could run into Eva and Marie. They always have good ideas. But if you don't see them, wait until I remove the wreath from my door. When you see it gone, this time it will mean I have something to tell you. And please don't come over here in the middle of the night again."

THE GHOST WHO SOUGHT REDEMPTION

CLAY WASN'T sure how long he had been standing at the entrance of the cemetery. There had been no moonlight to brighten the sky, no streetlights. Only an occasional headlight from a car passing by to break up the darkness. But now the sun was beginning to rise. He did not know where to find Eva or Marie, or if they were even at the cemetery. He started down one walkway when he heard a voice call out.

"Hey, it's you again."

Clay stopped walking and turned to the voice. The spirit he knew as Wesley stood some ten feet away.

"You're Wesley, right?"

Wesley approached Clay. "I understand you're trying to get the mediums to help you."

"Have you seen Eva or Marie?"

Wesley stopped walking, now standing about four feet from Clay. He shook his head. "No. The last time I saw them was at Marlow House. But they left. I don't know where they went. Not sure why you'd want to talk to either of them."

"I need their help."

Wesley scoffed. "You should move on. Aren't you just putting off the inevitable? You said you murdered someone. It's not like you can do anything to bring them back to life."

"And why exactly are you sticking around? What do you need from the mediums?" Clay asked.

"Let's just say I'm doing damage control, in case it's true that we're judged by our intentions and not actions," Wesley said.

TWENTY-THREE

Danielle sat with Walt in the parlor on Tuesday morning, going over their day's schedule while Danielle nursed the twins.

"If I could get out of here by nine, it will give me almost three hours," Danielle told Walt. "That should be plenty of time. You going to be okay alone with the twins?"

"Why is Walt going to be alone with the twins?" Marie asked as she appeared in the room.

"Morning, Marie," Walt greeted. "But I'm perfectly capable of taking care of Addison and Jack while Danielle goes out."

"I never said you weren't." Marie smiled down at Danielle, who had her hands full nursing the infants. "Where are you off to, dear? Isn't Lily coming home today? I thought you'd want to be here when she gets back with the baby."

"She is, but according to Ian, they probably won't discharge her until after lunch. There are a few things I want to pick up before she gets here."

Jack stopped nursing, and Walt leaned over to Danielle and gently took him from her. "I also think my wife wants to get away for a few hours by herself." Walt put Jack over his shoulder and gently burped the baby.

"Well, I can understand that." Marie looked to Walt. "While I understand you're perfectly capable, if you would like me to stay while Danielle is out, I'll be more than happy to."

Standing by the sofa, Walt continued to pat Jack. "I always appreciate an extra set of hands."

"Good." Marie smiled and glanced around. "I assume Ian is at the hospital. His car wasn't out front. Is Connor with him?"

"No. Connor's with his aunt Kelly," Danielle said. "She's going to bring him over here later this afternoon."

"When are you planning to leave?" Marie asked.

"I want to get out of here by nine, so in about fifteen minutes."

"Before you go, I wanted to tell you both, Clay tracked Eva and me down early this morning. The dream hop was not a success." Marie went on to tell them what Clay had shared with her and Eva, while Addison finished nursing.

Danielle adjusted her blouse before handing a now sleeping baby to Marie while saying, "Sorry to hear that, but can we deal with this later? I'd really like to get going so I'm back by noon."

"No problem, dear." Marie gently burped Addison. "Those young hooligans have time to mend their ways."

"Thanks, Marie." Danielle stood up from the sofa and adjusted her clothes. She walked over to Walt and kissed his cheek. "Love you."

Walt kissed her back. "Enjoy your time."

"What are you picking up?" Marie asked while Danielle gathered up her purse and cellphone from where she had set them in the living room.

"Old Salts, for one. We're out of cinnamon rolls. After all, Lily and I have to keep up our calorie intake for all this breastfeeding."

Marie laughed. "Sure you do, dear."

DANIELLE SAT ALONE in her Ford Flex, parked in her garage, the engine not running. She pressed the button on the remote clipped to her visor and watched as the garage door opened, letting in the morning sunlight. Instead of buckling her seatbelt or putting the key in the ignition, she leaned back in her car seat, took a deep breath, and enjoyed a few moments of solitude.

While she loved being a mother, there were times she felt overwhelmed. In those moments, guilt washed over her. After all, what did she have to complain about? She had a supportive and involved husband, a tremendous support system, and unlike so many young parents, she didn't have to worry about buying groceries or putting food on the table.

Perhaps it was the breastfeeding. Again, even asking herself that question brought a fresh wave of guilt. Danielle had always wanted to breastfeed when she had children. Yet she had always understood that not all women could produce enough milk, and for some women, it simply did not work out for other reasons.

When finding out they were having twins, she expressed disappointment to Lily that she wouldn't be able to breastfeed without supplementing with formula. But Lily told her she knew some mothers of twins had enough milk to nurse both babies without having to add formula, and perhaps she would be able to.

As it turned out, Lily had been right. She had plenty of milk. While Danielle was grateful, she sometimes felt overwhelmed at how much time she spent nursing, and she couldn't go anywhere for more than a few hours, or her milk would drop, and her bra would get soaked.

But then she would remember something Lily's mother had told Lily. She had reminded her that those first years of motherhood might seem overwhelming in that your entire life revolves around your babies—your toddlers. It's not like you can just take off and do whatever you want without first making plans for your children. Lily's mother had told her daughter that those early years of motherhood go so quickly, much quicker than she could ever imagine, and that while it might sometimes seem as if your life is no longer yours, before you know it your children are off living their own lives, and you look back on those early days and realize how it went so fast —too fast.

Danielle smiled at the sentiment. She wanted to enjoy every

moment of motherhood. And she was. Danielle took another deep breath and fastened her seatbelt.

A few moments later, she turned on the ignition and drove out of the garage. Once all the way onto the driveway, Danielle stopped the car and pressed the button on the remote again. Looking in the rearview mirror, she watched the garage door close.

Just as Danielle pulled into the alley, a voice said, "I need to talk to you."

Danielle slammed on the brakes and looked to the passenger seat. There sat Wesley, smiling at her.

"What are you doing here?" Danielle looked up the alley to make sure there were no cars coming before pressing on the gas and continuing down the narrow road.

"I wanted to see if there has been any progress with my wife."

"You mean your widow. Be honest, are you just jealous of your brother, or are you really concerned he's going to kill her?"

"I know my brother."

"Not sure what that means. But I don't know what you expect us to do."

"Do you remember that aunt who left Bonnie her estate?"

"I remember you telling me about it."

"Bonnie is finally listing her aunt's property. And when she does that, then my brother is that much closer to killing her. When that property sells, it's going to be a lot of money."

"What do you want me to do? Prevent the sale?"

"Hmmm. That's an idea. At least until we can figure out how to break them up."

"How will preventing a sale help?"

"You suggested it."

Danielle groaned. "Yeah, I suggested it facetiously. But why do you think it might slow your brother down?"

"If she sells the property and they put the proceeds in a joint bank account, it will be easier for him to keep the money if she mysteriously dies. But getting his hands on the real estate might be a little tricky."

"And how do you suggest I stop the sale?"

"She hasn't officially listed the property, but she's having Adam Nichols give her a CMA. She dropped off the key this morning."

"Adam?" Danielle glanced briefly at Wesley.

"You know him?"

"I'll tell you what, I'll go talk to Adam, see what I can do, but only if you let me do this myself. Now where is this house at?"

Wesley told Danielle the name of Bonnie's aunt, along with the location of the property. He then said, "He won't know I'm there."

Danielle put on her brakes and looked at Wesley. "I mean it. I want some time to myself today. I don't want you hanging around and annoying me. Just go and check back with me tomorrow."

"You mediums aren't very nice to ghosts."

"Yeah, right. I've heard that before. Now go!"

"HI, LESLIE, IS ADAM IN?" Danielle asked fifteen minutes later after entering the front office of Frederickport Vacation Properties.

Leslie, who sat behind one of the desks just inside the office, smiled up at Danielle. "Hi, Danielle. Here to see Adam?"

"Yeah, wondered if he was here."

"He is. Just got in about fifteen minutes ago. He's in his office, having coffee and reading the paper. Go on back."

A FEW MINUTES LATER, Danielle sat with Adam in his office, drinking a cup of coffee and eating a cinnamon roll he had offered her.

"I have to stop by Old Salts and pick up some of these," Danielle said before pulling off a bite of the roll and popping it in her mouth. She glanced at the newspaper on the desk and added, "I thought Walt was the only one who still read a newspaper?"

Adam, who sat behind his desk, shrugged. "I like to read the local newspaper." He took a sip of coffee and asked, "So what are you doing? Playing hooky?"

Danielle leaned back in her chair, a cup of coffee in one hand and a partially eaten cinnamon roll in the other. "Lily comes home from the hospital today. But not until this afternoon. I have a few errands to run before she gets there. And yeah, playing hooky a little." Danielle flashed Adam a smile.

"So how did I get on your errand list? Or do you just have super-cinnamon-roll radar?"

Danielle chuckled. "No. The cinnamon roll was a bonus. But I thought I would stop by and see if you have any interesting listings."

"You looking to buy?"

"Remember my former mother-in-law?"

"The one married to the medium?"

Danielle nodded. "Yeah. She hasn't been back since her first visit, but we talk frequently on the phone. She liked Frederickport and wondered what the current real estate market was like." It wasn't a complete lie.

"Not a lot on the market right now, to be honest. But I might be getting a new listing. I have to go check it out."

"Where is it?"

Adam stood up and grabbed a photograph off his desk and carried it to Danielle. She set her coffee cup on a table and took the picture from Adam.

Adam sat on the edge of his desk, several feet from Danielle. "It's on your side of town."

"I've seen this house."

"It's been empty for over a year. First, it was going through probate. The owner died. Between you and me, the whole thing was a mess."

"How so?" Danielle handed the photograph back to Adam.

Adam accepted the photo, glanced at it a moment, and then tossed it on his desk before saying, "It was owned by an elderly woman. I think Grandma knew her. Grandma knew everyone." Adam chuckled. "Anyway, she had two nieces, and one niece was her caretaker for the last couple of years of her life. But when she died, she left everything to the other niece."

"That must have made the niece who'd been taking care of her upset."

Adam nodded. "She contested the will. It looked like it was going to drag on, but then she just dropped her case. And the niece who hadn't been the caregiver inherited everything."

"Why?"

"Some rumors started going around about elder abuse, involving the niece who had been taking care of the aunt. But when she dropped her case, the rumors stopped."

TWENTY-FOUR

It was 11:45 a.m. when Danielle returned to Marlow House on Tuesday. During her morning outing, she noticed all the Fourth of July decorations displayed around town. She had almost forgotten Independence Day was on Thursday. With all that had been going on the last couple of months and the fact they had temporarily closed the bed-and-breakfast, she had given little thought to how they might celebrate the holiday. Fact was, the B and B's July Fourth celebrations, which also marked the grand opening of the bed-and-breakfast five years ago, didn't have a good track record for happy endings, so perhaps the Universe was trying to tell her something, she thought.

Sadie greeted Danielle as she walked from the garage through the yard to the kitchen door. The golden retriever followed Danielle into the house, where Danielle was greeted by Max, who wove in and out of her feet, purring.

Almost stumbling over the cat, Danielle made it to the kitchen table without dropping the bags she carried. After setting her packages on the table, she picked up Max, sat on a chair, and placed the cat on her lap. She stroked Max's fur while Sadie rested her head on Danielle's knee. The dog looked up into her eyes, her tail wagging.

"Well, this is quite a greeting," Danielle said with a chuckle.

"You're here," Marie said as she appeared in the kitchen.

Danielle looked up at the ghost and smiled. "Yes, I got quite the greeting from these two."

"They were a little miffed because I wouldn't let them come into the nursery with me. The babies are sleeping, and I was afraid they'd wake them."

"Where's Walt?"

"He's up in his office, doing some work. How was your morning?"

"Productive, I guess. Umm, has Walt had lunch yet?"

"No, he was talking about waiting for you to get back."

"Good, I picked up some lunch. I was going to pick up something for Lily and Ian too, but she texted me they had already eaten."

BY THE TIME Lily and Ian arrived at Marlow House with Emily Ann, Walt and Danielle had already finished lunch; the twins had been fed and placed together in the living room playpen. Earlier, Ian had brought Lily's rocking chair over and set it in Marlow House's living room.

Despite that, the arrival proved chaotic. As Ian pulled up in front of Marlow House and parked, Chris pulled in behind him with Heather, Hunny, and Bella. Danielle and Marie came outside to greet the new arrivals, leaving the front door wide open, while Walt stayed inside with the twins, looking out the front window.

They all exchanged greetings and hugs while Lily held on to her new daughter, Ian by her side, not wanting her to trip. Chris and Heather had come bearing gifts, and they carried those in with them as they all entered the house and headed to the living room.

But soon they were all settled down comfortably, with Hunny guarding the twins, and Sadie by Lily's side as she sat in the rocker with Emily Ann. After catching up on all the baby news and then opening gifts, Lily asked, "So what's going on with these two ghosts? Are they still hanging around? Are they here now?"

"Only Marie," Danielle said.

"Tell Lily her baby is beautiful," Marie said.

Danielle conveyed the message, and then Walt asked Lily, "Has Ian told you about the Bowman twins?"

"You mean about them getting arrested?"

Walt nodded. "And how their father wants us to help him convince his sons not to follow his path."

"Yeah. Ian said something about having Clay do a dream hop."

"According to Marie, the dream hop didn't work," Danielle said.

"The dream hop worked. But Clay's sons didn't believe he was really there," Marie grumbled.

"I woke up last night to use the bathroom, and when I was going back to bed, there was Clay, standing in the hallway." Heather gave an unladylike snort.

"Oh, my god!" Lily gasped. "That must have been terrifying."

"Fortunately, more annoying than terrifying," Heather said. "Now, if he had been alive, that would have been scary." Heather told them about Clay's dream hop and why it hadn't worked out.

"Now we have to figure out some way to convince those boys it wasn't a regular dream," Danielle said. "If we do that, they might listen to their father's advice."

"I'm not sure the Bowman boys will pay attention to what their father says, even if they understand it's him," Heather said. "Not from what I've heard about them. But if they at least listen to him, and Clay thinks he's done all he can, he might move on, and I won't have to worry about running into him in my hallway in the middle of the night."

"There has to be a way we can convince those boys it's really their father," Chris said.

They all sat in silence for a few moments, each one thinking of a way to convince the Bowman kids their father had visited them.

"Obviously, having them both in the dream didn't work," Ian said. "But how about getting someone else involved who isn't in the dream? Someone who can verify it was more than a dream."

Danielle looked at Ian. "What do you suggest?"

"Perhaps take a page out of Dickens's *A Christmas Carol*," Ian said with a chuckle.

"In what way?" Danielle asked.

Ian sat back in his chair, stretching his legs out while crossing his arms over his chest. He smiled a moment before answering, "Maybe a series of dreams. Tell them he is going to prove it's not just a regular dream and that the next morning they will be visited by…I don't know…"

"What? The ghost of Christmas past and future?" Heather asked with a giggle. She then added, "But actually, that's kind of an interesting idea."

"I agree," Walt said. "It might take just one night. He can visit the boys again, tell them someone will be visiting them the following day to deliver a specific message. If they still believe it's just a dream, he could visit them again the next night, same thing."

"Maybe Eva could keep an eye on the boys for a few days, learn their schedule," Danielle suggested. "If we know where they're going to be the next day, it'll be easier for someone to run into them and pass on whatever message Clay tells them to expect."

"But who is going to visit them, and what should they tell the boys?" Lily asked.

As they continued to discuss the topic, Marie wandered over to the playpen. She stood over it and watched the twins. Each baby wore a sleeper—Addison's pink and Jack's blue. They waved their hands and kicked their feet. Occasionally, the mediums would glance over at Marie and smile at her and the babies and then resume their conversation.

Something from the front yard caught Marie's eye. Moving closer to the window, she looked outside and saw Ian's sister and mother coming up the front walk with Connor. Marie turned from the window.

"It looks like Connor is home," Marie announced. "I'm going to take off. We don't need Connor asking me to play with him while his grandmother and aunt are here."

"Thanks, Marie." Danielle glanced at Ian. "Kelly and your mom are here with Connor. Marie is leaving."

"Goodbye, Marie," Lily called out before muttering, "I didn't know June was coming over with Kelly."

Chris offered to answer the front door because he was the closest one to the entry hall. A few minutes later, Kelly and June walked into the living room with the toddler while Chris trailed behind them. Connor immediately ran to his parents and new sister, with his grandmother following him. Kelly stood just inside the entrance, hands on hips, surveying the room.

"Wow, this place looks like a nursery. Cribs everywhere," Kelly said.

"Marlow House Bed and Breakfast now specializes in infants and toddlers," Danielle joked before the rest of the room exchanged greetings with Kelly and June.

June, now standing behind the rocker where Lily sat with the baby, glanced across the room at the playpen with the twins. She spied Hunny sleeping nearby and then looked over to Sadie.

"Is it such a good idea to have the dogs in here with the babies?" June asked.

"They're fine, Mom," Ian said.

"I know you said to come back tomorrow," Wesley said when he appeared in the middle of the room. "But I couldn't wait. Did you find out anything?"

"Clown!" Connor toddled toward the ghost.

"There he goes with that clown thing again," June said. Lily and Ian silently exchanged glances.

Connor reached Wesley and then plopped down on his bottom and looked up at the ghost. "Trick, pez?"

The mediums stared at the ghost but said nothing.

Wesley smiled down at Connor. "Hey, little buddy." The next moment Wesley grabbed hold of his own right hand, pulled it off, and tossed it in the air. The hand disappeared in midair and a moment later reappeared where Wesley had snatched it.

Connor started clapping and laughing. "Mo! Mo!"

Wesley grinned at Danielle. "I've learned some new tricks.

Pamela's been helping me. I think you know her. She told me you met."

"What is he doing?" June asked.

Kelly shook her head. "He never does this stuff when he's with us."

Ian walked over to his son and picked him up, intentionally walking through the area where he believed the ghost was most likely standing.

Wesley immediately backed up and started complaining while cringing repeatedly.

"Connor is just acting out a little, aren't you, buddy?" Ian said before giving his son a hug and kiss. He turned to his mother. "He had to move out of his room, and then his mom was gone for a few days, and we come back with a new sister for him. A lot for him to process. He's just trying to get some attention."

"I suppose you're right," June muttered.

The mediums sat quietly, saying nothing, silently observing while also keeping an eye on Wesley, who was now flapping his arms while circling the living room as if trying to get rid of whatever icky sensation Ian gave him when he stepped through his energy. Finally, Wesley said, "I'm going. I'll come back tomorrow, and when I do, I'd rather not be around anyone who can't see me. Clumsy clods!" He vanished.

Still in his father's arms, Connor reached out and said, "Clown go."

"Yes, Connor. The clown had to go," Heather told him.

June flashed Heather a quizzical expression and then turned to Ian and Lily. "We need to go too."

"Mom, we just got here," Kelly reminded her.

June looked at the sleeping baby in Lily's arms. "The baby's sleeping, and Connor seems to need a nap. Maybe tomorrow I can come back and hold that little angel?"

"Why don't you call first, Mom," Ian suggested. "Lily just got home from the hospital, and I imagine she'll need to rest tomorrow."

June glanced around the room at all of their friends sitting around but reserved comment.

"WHY DOES that clown ghost keep haunting Connor?" Lily asked after Kelly and June left.

"He's not really a clown," Heather said.

"To be honest, I doubt he was here to see Connor. He wanted to talk to me." Danielle then explained the encounter in the car and her visit with Adam.

"Wait a minute, that's the same Rylee who was my nurse?" Lily asked.

Danielle shrugged. "Apparently. According to Marie, he was talking to her in the hospital. Of course, just like you, she couldn't hear him."

"I can't believe it's the same nurse. She was too nice. I don't see her abusing her aunt."

"That's a totally different situation," Ian reminded her. "Caring for a family member can be a different dynamic."

"I'd think you'd be less likely to abuse a family member," Lily argued.

Ian shrugged. "I'm just saying family relationships are complicated."

"The thing I don't understand, if I was a nurse who was accused of elder abuse, and the accuser was willing to keep quiet for whatever reason, I certainly wouldn't take a job in the same town as that person. I'd want to stay far away from whoever had accused me," Heather said.

TWENTY-FIVE

Marie found Eva at the cemetery in an unlikely spot. The onetime silent screen star sat perched atop the Marlow family's stone mausoleum, chatting with the ghost of Pamela Beckett, who sat by her side. Before Marie approached her friend, she observed the pair for a moment. Eva, who had died young, had refused to move on because of her premature death, while Pamela had lived out her life yet had wasted those years and hadn't really lived, and because of that, she had also refused to move on.

After a moment, Marie approached her fellow ghosts, making her presence known. "Afternoon. Lovely day, isn't it? What are you two up to? You look so serious."

Eva turned to Marie and smiled. "We were discussing Pamela moving on."

"Really? You're ready?" Marie asked.

"I was thinking about it." Pamela shrugged. Her gaze moved over the rows and rows of headstones. "Eva pointed out that by staying here and not moving on, is that any different from all those years I stayed in my childhood home, not having a life of my own? It wasn't an actual ghost who helped cripple my spirit back then, but the residue of one because of a quilt my mother brought home.

THE GHOST WHO SOUGHT REDEMPTION

And is it any different now? I'm letting another spirit—Wesley—hold me here in some limbo."

"How is Wesley holding you here?" Marie asked.

Eva looked from Pamela to Marie. "Wesley was the first spirit Pamela met when she arrived. And in many ways, Pamela understood instinctively about the possibilities of her energy, while Wesley, who had been here longer, didn't even know how to change his shirt until Pamela explained."

"He's always been terrified of Eva, and I'm not sure why, but he doesn't seem to like you, Marie," Pamela said.

Marie chuckled. "It doesn't surprise me. We have a bit of history."

"I feel like my existence should be more than holding Wesley's hand. Not literally, of course. I need more."

"Before you go, can I ask you something?" Marie asked.

Pamela gave Marie a nod.

"What do you know about Wesley and his wife?"

"Just that he doesn't want his wife to marry his brother."

"Is it from jealousy?"

Pamela laughed. "I seriously doubt it. He doesn't say the nicest things about her."

"Supposedly, he's convinced his brother plans to kill her for her money."

Pamela nodded. "Yes. He believes that. But I don't think he wants to prevent the marriage to save her life. I mean, yes, he wants to save her life. But it's not because he's trying to be a hero or that he cares about her."

"Then why?" Eva asked.

"He's rather terrified of moving on. For some reason, he thinks stopping the marriage will save her life, which he feels will minimize whatever judgment he might face when he does pass over."

Marie shook her head. "What's with these two meddlesome spirits? Running around frantically trying to earn some last-minute brownie points to make up for a lifetime of misdeeds. We know what Clay's misdeeds are, but what did Wesley do?"

Pamela shrugged. "I don't know if he's done anything."

"Do you know why he's convinced his brother plans to murder his wife?" Marie asked.

Pamela shook her head. "No. Do you have any other questions?"

Marie thought about it for a moment before answering, "No."

Pamela smiled at Marie and Eva. "Then tell Wesley I've gone."

And just like that, Pamela Beckett moved on in her journey.

"When she said gone, did she mean..." Marie started to ask.

"Yes, she moved on," Eva finished for Marie as she floated down from the headstone.

"I just wish Clay and Wesley would move on." Marie then told Eva what had been discussed over at Marlow House that afternoon.

After Marie finished, Eva asked, "Did I ever tell you when I played the Ghost of Christmas Past in a rendition of *A Christmas Carol* right here in Fredrickport? I was just fifteen at the time..."

"Yes, dear, you can tell me all about it after we go check on the Bowman twins and see if we can figure out what they might be doing tomorrow."

"WHY CAN'T we go to the beach tomorrow?" Zack asked his mother. He stood next to her at the kitchen sink in the garage apartment as she washed dishes.

"Go grab a tea towel and dry these dishes," she told him.

In the living room, his brother sat at the card table his mother had squeezed in one corner. White typing paper and colored markers were scattered across the table, with some pieces of paper already drawn on. Eric listened to his brother while he colored in his picture. It was a monster eating a man. Earlier, when Zack had asked who the man was, Eric told him, "Chief MacDonald."

"If I dry the dishes, can we go to the beach tomorrow?" Zack asked his mother.

The next moment, Eva and Marie stood in the middle of the apartment.

Zack's mother turned to him, hands now on hips, and said

THE GHOST WHO SOUGHT REDEMPTION

angrily, "No, you cannot go to the beach tomorrow. And you can't go the next day. You are both under house arrest, and until this matter is settled, and you boys show significant regret, you won't be going anywhere."

"Are you going to keep us in this house forever?" Zack whined.

"I suppose that's up to you. Now dry these dishes and put them away."

Marie and Eva quietly observed the encounter, each noticing the other brother stayed quiet, keeping his head down and focusing on whatever he was drawing.

"It looks like we have our answer. The boys are going to be here in this apartment for a while," Eva said.

Marie watched as Zack's mother grabbed a towel from the counter and tossed it at him before storming off to her bedroom and slamming the door behind her. Reluctantly, Zack started drying the dishes. "Why don't you come put these away for me?"

Eric looked over at his brother from the card table. "Mom asked you to do it."

"You butt."

"Charming boys," Eva muttered from the sidelines.

"We can't have someone knock on the door and deliver Clay's message," Marie said. "I envisioned something more like the boys being at the library, and we get Olivia to hand a note to the boys and say, 'This is from your father.'"

"Yes, dear, while that is all very dramatic, and you know I love drama, perhaps we should go for something a little more direct and immediate. Get this done now."

Marie looked at Eva. "What do you mean?"

"You can harness energy. Go over there, pick up one of those markers, and write them a note. If you want some drama, make sure they see you writing the note. Well, not you exactly, but you know what I mean."

Marie stared at Eva for a moment. "You're right. We were all overthinking this."

"Do it now, while their mother is in the bedroom. No reason for her to get more upset than she already is. After all, her late husband is a murderer, and her two sons seem to be following in his footsteps. Did you notice that picture the one at the table is coloring?"

Marie moved over to the card table and looked down at the picture, her attention drawn to the bright red blood dripping from the monster's sharp fangs. "Who do you suspect the monster is eating?"

"Does it matter?"

Marie shrugged and then reached for a marker.

ERIC CHEWED on his lower lip as he focused on his picture, when he decided to add a few red slashes across the man's throat. He looked up from the drawing, searching for a red marker, when he spied a black marker float up from the table. He froze as his eyes widened at the sight.

As the marker hovered above the table, a blank piece of paper drifted up in the air and floated toward him, landing atop his drawing. Unable to move, he stared down at the blank piece of paper covering his drawing and failed to see the cap coming off the black marker. The next moment, the marker wrote across the paper. The words slowly appeared: *That was not a twin dream. Your father was there. Listen to him next time.*

The marker dropped to the table, and Eric let out a scream and jumped up from his chair.

Zack turned from the sink and saw his brother pressed against the wall, staring at the card table.

"What are you doing?" Zack asked.

Eric pointed to the table but didn't move.

Zack rolled his eyes, tossed the damp tea towel on the counter, and walked over to the table. "What, is there a spider or something? You scared of spiders now? Can't you just smash it instead of acting like a stupid girl?"

"Look!" Eric's right hand quivered as he pointed to the table.

Zack walked over to the table and looked down at the pieces of paper. He spied the note, picked it up, and then read it. After reading the note, he tossed it on the table and looked at his brother. "Funny. Ha ha. You are so lame."

"I didn't write that!"

"Sure you didn't. Stop being such a jerk."

Just as Zack turned back to the card table, prepared to walk around it en route to the kitchen, he froze when a piece of blank paper floated up from the table and landed on the paper Zack had just tossed there. As Zack stared down at the paper, the black marker lifted from the table.

"Look!" Eric shouted, pointing at the marker.

Zack looked from the blank paper to the marker and watched as the marker floated toward him and then stopped above the piece of blank paper. Zack's mouth fell open as he watched the marker write: *Your brother did not write that note. Your father will visit your dream again.*

TWENTY-SIX

After Chris and Heather dropped by Marlow House after lunch on Tuesday, to see if Lily and the baby were home from the hospital, they ended up staying for a couple of hours, but eventually returned to the office. It was after five when Chris and Heather left the office for home. As they did most days, they carpooled to work, taking turns. Chris had driven today, and when he reached Heather's, he pulled up in front of her house to drop her off. After she got out of Chris's car, she slammed the passenger door shut and waved goodbye to Chris. She stayed a moment on the sidewalk in front of her house as she watched Chris drive up the street to his house.

Heather turned from the street and started up the walkway to her front door. When she was about halfway there, she started when Eva and Marie suddenly appeared.

On reflex, Heather jumped back. "You guys scared me! Where's the snowflakes or glitter?"

"No time for that," Eva told her. "We're on our way to Marlow House, but we needed to stop here first and tell you to remove the wreath."

"Remove the wreath? You have something you want me to tell Clay?"

"Yes." Marie quickly recounted what had happened over at the garage apartment. When she was done, she asked, "Do you need us to stay with you until Clay shows up, if you would rather not be alone with him?"

"I'd rather not see him at all, but that's beside the point. But no, if you're on your way to Marlow House, you don't need to babysit me. Brian's going to be here pretty soon, anyway. Not that he can see Clay. And who knows when Clay will notice I've removed the wreath. He might not stop by until tomorrow."

Marie nodded. "True."

"When you told his sons they'd have another dream, did you say tonight? Because if Clay doesn't show until tomorrow, it obviously won't be tonight."

"Don't worry about that. We didn't specify when they'd have another dream," Marie told her.

"Okay. I'll let you know when he shows up." Heather walked the rest of the way to her door and immediately removed the wreath. When she glanced back to tell Marie and Eva something, they were already gone. "Well, goodbye to you too," Heather muttered.

Wreath in one hand, Heather dug her house key from the purse hanging over her shoulder. She then used it to unlock the door. The next moment, she walked into her house with her wreath and was greeted by Clay Bowman, who stood in her entry hall, looking at her. Once again Heather startled in surprise.

"Crap. Do you have to pop in like that?" She shut the door and then set the wreath on the entry table.

"You removed the wreath. I thought that meant you wanted to talk to me."

Heather turned back to Clay. "It does, but I didn't think it worked like some freaking pager. How did you get here so quickly? Have you been stalking outside and creeping on my house?"

"Do you have something to tell me or not?"

Heather glanced around. She didn't see Bella and suspected the cat was in hiding. The other night, Walt had explained Clay to Bella, assuring the cat Clay couldn't hurt Heather or Bella. Of course, that didn't mean the cat wanted to hang out with the ghost. But then Heather spied Bella crouching on a curio shelf down the hall.

"Let's go in the kitchen. I want to get something to drink."

Clay followed Heather toward the kitchen. He failed to notice the cat watching him, and just as he walked by the curio shelf, the cat let out an unholy screech and leapt on the ghost, falling through Clay's head and then body to the floor.

Clay came to an abrupt stop and looked down in time to see the cat racing out of his foot and down the hall into the kitchen. "What the hell was that?"

"Bella. She doesn't like you."

"And I don't like how that felt. Tell her not to do that again," he snapped.

"She's a cat. Obviously, you've never had a cat. You can't tell a cat what to do. Well, not unless you're Walt."

"What's that supposed to mean?" Clay grumbled as he rolled his shoulders uncomfortably, trying to shake off the unpleasant sensation. He followed Heather.

Once in the kitchen, Clay watched as Heather set her purse on the kitchen table and then walk to the counter to prepare a glass of iced green tea.

"You going to drink that this late at night?" he asked.

Heather frowned at Clay. "Why not?"

"You can't drink caffeine this late and still have a good night's sleep."

"Do you get a lot of good sleep now that you can't drink caffeine?" Heather smirked.

"I don't sleep." Clay didn't sound happy.

"Sucks to be you." Heather grabbed her glass of iced tea and headed for the kitchen table. She sat down and pointed to the empty chair across from her for him to sit in. Reluctantly, he sat, and when he did, Heather told Clay about Marie and Eva's visit to see his sons.

"I wonder what the boys thought when they saw that pen writing on its own."

Heather glanced over toward the refrigerator and spied her cat hunched atop the appliance. Maybe Heather couldn't read the cat's mind like Walt could, but she had a fairly good idea Bella was trying to figure out if she could leap all the way to Clay.

So engrossed in Bella's possible shenanigans, Heather momentarily forgot what she and Clay had just been talking about. "What?"

"I said, I wonder what the boys thought when they saw that pen move on its own."

"Ahh, I don't know." Heather glanced from Clay to her cat, back to Clay.

"Do you think my boys will listen to me now?"

Heather shrugged and took a sip of tea before saying, "All you can do is try. But answer me this: do you think your sons will heed your advice even if they believe it's really you?"

Clay considered the question for a moment. Finally, he said, "I'm not really sure. I hope so."

Heather set her glass of tea on the table and studied Clay for a moment.

Clay frowned at her. "What?"

"You were horrible when you were alive. Nasty. Why?"

Clay shrugged. "I don't know. I guess I had goals, and people were in the way."

"How was I in the way?"

"I suppose you weren't in the way as much as you were convenient."

"Convenient?"

"Someone to take the fall for Camilla's murder. And I suppose, before I even knew Camilla was back in town, getting rid of someone like you seemed like a good idea if I wanted to show my brother-in-law I was serious about cleaning up Frederickport. It had a uniquely high capital crime rate."

"Which you increased."

"And here I am."

Heather glanced back to the cat again, concerned Bella might hurt herself attempting to jump all the way to Clay

"Can you do me a favor? Stand up a moment."

Clay frowned. "Why?"

"Come on, just do it. You owe me. After all, you did try to kill me."

Reluctantly, Clay stood. "Now what?"

"Move back a few feet," Heather said while giving her hand a little wave toward her refrigerator. Clay moved a few feet back. "More." He moved a few more steps back. "Okay, just another foot and then stop."

Clay let out a grunt but moved back a step and stopped. Just as he was about to ask Heather why she wanted him to stand there, Bella jumped atop his head, falling through his body as she hissed and batted her paws in all directions, claws fully extended. Just at that moment, Brian walked into the kitchen from the back door. He stopped in his tracks and watched the cat, who looked like a mini hissing tornado. When Bella's paws touched the floor, she raced off, this time back into the living room.

"What the hell was that?" Brian asked.

Heather couldn't help but giggle, especially now that Clay was jumping around, flapping his arms, trying to shake off the disagreeable sensation. "Bella doesn't like Clay."

"What does Clay have to do with it?" Brian asked.

Heather pointed to the ghost. "Clay is standing right there. Actually, he's more like jumping around like someone who stepped in a pile of dog poop and is trying to shake it off."

"He's here?"

"Yes, but he should probably be going. He has things to do."

The next moment, Clay disappeared.

"He's gone," Heather announced.

"What's going on?"

"I'll explain everything in a minute. I need to call Danielle and Chris." Heather grabbed her purse and looked for her cellphone.

"WHAT'S WRONG WITH YOU BOYS?" Debbie Bowman asked her sons. They had been quiet all evening, ever since she had come out from her room after she told Zack to dry and put away the dishes. While he had dried the dishes, he hadn't put them away, for which she had immediately scolded him. Yet instead of arguing with her, as was his normal behavior these days, he went straight to the kitchen and started putting the dishes away, and what surprised her even more, Eric helped him.

After they finished with the dishes, the boys had returned to the living room, and each picked up a book, sat on the sofa, and began reading. With her homeschooling, she required they read before dinner, yet normally she had to nag them to each pick up their book, yet not tonight.

When dinner came, they sat at the table, quietly eating, until she could no longer stand the silence. She repeated the question, "What is wrong with you boys?"

Zack looked up at his mother. "I think this place is haunted."

"And we think it's Dad," Eric added.

Their mother arched a brow. "Haunted?"

Zack nodded furiously and then jumped from the kitchen table, ran to the card table, and grabbed the two notes. He handed them to his mother.

She accepted the two sheets of paper and looked at each one. She frowned. Both notes were written in cursive, and while she had taught her sons to read cursive, neither one could write it very well. This was not their handwriting.

She looked up at the twins. "Who wrote this?"

TWENTY-SEVEN

Debbie didn't open the sofa bed on Tuesday evening. Instead, she told Zack and Eric they could sleep in her bed, and she would stay in the living room on the couch. She left the door to the bedroom partially open, and in the living room kitchen area of the garage apartment, the only lights on were the two lamps sitting on the end tables on either side of the sofa.

Dressed in a pair of sweatpants and one of Clay's old T-shirts, she sat on the sofa and called her sister, Robyn, on the cellphone.

"Hey, Deb, what's up?" Robyn answered the call.

"Can you come over? I need to talk to you, and the boys are already in bed."

"Why don't you just walk over here? The boys will be okay, and I might wake them up walking through the living room."

"They aren't in the living room. I put them in my room for the night."

"You aren't sleeping on the sofa bed, are you?"

"No. I'm not going to pull it out. I'm just going to sleep on the couch. Not a fan of pull-out beds."

"Then why are the boys sleeping in your room? They don't mind the sofa bed."

"I'll explain it when you come over."
"Okay. Now you have me curious."
"One more thing."
"Sure, what?"
"Do you have any wine?"
"Deb, you don't need any wine."
"Yes, I do. Please, Robyn."

ROBYN AND DEBBIE sat side by side on the sofa, each with a glass of wine in hand, and the partially empty bottle sitting on the coffee table, with their stocking-clad feet propped up on said table.

Robyn held her glass of wine in one hand while her other hand held the two sheets of paper with the notes written in cursive. She studied the top sheet and leaned forward, setting her wineglass on the coffee table so she could shuffle both sheets in her hands, to better examine and read the notes.

Robyn shook her head. "Are you sure the boys didn't write these?"

"No way. Their handwriting is horrible."

"But they had to. They're pranking you."

"You didn't see how upset they were. Afraid. They're certain this place is haunted, and they wonder if it's their dad."

Robyn dropped the pages onto her lap, leaned forward, and picked up her wineglass. She took a sip and looked at her sister. "What do you think?"

"I haven't seen anything unusual around here. Other than these notes. I certainly didn't see a pen write it like they claim."

"Well, we know one thing." Robyn took a gulp of wine and then turned back to Debbie. "The boys are either telling the truth and this place is haunted, or Zack and Eric are trying to freak you out. It would be one thing if the boys claimed to have found the notes. We might then assume someone broke into the apartment and left the notes maliciously, maybe to get us to leave. But since they claimed to have seen the pen write it, then that means they're in on it. Do you know who they might have gotten to write the notes for them?"

"They didn't have anyone write those notes."

"Then you're saying my garage apartment is haunted." Robyn downed the remainder of her wine.

ZACK HAD SMUGGLED his mother's iPad into the bedroom with them. Too afraid to go to sleep, the boys pulled the sheets over themselves and found a movie to stream, using a pillow to prop up the iPad so they could watch without having to hold it. They shared a pair of wired headphones, with Zack using the right earbud, and Eric the left.

After Robyn left, Debbie went to get her iPad and found it gone from its regular place. She knew immediately who had it. Debbie slipped quietly into the boys' room and found them both asleep, with the sheets and covers now kicked off their bodies, the iPad streaming a Disney movie, with one earbud in Zack's right ear, while the other earbud lay by Eric's head. She carefully removed the earbud from Zack's ear, picked up the iPad, turned it off, and then covered up the two sleeping boys.

ERIC LOOKED AROUND THE ROOM. He was alone in Police Chief MacDonald's office, sitting in the same chair he had been sitting in the other day. How did he get here? Why was he alone? The next moment, he heard his brother say, "What are we doing here?" Eric turned to see a confused Zack sitting on the chair next to him.

"You weren't here a minute ago," Eric said.

"Is this another dream? We were in bed, watching a movie, and now we're here."

"Hello, boys," a new voice said. They turned to the voice and found their father sitting at the police chief's desk.

"This is a dream," Zack said.
"You read the notes, didn't you?" Clay asked.
"Did you write them?" Eric asked.
Clay shook his head. "No. Someone wrote them for me. I can't move things." Clay then picked up a pen from the desk, looked at it, and then let it drop to the floor. He looked back at his sons and smiled. "I take that back. I guess I can move things in a dream. But that's about all."
"Why are you here? Are you really here?" Eric asked.
Zack shook his head. "It's a dream."
"Then explain the notes," Clay challenged.
Zack looked at his father. "Okay, let's say you're really here. Why? Why did you bring us here to your old office?"
"This was never really my office. I was covering for Chief MacDonald, and I was using his office. But it was never really mine."
"You said it was," Eric said. "You said you were going to be the new police chief."
"And then you got arrested," Zack said.
"But you came back," Eric added.
"And then someone killed you," Zack whispered, his gaze focused on his father. "And you've come back again."
"I came back because I love you both. I ruined my life, your mother's. At the time, I didn't realize what I was doing. Back then, I was just so focused on getting what I wanted. It didn't matter how it might hurt others, or what I was teaching you. And if I'm honest, back then I thought I was teaching you how to go after whatever you wanted, no matter the cost. Even if it meant hurting others. It didn't matter as long as I got what I wanted. But I was wrong."
Eric studied his father for a moment and then asked in a serious voice, "Dad, if you hadn't been caught, would you still be telling us this?"
Clay leaned forward, placing his elbows on the desk. He looked across it at his sons. "If I hadn't been caught, and then got everything I wanted, and continued to hurt others, yet ended up living a

long life, and I died wealthy and powerful, happy, even…would I still come back and try to warn you?"

"Would you?" Eric prodded.

Clay nodded. "Yes, but by then, it would be too late. You'd be grown men."

"But what if we were just like you? And never got caught, not like we got caught breaking into the hobby store. What if we never got caught, and got really good at it," Eric asked.

Clay let out a sigh. "You see, that's the thing. You will eventually die. Like I did. We all die. That's something none of us can avoid. Some of us, like me, die sooner than others. But you see, when that time comes, how you lived here will determine how you feel after you move on."

Zack shook his head. "I don't understand."

"There's an emptiness. Unlike anything I've ever experienced, and I don't think I can adequately explain. And I know instinctively it has nothing to do with the fact I was arrested and then killed. The emptiness I feel right now…" Clay shook his head. "I can't explain."

What looked like snow fell from the ceiling. The boys looked up. "What's that?" they chimed.

The snow landed on the desk and swirled, resembling a twister, and from the twister emerged an image of a young woman who looked as if she had come from the early 1900s. Once her image was fully visible, the snow vanished, and her effervescent image hovered above the desk.

"Eva," Clay muttered.

She nodded at Clay and turned to the boys. "My name is Eva Thorndike, and I thought perhaps I might be able to help your father."

"You're beautiful," Zack muttered, his eyes wide as he stared at the apparition.

"Why, thank you." Eva smiled. "Your father loves you. That's why he's here. He wants to spare you the pain he's currently experiencing."

"He's in pain?" Eric asked.

Eva nodded. "You boys are alive. You have a spirit and a body.

Your father and I, we are no longer of the world you live in. We only have our spirit—some call it a soul."

"You and Dad have bodies," Zack argued.

Eva shook her head. "No, what you see is only an illusion we create with our energy. And when you die, your spirit will leave that body and move on, like your father did. But the body and the spirit have something in common."

"What?" the boys chorused.

"They must each be fed to grow and survive. The food you eat affects the health of your body, even how you feel. Have you ever eaten an entire bowl of candy or two pieces of cake and then afterwards felt sick?"

"You mean like when Mom tells us junk food is bad for us?" Eric asked.

Eva nodded. "Exactly. Well, your soul—your spirit—also needs to be fed in order to grow and feel healthy."

Zack wrinkled his nose. "What does a soul eat?"

"How you live your life, how you treat people. Those are the things that feed your soul. But for some people, they don't truly appreciate their poor diet until after they die—and then it hits them. That's what has happened to your father. That empty feeling he can't quite explain. It can be overwhelming. Something you can't avoid. What makes it worse is realizing someone you love may be facing your same fate. He's here to help you boys. He doesn't want you to feel how he does, nor to face what he's ultimately facing."

"What do you mean, ultimately facing?" Zack asked.

Eva looked at Clay, waiting for him to explain.

Clay sighed and looked from Eva to his sons. "I must eventually move on. I'm sort of in a limbo state. But when I move on, well, I'm not sure what awaits me. I just know I'll be held accountable for any wrongs I've committed during my life. Just because you don't get caught when you're alive doesn't mean it won't catch up to you."

Zack's eyes widened. "Dad, are you saying you're going to hell?"

Clay shrugged. "I don't know."

The boys looked anxiously at Eva, waiting for an answer.

Eva smiled down at the boys. "Not in the way you imagine."

"Boys, look at me," Clay asked. They did. "I want you to ask your mother to let you talk to Police Chief MacDonald again. And when you see him, tell him you want to try, and that you want to make better decisions. Promise me. He is a good man and a good father. He can help you. But you have to be willing to try."

"We promise," the boys said.

TWENTY-EIGHT

Having been an only child, Danielle had never experienced what it was like to grow up in a big family. The same could be said to be true of Walt. Of course, there had been her cousins, Cheryl and Sean, who had always been around when she was growing up. But they were gone, as were her parents. But here she was now, a family of sorts, with three infants and a toddler. One child per adult. But even that could seem overwhelming. Danielle told herself that she would one day refer to this moment in time as cozy chaos.

The Marlow household had gotten up a little earlier than normal that morning. It started with Connor having a bad dream. After he found his parents, he inadvertently woke his baby sister, who proved to have a healthy set of lungs.

Sadie, who had been sleeping in the hallway, woke from the crying. But since Connor had shut the bedroom door when entering his parents' room, Sadie could not investigate the problem. The golden retriever, believing it was her duty to wake Walt so he could save the infant from whatever had befallen her, started barking. The barking worked to wake Walt, along with everyone else in the house, including the twins.

It was now 7:00 a.m., and the household was just settling down. Crying infants had been fed, and a cranky toddler sat in his highchair, angrily throwing dry cereal onto the floor in protest. Loyal Sadie sat by the highchair, ready to handle toddler cleanup.

The young mothers sat together at the kitchen table, finally getting to enjoy their morning coffee. Ian held a fussy Emily Ann in his arms as he circled the kitchen floor while gently patting the infant's back. Walt had successfully strapped the twins into their swings, and he turned his attention to Connor, trying to distract him by using his telekinetic abilities to animate the silverware and cereal box. His efforts appeared to work. The toddler started giggling, and instead of throwing cereal onto the floor, he ate it.

While chatting with the other adults in the room, Danielle sipped her coffee and absently fiddled with her phone, checking her emails and messages. One message caught her eye, and she set her mug on the table and looked closer at the phone. After a moment, she said, "Adam sent me a message last night. He asked me if I wanted to see that house he might be listing."

Ian, still circling the room, paused a moment and looked at Danielle. "Is that the house Rylee's aunt owned?"

"I still don't believe Rylee abused her aunt," Lily chimed. "She was so nice to me."

"Yeah, it's the same house." Danielle set her phone back on the table. "Adam's going over there to take some pictures. He told me he's going early this morning, before he goes into the office, and if I'm up, I can meet him over there."

"Does he really think you're interested in the house?" Lily asked.

"I might have led him to believe Madeline might be interested." Danielle flashed Lily a guilty grin.

"Poor Adam. He has no idea what's going on around him." Lily snickered before taking another sip of coffee.

"You going?" Walt asked.

Danielle looked at Walt. "If I go, it means I have to leave in about fifteen minutes. You okay with that?"

"If Adam is getting ready to list the property, maybe he knows more about Wesley's widow," Walt suggested. "She could have mentioned a pending wedding or something about what's going on in her current life."

"You'll be okay here with the babies?" Danielle asked.

Walt flashed Danielle a grin. "What do you think?"

"Then I guess I'll go. I'll text him and tell him I'll meet him over there." Danielle looked back at her phone and sent Adam a text.

AS DANIELLE GATHERED up her purse and shoes before leaving, she felt a twinge of guilt for leaving Walt and the others with all the little ones. Yet before she left, Lily, who wanted to go back to sleep, talked Connor into lying in bed with her and watching a Disney movie while she napped. That left Walt and Ian in charge of the three infants. She no longer felt guilty.

Danielle had just pulled out of her garage and was heading down the alley when she spied Heather standing in her driveway, talking to someone. Danielle assumed Heather was on her way to work, but just as she was about to drive by Heather's house, she recognized who Heather was talking to: Clay Bowman. Without thought, she made an abrupt right and turned into the driveway, parking behind Heather's car. Both Heather and Clay looked at Danielle in surprise.

Danielle got out of her car and walked toward the pair. "Everything alright, Heather?"

"I suppose I should be grateful he didn't mess up my morning run," Heather said as Danielle got closer.

Clay turned to Danielle. "I understand I'm probably the last soul you and Heather want to see."

Heather glanced at the time on her cellphone and then looked back to Danielle. "I need to pick up Chris. It's my day to drive. But Clay stopped by and wanted to tell me the dream hop seemed to work. At least, his sons no longer believe it was just a dream."

"I need one of the mediums to talk to Chief MacDonald," Clay said.

TEN MINUTES LATER, Danielle was back in her car on her way to meet Adam at the house. With her phone already synced to her car, she placed a hands-free call to MacDonald as she drove.

"You're up early," the chief said when answering the phone.

"It's been a crazy morning. You at work yet?"

"No. I'm leaving in about ten minutes. What's up?"

Danielle told the chief about seeing Clay that morning and about the dream hops with his sons.

"And he trusts me to help with his sons?" He sounded lightly amused at the idea.

"Apparently, one's vision can become clearer when they move to the other side. Although, that hasn't been my experience with every spirit I've encountered."

DANIELLE GUESSED the old Craftsman home she had come to look at was about ninety years old. She pulled up in front of the property and parked. It was obvious the house had been vacant for some time, considering the condition of the yard. Along the northern border of the property, a row of arborvitaes served as a privacy fence separating this house from its neighbor. Several of the plants had died and needed to be removed, while the height of the overall row needed trimming a few feet. An overgrown hydrangea blocked a portion of the sidewalk, while the front lawn was a patchwork of green and brown.

She didn't bother getting out of her car since Adam hadn't arrived yet. He said he wanted to take some pictures today, but after seeing the front yard, she doubted he meant listing pictures. He probably wanted to assess the condition of the property and make suggestions on what needed to be done before putting the house on the market.

Danielle picked up her phone and was just texting Walt, telling him she had arrived at the house and Adam wasn't there yet, when

Adam pulled up behind her. She quickly rewrote her text, sent it to Walt, and then got out of her vehicle.

"Looks like the yard needs a little TLC," Danielle said as she slammed her driver's door shut and walked to Adam.

"Yeah, I noticed that when I drove by the other day. I haven't been inside yet." Adam held a yellow legal pad of paper and pen in one hand and a ring of keys in the other.

They both turned to the house. "Was it this neglected when Cordelia was living in it?" Danielle asked. She stood with Adam on the sidewalk, looking up at the house. "If her niece wasn't taking proper care of her aunt, I can understand the property getting neglected."

"No. It was actually in pretty good shape." With his hand holding the keys, Adam pointed to a house down the street. "I sold that house about a month before she passed away. I remember my buyer commenting on this house. He liked the use of the arborvitaes as a privacy fence. At the time, this front yard was well tended. I seem to remember there were some rose bushes over there." Adam pointed to a dirt area in the front yard. "But it looks like someone took them out."

"You mentioned what this property was probably going for. I understand prices have gone up, but I don't see how this is worth that much."

"It's the lot." Adam pointed to the vacant land on the side without the arborvitaes. "That's part of this property. It's a little over an acre."

Danielle arched her brows. "Really?"

"Come on, let's go look inside."

"Why do you think the owner has neglected this place?" Danielle followed Adam to the front door. Together, they walked around the intruding hydrangea bush.

"She never lived in it. And then after the lawsuit with her cousin, she had to wait for it to go through probate."

"Lily knows the cousin. She's a nurse in the maternity ward. According to Lily, she was really sweet to her."

Now at the front door, Adam tucked the pad of paper under his one arm while he shuffled the keys to find the right one. "How is Lily?"

"When I left the house, she was taking a nap with Connor. Or should I say, she was napping while he was watching *Lady and the Tramp*. But she's doing good."

"Got it!" Adam announced before pushing the door open. They stepped inside the house, and Adam tried the light switch. Nothing happened. "Damn, I told her the utilities needed to be on."

Danielle walked over to the front window and pulled open the blind. Sunlight spilled into the living room.

"First thing on the list, turn on the utilities," Adam grumbled while jotting a note on his pad of paper.

"The living room looks much better than the outside. Just a little dust, but not bad."

Adam surveyed the room. "Looks like a little old lady lived here."

Danielle laughed. "A little old lady did live here."

"You think your mother-in-law might like it?"

"You mean former mother-in-law? But maybe."

They walked into the kitchen, and Adam noticeably sniffed. He looked around. "This place needs to be aired out." He wrote another note on the legal pad.

They continued walking through the first floor and came to a doorway. When Adam opened the door and looked in the room, he said, "This must be what Bonnie called the parlor."

Danielle followed Adam into the room but stopped abruptly when she saw an elderly woman with white hair sitting on one of the two wingback chairs in the room. She stared at Adam and Danielle but said nothing. Danielle looked from Adam to the elderly woman and back to Adam.

"This is not something you see every day in Frederickport," Adam said.

For a moment Danielle thought Adam saw the woman. He stood facing the wingback chair, but then she realized he wasn't looking at the woman in the chair, but the bars on the window behind the chair. "She needs to remove those bars."

Adam turned from the window and said, "Look at this."

Danielle looked over to where Adam now stood by the desk and pointed to a collection of knives hanging on the wall. They looked like something ancient warriors carried into war. There was also one knife sitting on a display stand on the desk.

"I have a feeling this knife collection belonged to the aunt's husband," Adam said. "She'll need to move these before we list the house. They're probably valuable, and that one on the desk looks dangerous. I can just see some prospective buyer looking at the house and their kid picks up that knife and cuts their damn arm off." Adam jotted down another note.

Danielle looked from the knives to the portrait hanging over the desk above them. She then looked over at the elderly woman. The woman in the portrait looked like a much younger version of the one sitting in the wingback chair. Danielle looked back to the portrait and asked, "Hey, Adam, any idea who this is?"

Adam glanced up at the portrait. "That must be Bonnie's aunt. She mentioned there was a portrait of her in here."

Danielle looked back to the woman in the corner. "You can see me, can't you?" the woman asked.

TWENTY-NINE

While Danielle was on her way to meet Adam, Chief MacDonald, who had just gotten off the phone with her, was in his kitchen, rinsing out his coffee mug and setting it in the sink. His teenage son, Eddy, walked into the room.

"Are we still gunna go to Beach Taco today?" Eddy asked his father. The night before, MacDonald and his sons had discussed having lunch together. In their tentative plan, the boys would ride their bikes to the police station and meet their father at 11:30, where they would leave their bikes and then drive to Beach Taco with their dad.

"Sure. But make sure your brother wears his helmet. You too."

"Okay."

"Don't forget, the guitar lessons are this morning."

Thirty minutes later, the chief sat in his office, having his second cup of coffee for the day. While sorting through some papers on his desk, he heard a knock at his open door. He looked up to see Brian standing in the doorway. He waved Brian in.

"Did Danielle get a hold of you?" Brian asked in a low voice when he reached the chief's desk.

MacDonald leaned back in his chair and looked up at Brian. "You mean about Clay?"

Brian nodded and took a seat in a chair facing the chief. "Heather called me this morning on her way to work. Told me Danielle was going to give you the heads-up, but I think she's worried Danielle might not get ahold of you, and with all that's going on over at Marlow House these days, she was afraid Bowman's wife and kids might show up and you wouldn't know what's going on with the boys. Sounds like their attitudes might be improved compared to the last time they were in here."

The chief's desk phone rang. He motioned to Brian to hold that thought before answering the phone. It didn't take long for Brian to figure out who was on the other end of the call. When he hung up, Brian said, "That was Debbie Bowman, wasn't it?"

"Yeah." The chief let out a sigh. "She asked me if she and the boys could come in this morning and talk to me about the boys' legal problems. She also apologized for their attitude the other day and promised me they wanted to do better."

"When are they coming in?"

"11:30." The chief paused a moment and cringed. "Oh crap, I'm supposed to meet Evan and Eddy here at 11:30. I told them I'd take them to Beach Taco for lunch."

"Give them a call and have them come at noon. I don't imagine your meeting with the Bowman boys will take more than half an hour."

The chief glanced at the clock. "I'll have to call them later. They're at guitar lessons right now."

Brian arched his brows. "Guitar lessons?"

The chief chuckled. "Yeah, one of our neighbors down the street is a music teacher at the high school. He teaches piano and guitar during the summer. Eddy wanted to take guitar, and of course, then Evan wanted to."

"They don't want to take piano?" Brian teased.

"It's not as cool. Plus, we don't have a piano. But I did have a couple of old guitars that have been sitting in the garage."

"From your rock and roll era?"

The chief laughed. "Yeah, something like that."

DANIELLE SAT on the sofa in the living room, nursing the twins, Walt by her side. Across from them on the sofa sat Lily, holding a sleeping Emily Ann, while Connor played on the floor with his father, helping him build a house from Lincoln Logs. Sadie sat near Connor and Ian, eyeing the Lincoln Logs, while Max napped on the back of the sofa behind Danielle.

"And you didn't get to talk to her?" Lily asked Danielle.

"I couldn't start a conversation with Adam there. He would think I was talking to the chair."

"I wonder why she's still here," Walt said.

"I don't know. I remember Marie didn't even know she'd passed away. I imagine she's been in that house since she died." Danielle glanced around. "Where is Marie, by the way? I haven't seen her or Eva all morning."

"They stopped by when you were with Adam," Walt explained. "They felt Clay was handled, so they were off to see to the other problem."

"You mean Wesley's wife?" Danielle asked.

"From what they told Walt," Lily said, "sounds like they're doing some ghost eavesdropping."

Ian looked over to where the other adults sat. "It'll be a good way to find out if Wesley is right. Is his brother planning to murder his widow?"

"I think you should go back over to that house and talk to the ghost," Lily said.

Danielle looked at Lily. "There are a few things I'd like to ask her. Why do you want me to talk to her?"

"Ask her about Rylee. Did she really abuse her? I can't believe the nurse who took such good care of me could turn around and abuse a vulnerable old woman."

"Eva and Marie could go over and talk to her, but not sure how Danielle can go over there without Adam," Ian pointed out.

"They're kind of busy right now. And I'd like to talk to her myself." Danielle glanced down and noticed Jack had fallen asleep. She motioned to Walt, who gently took his son, leaving Addison to nurse.

"You planning to break into the house?" Ian teased. "Wouldn't be the first time."

"No. While I understand Adam can't let me go to the house without him, I could ask him to meet me over there so I can take some photos to send Madeline. Someone can go with me, like Chris or Heather, and they can keep Adam distracted while I talk to her."

"Chris would be a good one to take. All Chris has to do is mention he's considering buying something and he'll have Adam's full attention," Lily snarked.

THE DAY GOT AWAY from Chief MacDonald, and he forgot to call Eddy to tell him to come to the station a little later. The boys arrived ten minutes early. He gave them a brief synopsis of what was going on and asked them to wait in the break room, promising them that as soon as he was finished talking with the Bowmans, they would go to lunch. Since both Eddy and Evan were curious to learn more about the Bowmans, especially after their father mentioned the dream hop, they were more than willing to wait in the break room.

Debbie Bowman arrived at the designated time, her sons by her side. Colleen took her to the chief, but once they stepped in the office, Debbie said, "Chief MacDonald, before my sons talk to you, I was wondering if we could have a private word."

Chief MacDonald, who was now standing beside his desk, looked over at Colleen, who lingered in the doorway, listening. He glanced at Colleen, gave a nod, and she said, "Boys, why don't you come with me while your mother talks to the chief?"

"I'll call you when I'm ready to talk to them," the chief told Colleen. She nodded and led the boys out of the office.

THE CHIEF DIDN'T SAY what he wanted her to do with the boys while he talked to their mother, so Colleen took them to the break room. She had baked some cookies the night before and had left them in the break room for her co-workers and decided that would be a good way to keep the boys occupied. Feed them cookies.

EVAN AND EDDY sat in the break room, eyeing the cookies someone had left on the table, when the door opened and in walked Colleen with the Bowman twins.

"Oh, Eddy and Evan, I didn't know you were here," Colleen greeted. She looked at the Bowman twins and said, "This is Evan and Eddy MacDonald, Chief MacDonald's sons." The Bowman twins remained silent, standing awkwardly next to Colleen. "Their mother is talking with your dad right now, and they're waiting in here." She looked at the Bowman twins and pointed to two empty chairs. "You boys can go ahead and sit down. If you want, you can have a couple of cookies. I made them. They're chocolate chip." She looked back at Evan and Eddy and said, "You can have some, too."

"Umm, thanks," Eddy said.

Evan flashed her a smile yet said nothing, his attention on a figure that had appeared behind her. Clay Bowman. Colleen told the Bowman twins to wait in the room until she came for them, and then she turned to leave, almost walking through Clay, yet he managed to jump out of her way.

A few minutes later, the four boys were alone in the break room save for the ghost that only Evan could see or hear. Zack leaned to the plate of cookies, snatched two, and handed one to his brother. Eddy silently watched the twins while Evan watched their father.

Clay looked at Evan. "Tell them I'm here."

Evan's eyes widened. He looked nervously from Clay to the twins.

"Please tell them. I want them to know that when they talk to your father, I'll be with them."

Noticing his brother's odd expression, Eddy whispered, "What's wrong, Evan?"

Glancing from the ghost to his brother, he said, "He's here."

Eddy frowned. "Who's here?"

Evan nodded toward the twins before looking to the spot where the ghost stood. Zack and Eric both noticed this gesture. They frowned at Evan but said nothing.

"Who's here?" Eddy repeated.

"Their dad," Evan hissed under his breath.

"What did you say?" Zack asked, his expression dark.

Evan let out an exasperated sigh, stood up, marched to the door, closed it, and looked back at the other three boys. "I will deny saying this if you tell anyone. But your dad is here. He wants me to tell you something."

Zack threw what remained of his cookie on the table and stood up. "You're a jerk."

"Remind him about the dream," Clay urged.

"You dreamt about your dad the last two nights." Evan spoke quickly, trying to get the words out as fast as possible. He wasn't scared of the twins, after all, they were younger than him, and he had his older brother with him. But considering his father was trying to help the boys, getting them so angry that they might do something stupid wouldn't help their situation.

"Who told you about the dream?" Eric asked.

"This sounds crazy, but I can see ghosts. Your dad's here. He wants to move on, but he can't until he knows you're okay. He's standing right there." Evan pointed to where Clay stood.

"Ask him something," Eddy suggested. "Something only your dad and you know."

Eric looked at Eddy before turning to Evan. "What's my dad's favorite movie?"

Evan looked at Clay.

Clay smiled. "*Batman*."

Evan wrinkled his nose. "Really? *Batman*?"

Eyes wide, Zack fell back into his chair.

"What kind of dog did my dad have when he was a kid?" Eric asked.

"I didn't have a dog."

"That sucks," Evan said.

"What did he say?" Eddy asked.

"He didn't have a dog."

Zack stood up. "Is our dad really here?"

Evan nodded. "He is."

"Tell them I love them. I love their mom. And I will always regret how I hurt my family. But tell them they are better than me. Show the world how much better they can be."

After Evan repeated the words, the door opened, and Colleen looked in the room. "Chief MacDonald will see you both now."

THIRTY

While the Bowman twins were alone in the break room with Eddy and Evan, Debbie Bowman was with Chief MacDonald, candidly sharing with him her sincere concerns regarding her sons.

"I'm worried about them, not only because they broke into a local shop—which is a horrible thing. I'm not trying to gloss over that. I understand they need to be held accountable. But I am more concerned about their mental health."

"I understand, and I imagine the court will recommend counseling, especially considering your husband's recent death and the circumstances surrounding it. That's a lot for two small boys to take in. I can relate. My youngest is only a little older than your boys."

"It's more than that." Debbie paused and glanced over to the open doorway leading to the hall. Wanting more privacy, she stood and walked to the door and closed it. After she did, she turned back to the chief. "I'm ashamed to admit it, but I haven't been the mother they need. Since their father's death…well…" Debbie looked down but didn't finish the sentence.

"It would probably be a good idea for you to get counseling, too."

Debbie looked up at the chief. "It might be my fault. I've sort of checked out these last few weeks. The boys have found a way to conjure up one parent, since their other one who's actually with them hasn't been present."

The chief frowned. "I don't understand what you're saying."

"They are convinced their father has been visiting them in their dreams."

"That's not so unusual. My boys lost their mother, and they sometimes dream about her."

Debbie returned to her chair and sat down. "No. It isn't like that. They said…well…that his ghost comes to their dreams and visits them. They insist they're having the same dream at the same time. Which actually is totally possible if some of those articles I've read about twin dreams are true. But that's really beside the point. They're convinced their father is coming to them, speaking to them."

"Is that such a bad thing? Although I guess it depends on what he's saying to them."

"They claim their father has apologized. Supposedly, Clay has taken total responsibility for his actions and doesn't want his sons to treat people like he did."

"Like I said, is that a bad thing?"

Debbie reached down to the floor and picked up her purse, which she had set by her feet when first sitting down in the chair. She set the purse on her lap and opened it. From the purse, she pulled two sheets of wrinkled paper. She stood up and handed the papers to the chief.

With a frown, he leaned across his desk and accepted them. "What is this?" He unfolded each one and read the cursive handwriting.

"The boys insist a ghost wrote those notes, telling them it was really their father in their dreams. They even claimed the marker moved on its own. They're making up these fanciful stories, and I honestly feel they think everything they're saying is true."

"Are you suggesting your boys wrote these notes?"

Debbie shook her head. "No. They can read cursive, but they aren't very good at writing it."

MacDonald dropped the pages on the desk. "What are you saying? Someone else wrote these for them?"

"I don't know what I'm saying!" Debbie broke into tears and started sobbing.

MacDonald sat there quietly for a moment as she cried. He stood up, grabbed some tissues from a box on his desk, and walked over to her. He handed her the tissues, which she accepted before blowing her nose.

Instead of returning to his desk, he sat down in a chair next to her. In a quiet voice, he said, "Why don't we not worry about the notes or the dreams right now?"

Wad of tissue in hand, Debbie looked up to the chief and sniffled. She wiped her red nose and asked, "I shouldn't be worried about the notes? My sister insists Eric and Zack are pulling an elaborate hoax. But my sons didn't write those notes. I don't understand what's going on."

"If they're pulling a hoax, so what? It could be their way of comforting you."

Debbie frowned. "How so?"

"Perhaps they've come to the realization their father made mistakes. He loved them, but he made mistakes. By saying their father is claiming full responsibility for how things turned out, it could be your sons' way of telling you they don't blame you. And they're willing to do better."

Debbie sniffled again, dabbed her nose with the wad of tissue, and said, "You think?"

The chief nodded. "Now why don't we have them come back in? No reason to mention their dream. If they want to tell me about it, okay? But let's not bring it up. Instead, I would rather discuss types of community service that might be appropriate for someone their age and considering what they did."

"Community service? Like picking up trash on the beach?"

"No, something where they're more involved with the community. Millie Samson from the museum mentioned they're looking for a couple of helpers over the holiday weekend. They're opening a new exhibit tomorrow, and they're planning some special events over the weekend. She asked if my boys might be interested. Several of the normal volunteers are going to be out of town for the holiday. So perhaps that might be an idea."

"The boys liked the museum, but I'm not sure Millie would welcome them." She added with a whisper, "They took those keys."

"It could be a way for them to make it up to the museum. I was also considering having them help with the pet adoption fair that's scheduled next week. What do you say? Shall we bring the boys back in here and talk to them about it?"

AFTER COLLEEN RETURNED the Bowman boys to the chief's office, they stood quietly on either side of their mother while she sat in a chair and the chief sat behind his desk. When Colleen left the office, she closed the door, and Debbie started the conversation with, "Boys, did you want to tell the chief something?"

"We're sorry," they chorused.

"Can you explain what exactly you're sorry for?" the chief asked.

The boys exchanged a glance. Eric gave his brother a silent nod and mouthed something the chief couldn't see before looking back at him.

"We're sorry for being butts," Zack began.

"Zack!" Debbie scolded. "Your language."

"Let him go on," the chief urged.

Zack took a deep breath and looked at the chief. "We're sorry for breaking into that store. It was wrong. And we promise we won't do something like that again."

"And we're sorry for how we acted the last time we were in here," Eric added.

"Our dad told us you're a good guy, and we can trust you. Eric and I don't want to get in trouble anymore," Zack said.

The chief arched his brows. "Really?"

Both boys nodded.

ACROSS TOWN, while Danielle and her friends made plans to revisit Adam's listing, and MacDonald finished up his meeting with the remorseful delinquents and their mother, Eva and Marie were busy surveilling Wesley's widow and his brother, with Eva watching the widow, and Marie the brother.

The only thing Marie had learned thus far about Wesley's brother was that he had an incredibly boring job working at the auto parts store, where he spent most of his time on the phone or at the service counter, discussing spark plugs and other dull topics. It didn't take Marie long to realize surveilling him at his work was a waste of time, and she wasn't learning anything useful about him. Instead, it would probably be better to watch him when he was with Bonnie, and if she was lucky, he would try killing Bonnie while Marie was there—if he had homicidal intentions—Marie could save the woman, Adrian could be arrested, and Marie's job would be done, and she could do something more enjoyable, like spending time with the new babies.

Marie was considering leaving and finding Eva to suggest another strategy when Adrian's cellphone rang. He was only on the call for a minute, but as soon as he got off the phone, he told the other employee he was taking his lunch break early, and then he promptly left. Curious to see where he was going, Marie followed him.

Adrian walked down the alley and entered the local florist shop from the back service entrance. Marie followed him inside and, to her surprise, found the lovely widow Pierson, owner of the flower shop, waiting for him. As soon as he was in the back room, alone with widow Pierson, he closed the door, and the two embraced.

"Oh my," Marie muttered. Wanting to blush at the amorous encounter, Marie moved to the front of the flower shop and found it empty. Fortunately, there were no employees or customers to walk in on the hanky-panky currently taking place in the back room. She moved to the front of the flower shop and noticed a sign hanging on the outside of the glass door, but she couldn't see what it said. Moving outside the building, she read the sign: *Closed for lunch. Will be back at 1 p.m.* Marie tested the door with her energy. As she expected, it was locked.

As she was about to go back into the flower shop, she heard someone say, "Hi, Marie." She turned to see Evan MacDonald walking with his father and brother.

"Where is she?" MacDonald asked in a low voice.

Evan stopped in front of the flower shop and pointed toward the door. "Right there."

"Afternoon, Marie," Edward said, as if it was perfectly natural to say hello to something none of them but Evan could see. "And thank you for helping with the Bowman boys. The dream hop seemed to work, and I met with them today. Their attitudes are much improved, and I'll be working with them."

"Tell your father I'm happy to hear that," Marie said.

Evan repeated Marie's words, and Eddy shook his head. "I doubt I'm ever getting used to this."

MacDonald chuckled and gave his eldest son a pat on the back. "Welcome to the club, bud."

"We're going to lunch at Beach Taco," Evan told Marie.

"That's nice." Marie glanced toward the flower shop, wondering how the lovers were doing.

"Why are you here?" Evan asked.

"Evan, you shouldn't be standing there talking to a door," Eddy said under his breath.

"I'm not talking to a door."

"I get it, but they don't." Eddy nodded to a group of older teenagers who had walked by and were now looking back at the three of them standing a few feet from the entrance of the flower shop while his younger brother seemed to be in a conversation with the door.

"We should probably go," the chief said, placing a hand on Evan's right shoulder.

"Wait, before you do, tell your father something for me."

Evan looked at his father. "Marie wants me to tell you something."

"What?"

"Tell your father…umm…Wesley may be right. His brother isn't acting like someone who is marrying for love."

Evan repeated Marie's words.

The chief frowned. "What do you mean?"

"It seems he has another friend," Marie said.

"What do you mean he has another friend?" Evan asked.

Marie opened her mouth, about to say something, but changed her mind. She glanced back at the closed door of the florist shop. She looked back at Evan and said, "Tell your father I'll explain later." Marie vanished.

THIRTY-ONE

Marie returned to Marlow House late Wednesday afternoon and found the young parents in the living room, discussing the day's events while the two mothers nursed, and Connor sat at the coffee table, coloring with his father.

"I'm glad you're all here," Marie said when she appeared in the room.

"Marie's here," Danielle announced for the non-mediums just before Connor waved a red crayon at the ghost.

"It looks like one of your problem ghosts may be taken care of, which will make Heather happy," Marie announced.

"I assume you're talking about Clay," Walt said.

"I am."

"If it's about the successful dream hop and the boys seeing the chief this afternoon with a much-improved attitude, the chief already called me about it a little while ago, and we were just discussing it," Danielle told Marie.

"I also have news about the other ghost issue," Marie said.

"I sorta do too, but you go first," Danielle said.

"You sorta do what?" Lily asked.

"We're talking about Wesley now," Danielle explained.

Lily nodded. "Ohhh."

"While I have nothing to support Wesley's claim that Adrian intends to murder his widow, he is right about one thing. His brother is not that committed to Bonnie."

"Why do you say that?" Walt asked.

"He took a break this afternoon from work, visited the local florist. It was a personal visit."

"What do you mean, a personal visit?" Danielle asked.

"Let's just say Mrs. Pierson closed her flower shop for an hour while she entertained in the back room."

"The woman who owns the florist shop, she and Adrian?" Danielle asked.

"Okay, this is getting good. Does that mean what I think it does?" Lily asked.

Marie looked at Lily. "If you mean is there hanky-panky going on between Adrian and Mrs. Pierson in her storage room, yes."

Danielle repeated Marie's words for Lily and Ian.

"I wonder what Mr. Pierson would think about this," Walt said.

"There is no Mr. Pierson," Marie told Walt. "He died about ten years ago."

"I want details!" Lily demanded.

Marie recounted what she had observed, which Danielle repeated for the non-mediums. After they finished, Lily said, "Well, you guys handled Clay's problem, and it looks like this one is about to be handled, too."

"How does Adrian having someone on the side take care of Wesley's problem?" Danielle asked.

"It's easy. Once Bonnie finds out Adrian is seeing someone else, she's not going to marry him. And if she doesn't marry him, Adrian has no reason to kill her, because killing her alone won't give him access to her bank account. Wesley says it's her money he wants, not to see her dead."

"True, but how do we go about doing that?" Danielle asked. "First of all, none of us have witnessed anything, aside from Marie. And I doubt Bonnie will listen to Marie."

"Obviously, Marie can't tell her," Lily agreed.

"But even if one of us saw them together in a compromising position, I don't want to go up to a virtual stranger and tell her that her boyfriend is fooling around with another woman. Would you want to?" Danielle asked.

"I wouldn't even want to tell an acquaintance or friend that," Lily grumbled.

"Not sure about the rest of you," Ian began, "but I'd like Wesley to move on. He keeps barging in on my family and complicating things with Connor."

Danielle looked at Ian. "He's annoying, but Connor's not even afraid of him. If anything, he's entertained by the guy."

"Yes, but that's the problem. I don't need to deal with my mom constantly asking why Connor is acting so strange. Because, while Wesley might not directly hurt Connor, my mother's reaction to Connor's interaction with the ghost could eventually psychologically hurt my son."

"I understand what Ian's saying," Walt chimed in.

"Okay, so what do you guys suggest? Can we use this information someway to break up Adrian and Bonnie, which could lead to Wesley moving on?" Danielle asked.

"By the way, right before Adrian left the florist shop, he and the good widow made a date for their next rendezvous. They're meeting again at the florist's on Saturday morning before it opens. Apparently, Bonnie's going to Portland on Saturday morning with some friends."

Danielle repeated Marie's words, to which Lily asked, "I'm assuming Marie knows about Bonnie going to Portland because Adrian told the florist lady when they were making their next date. So the woman knows she is fooling around with a guy who is supposed to be in a committed relationship with another woman?"

"Tell Lily that's exactly what it means."

Danielle gave Lily a nod.

"I wonder, does that also mean the woman knows Adrian plans to marry Bonnie for her money and kill her? If so, that makes her an accessory," Lily pointed out.

"People marry for money all the time, and it doesn't mean they plan to kill their spouse," Ian reminded her.

"When Jack and I operated the Eva Aphrodite, several regular patrons were men who'd married wealthy women. Those marriages were never about love, and infidelity was common. Their mistresses were aware of the wives, and I suspect many of the wives knew about the mistresses," Walt said.

"True, but I doubt Bonnie would marry this guy if he already has someone on the side," Marie said.

Once again, Danielle repeated Marie's words.

"Okay, let me get this straight," Lily began. "Adrian is probably pursuing Bonnie for her money, not love. His current lover knows about Bonnie, and while that may not mean either has homicidal intentions, we are fairly certain if Bonnie learns of these extracurricular activities, she will end the relationship, therefore freeing Wesley's imagined obligation to stick around, so he can move on and stop visiting Connor. Right?"

"That pretty much sums it up," Danielle said. "But there is still that pesky part of how we inform Bonnie so she will believe the information without us looking like jerks."

They contemplated the situation for a moment. Finally, Ian said, "There's one way to inform her of the cheating. Take a picture of the two together and send it to Bonnie. It doesn't need to be too explicit, and it's unnecessary to take a picture that can identify the woman, only Adrian. Frankly, it's sleazy sending a compromising photograph of a woman to someone."

"And how do we get a picture?" Lily asked.

"Marie can take it on Saturday when they meet up."

Danielle chuckled. "They might notice a cellphone floating around the room."

"Not if they're preoccupied." Ian smiled. "And it wouldn't be a cellphone. More like an inexpensive digital camera. After Marie gets the photos, I can text them to Bonnie from a throwaway cellphone so we can send them to her anonymously."

"Where are you going to get a phone like that?" Danielle asked.

"Chris."

Danielle frowned. "Chris?"

Ian shrugged. "Chris has connections."

"Tell Ian I like the idea, but I have a few questions," Marie said.

"What are your questions?" Danielle asked.

"Maybe they won't notice me taking pictures, but I'm not sure how I'll get the camera to the florist shop without someone seeing it. A floating camera might draw attention."

Danielle chuckled and repeated the question.

Once again, the room grew quiet while they considered Marie's question. Finally, Walt said, "We can go down there Friday night, pick up food at Beach Taco. I'll take the camera with me, and when we walk by the florist shop, when no one is looking, I can set it safely on the roof for Marie to retrieve the next morning. When she's done, she can put it back on the roof for us to retrieve, with her help, when no one is around, of course. So, no reason for the camera to be floating around town."

"We'll need to put it in a plastic bag or something so it doesn't get wet," Danielle added.

"That might work," Ian said.

"There's only one problem with this plan," Danielle said.

"What's that?" Lily asked.

"There's no guarantee Bonnie won't forgive Adrian, and still marry him."

Lily nodded. "True."

"There is actually another problem with this plan," Marie said.

"What's that?" Walt asked.

"I might walk through walls, but I can't take a camera with me."

"You could enter the shop with Adrian and stay close behind him, perhaps holding the camera next to his back, where he won't see it, and when inside, move it before the good widow sees it," Walt suggested.

"Okay, I'll try. The worst that can happen is they'll see the camera and get all confused," Marie said.

Once again, Danielle repeated Marie's words for the others.

"Now, dear, what was your news regarding Wesley?" Marie asked.

"Oh, that. I almost forgot." Danielle then recounted her experience over at Cordelia's house.

"So that's why I haven't run into her. She hasn't left her house. I wonder if she's stuck there, like Walt was. I suppose you want me to go talk to her?" Marie didn't sound excited about the prospect.

"It's not necessary right now. I doubt Cordelia knows anything about Bonnie and Adrian, and from what Bonnie told Adam, she hasn't stepped into that house since her aunt died. Although, I wouldn't mind talking to her myself, but right now we need to focus on breaking up Adrian and Bonnie, and tomorrow is the Fourth of July, and Walt and I are attending the opening at the museum."

"Do you still want me to help with the little ones while you go?" Marie sounded more enthused about spending time with the babies than talking to Cordelia's ghost.

"Definitely," Danielle told her.

LATER THAT EVENING, over at the Lyons' garage apartment, Zack and Eric snuggled under a pile of blankets on the pull-out bed in the living room while their mother was in the bathroom, taking a shower. The only light in the room came from the fixture over the stove in the small adjacent kitchen.

"Hey, Zack, I've been thinking of those soup cans."

Zack let out a deep sigh. "Yeah, me too."

"We can't keep them."

Zack looked at his brother. "What do you want to do?"

"I figure we just need to put this right. We haven't taken anything out of the cans. Everything is still there. If we put it all back without hurting anything, we should be good when we die."

"Maybe we should just give them to the chief? Tell him what happened. Let him put them back," Zack suggested.

Eric shook his head. "No. I thought about that. But the chief, he's going to be talking to the judge about us. If we tell him we broke into that house and took stuff, well, he's gunna have to tell the judge. And that stuff in the cans, it's worth a lot of money. I remember Dad once saying that when you steal something over a thousand dollars, they can lock you away for a long time. I don't wanna go to jail for a long time."

"Mom wouldn't like that either. She's already so sad ever since Dad died."

"We just have to put the stuff back, and don't say nothing to nobody."

"When are we going to do it?"

"I'm not sure. Tomorrow, we promised to help at the museum. And getting away from mom for an hour is going to be a little more difficult than it has been. She's been watching us much more, ever since we got arrested."

"Yeah. But it is kinda nice. She's having dinner with us again."

THIRTY-TWO

The American flag, its pole secured in the flagpole holder on the front porch, waved proudly by the front entrance of Marlow House, as it did on most days. But today was Thursday, July Fourth, and typically the residents of Marlow House adorned the exterior of the property with additional patriotic decorations, especially on those years when they held events not just celebrating Independence Day, but the anniversary of Marlow House Bed and Breakfast's grand opening.

Unfortunately, this year's decorations were overlooked since the residents were preoccupied with the growing population on Beach Drive, namely the Marlow twins, and the Bartleys' new daughter. Yet this didn't mean some of them wouldn't be doing something special for the holiday.

"I feel guilty going without you," Danielle told Lily. "I understand why you don't want to come. But are you sure you're okay with us leaving the twins?"

Lily, who lounged on the sofa in the living room, glanced over at the three portable cribs lined up by the wall. Two of the cribs held sleeping babies, while a third, Jack, floated lazily around the room.

Lily smiled at the orbiting baby and looked back at Danielle. "We'll be fine."

"Yes, we will," Marie, who paced the room with a fussy Jack, called out.

"Marie agrees." Danielle chuckled.

"I also have Ian and Connor, yet not sure how Connor will help." Lily giggled. "But when I have more energy, I'll go to the museum with Ian and check out the new exhibit. But I'm too tired now, anyway. I just want to sleep."

WALT AND DANIELLE arrived at the museum a little after ten in the morning. The front parking lot had more cars than normal at this time of day. The moment they entered the building, Millie Samson, dressed in a long blue skirt and a red and white blouse, greeted them by asking, "You didn't bring the twins?"

Danielle stood in the front entrance of the museum with Walt by her side. She smiled at the elderly woman. "No, they're home in expert hands. How's the exhibit going?"

"I was expecting more people, but it's early still." She motioned toward the main exhibit area. "But go on in. There are a few of your friends already here."

They chatted a few more minutes before Walt and Danielle moved on to the exhibit area. Once inside the large room, they noticed a table set up with refreshments and two young boys standing behind the table, handing out napkins and paper cups.

"Are those the Bowman twins?" Walt whispered to Danielle as they walked all the way into the room.

"Yes. Remember, the chief told me he's having them volunteer as their community service."

"Edward has something against Millie?" Walt teased.

Danielle playfully elbowed her husband. "Walt!" She giggled.

The next familiar faces they noticed were Adam and Melony standing next to the new tunnel exhibit, speaking to someone they didn't recognize. They walked toward the new exhibit.

"Oh, Walt, Danielle, I wondered if we'd see you," Adam greeted, while Melony gave Danielle and Walt each a quick hello hug. Adam then introduced the couple he and Melony stood with. They were Adrian Sadler and Bonnie Sadler. Bonnie was the owner of the property Adam had taken her to see, and Adrian was Wesley's brother, but since Adam didn't mention showing Bonnie's house to her, Danielle said nothing and smiled politely while extending a generic greeting.

As Adam explained to Bonnie and Adrian, Walt and Danielle's connection with the tunnel—aka the new exhibit everyone had come to see today—Danielle quietly assessed the pair. She wasn't surprised Adrian and Wesley weren't blood brothers, considering they looked nothing alike. Adrian, far better looking than Wesley, looked a bit like a poor man's, Ryan Gosling, while Bonnie, at least four inches shorter than Adrian, was a rather plain, not unattractive, but forgettable-looking brunette with short curly hair and hazel eyes.

Bonnie clung to Adrian's side, holding onto his right arm as if it were a lifeline, while she kept smiling up to him, her grin widening every time he said something to Adam or Walt, as if Adrian were indeed the cleverest man she had ever met.

"Adrian and Bonnie were sharing their good news with me before you walked up," Adam told Walt and Danielle. Before Adam had a chance to announce the good news, Bonnie abruptly stuck out her left hand to Danielle and Walt, showing off an engagement ring.

"Oh, when's the big day?" Danielle asked.

Bonnie took back her left hand, looking at it one last time before letting it drop back to her side. She looked at Danielle and grinned excitedly. "We haven't set a date yet. But we'll probably elope."

"No big wedding?" Melony asked. She had been in the bathroom when Bonnie and Adrian had first broken the engagement news to Adam. She had returned moments earlier, so she, like Walt and Danielle, was hearing the news for the first time.

"We don't really have any family," Adrian said. "So no reason to go to all that fuss."

Bonnie hugged Adrian's arm and looked up at him lovingly. "The important thing is that we'll be together."

Adrian smiled down at his fiancée and, with his free hand, gave her hand holding his other arm a little pat.

They chatted a few minutes longer before Bonnie and Adrian wandered off to look at the other exhibits.

DANIELLE AND MELONY stood alone in one corner of the exhibit area, each sipping a glass of punch and people-watching while Walt and Adam mingled throughout the small crowd.

"If I know Adam, he's going to leave today with at least two listing leads." Melony chuckled and took a drink of her punch.

Danielle noticed Adrian and Bonnie leaving the exhibit area, presumably leaving the museum. She looked back at Melony. "Did Adam tell you about me looking at Bonnie's house?"

"He did. So your former mother-in-law might really be interested in buying property in Frederickport?"

Danielle shrugged. "We've discussed the possibility. I was going to ask Adam if I could go over there and take pictures so I can send them to her."

"I'm sure he'll be fine with that. But the house isn't officially listed yet. She needs to fix some things first before they put it on the market."

"Like the front yard?"

"Adam mentioned the yard looked like it hadn't been touched since Cordelia died. Which is a shame. I remember Cordelia used to take good care of her house. Oh, she didn't do the yard work herself, but she didn't have a problem paying someone to do it."

"You knew her?" Danielle asked.

"Yes. Mom and she were both members of the local Women's Club, back in the day." Melony finished the last of her punch and held the empty cup in her hand.

"What was she like?"

"Mom used to say she came from one of the poorest families in town. But Cordelia married money. Didn't have any kids. She had a brother and sister, who never seemed to do much better than their parents had. From what Mom said, her sister, Bonnie's mother, resented the fact her sister had it so easy because she married money. But to Cordelia's credit, she seemed to be generous with her two nieces. That's what my mom always said, anyway."

"I understand Bonnie's cousin, Rylee, took care of her aunt for the last couple of years of her life. But when she died, she left everything to Bonnie."

Melony nodded. "Yeah. I was surprised. As for Bonnie not helping care for her aunt, while Bonnie has always been sweet, she doesn't do well around sick people." Melony chuckled and added, "Those are her words, not mine. Phobia, perhaps. I'm not sure. But because of that, she never really helped Rylee take care of Cordelia, and from what I understand, she rarely visited her."

"Do you have any theories on why she left her estate to Bonnie?"

Melony absently looked down at the empty cup in her hands as she considered the question. "From what I understand, Cordelia rewrote the will not long before she died, leaving everything to Bonnie. There were rumors it had something to do with Rylee's treatment of her aunt when she was taking care of her. But I don't believe that. One theory: she left it to Bonnie because she needed it more, and Rylee would be okay without her money."

Danielle frowned. "Why would she need it more?"

"I doubt you ever met Bonnie's first husband. Who, by the way, was Adrian's brother. Keep it all in the family." Melony chuckled before continuing, "They look nothing alike because they were both adopted. I have to say, Bonnie did better in the looks department this time around, but I'm not sure Adrian is any more of a prize than Wesley."

"You didn't care for her first husband?"

Melony shrugged and looked up from her hands at Danielle. "It wasn't like he abused Bonnie or anything. I guess the best way to describe him, mediocre. While he had a job, he wasn't that good at it. Bonnie never worked. She always needed to be taken care of.

Rylee, on the other hand, was always independent. Put herself through nursing school. Her parents weren't able to help her, and supposedly her aunt offered to pay for her school. But Rylee wouldn't accept the money. It's possible she left Bonnie her estate because she was annoyed Rylee refused her generous offer. One thing I've noticed over the years, wealthy people often use their money more to control rather than help family members."

"So Cordelia thought, well, you were too proud to accept my offer, so I guess you don't want to inherit anything?" Danielle suggested.

Melony shrugged. "That's possible. And it was no secret Rylee was paid to care for her. It was her job. So I guess Cordelia didn't feel obligated to leave her estate to Rylee."

"I wonder why she didn't leave her estate to both nieces," Danielle said.

"I don't think she ever planned to do that. Not long after Cordelia died, before anyone knew about the will, I ran into a friend of my mother's, another Women's Club member. She asked me if I heard about Cordelia, and then said something about Rylee now being set up for life. Apparently, Cordelia had told her she was leaving everything to Rylee."

"But she didn't."

Melony shook her head. "No. We learned later she changed her will the month before she died. It's possible something else happened that month."

"If she had to change her will, wouldn't her attorney know why she made the change?"

Melony smiled. "My father was her attorney, and when he died, Clarence took over his account. But when all the crap hit the fan regarding Dad's law firm, instead of finding a new attorney, she started using a paralegal in Astoria, who, I understand, was recommended by Wesley. Anyway, rumor has it she changed the will when Rylee took a few days off. It was one of the few times Bonnie agreed to stay with her aunt."

"Wait a minute, you're saying she changed the will when Bonnie was there? Didn't anyone find that suspicious?"

"Sure. It's why Rylee contested the will. But according to the paralegal, Cordelia called her to the house and asked her to come over the weekend Rylee would be gone. The paralegal claimed that was the first time she had met Bonnie, and Bonnie didn't know the paralegal was coming over. Supposedly, Bonnie was as surprised as anyone when she discovered her aunt had left her everything."

"Wow."

"According to Bonnie, her aunt told her the paralegal was there because she had some papers to sign and said nothing about revising her will. Both the paralegal and Bonnie said Bonnie wasn't in the room when her aunt met with the paralegal that day, and she wasn't told about any changes to the will until after the aunt died."

THIRTY-THREE

Walt and Danielle only stayed at the museum for a couple of hours on Thursday. But before they said goodbye to Adam, Danielle asked him if he would let her go over to the house the next day so she could take pictures of the property and send them to Madeline. She felt a little guilty telling the white lie, and so as to not find herself caught in it at some future date, she decided she would send the photos off to Madeline and write something like: *you once mentioned you might be interested in Frederickport property, so I thought I'd give you a sample of what's currently on the market.* She wanted to cover her bases, because if Madeline ever visited her in the future, and she saw Adam, he would mention the property.

"I WISH you could come with us," Walt told Danielle Thursday evening as he and Ian prepared to take Connor to the firework show along the beach. They had finished dinner twenty minutes earlier, and together Walt and Ian—with the help of Walt's telekinetic gift—cleaned up the dinner dishes.

Danielle and Lily sat together on the sofa, each holding their daughters, while Jack napped between them. Danielle looked at Walt and smiled. "Next year. I really have no desire to go to the firework show tonight."

"Neither do I," Lily agreed.

"You boys go, have fun. Take Connor for ice cream afterwards," Danielle suggested.

Connor perked up. "Ice keem?"

Ian laughed. "Now we'll have to take him."

Danielle flashed Ian a mischievous grin. "I imagine Walt wants to go for ice cream, anyway."

"She's right." Walt winked at his wife. They chatted a few more minutes while Ian changed Connor's diaper and gathered up what they needed to take. When they were ready to leave, Walt walked over to the sofa, gave Danielle a kiss, and dropped a kiss on the foreheads of his son and daughter. For good measure, he ruffled Lily's hair, as if she were an obedient dog, and ran a gentle finger over Emily Ann's forehead.

Lily laughed at Walt and absently brushed her fingers through her hair. "Gee, thanks, Walt," she said, still laughing.

"You know I love you." Walt gave her a wink and started for the door.

With Connor now in his arms, Ian walked to the sofa and gave his wife a kiss, but spared Danielle the same attention Walt had given Lily, considering both his hands were occupied. Sadie followed them all to the front door.

A few minutes later, after Danielle and Lily heard the front door open and close, Sadie returned to the living room and lay down in front of the sofa.

"This will be good for Connor, spending guy time with Walt and his dad. Plus, I really didn't want to go tonight," Lily said.

"Me either."

"When Ian was changing Connor, it reminded me I need to start potty training that boy," Lily said.

"They always say you shouldn't start potting training a boy until he's two and a half."

"Yeah, that's what my mother always told me. But I recently

read an article that claimed the study advocating later potty training was funded by companies that made diapers."

Danielle arched her brows. "Really? So it would be a financial incentive for those companies to keep toddlers in diapers longer. Sort of like how they marketed baby formula, and many women stopped breastfeeding."

"Exactly. But to be honest, I'm not really sure the story about the diaper companies funding the studies is true. After all, I saw it on social media."

They both laughed.

"But I'm considering giving potty training a shot with Connor after he turns two. If it becomes a major deal with him, and he's not mature enough, I'll back off."

"Look at us, Lily, all this baby and mommy talk," Danielle teased.

They both laughed again.

"Okay, enough about diapers and breastfeeding. So that player Adrian has actually asked Bonnie to marry him? All the while, he's planning to hook up with another woman?"

Danielle shrugged. "It looks that way. I feel sorry for Bonnie. She seems totally over the moon for this guy. I hate breaking her heart."

"It's better than letting her marry that jerk. And if Wesley is right, we might be saving Bonnie's life."

"True. Wish we could come up with something else. But aside from catching him cheating, Eva and Marie haven't come across anything that might substantiate Wesley's claim about his brother."

"Are you really going back to that house tomorrow?" Lily asked.

"Oh! I almost forgot; I need to call Heather."

"Why?"

"Remember, I need to take either her or Chris with me so I can talk to the ghost. I was going to call Heather tonight and ask her." Danielle reached over to the side table and picked up her cellphone. Lily sat quietly and listened to Danielle's side of the conversation. When Danielle hung up, she said, "Heather's going to go, but she's calling Chris to see if he wants to go too."

THE GHOST WHO SOUGHT REDEMPTION

CHRIS AND HEATHER showed up midmorning on Friday to drive Danielle to Cordelia's house. Chris had Hunny with him, but he left the dog at Marlow House. After Danielle climbed into the backseat of Chris's car and slammed the door shut, Chris asked, "How's it going with having a second family living with you?"

Putting on her seatbelt, Danielle looked to the driver's seat. "It's been going great, actually. It's nice having Lily's company. And what's one more baby and a toddler?"

"Plus, Walt and Ian are waiting on Lily and Danielle like princesses," Heather snarked but added, "As they should."

Chris laughed and put his car in drive. He pulled out into the street and asked, "Did you tell Adam we're coming with you?"

"No. He offered to pick me up, but I told him I was going to be out running errands, so it wasn't necessary. I figure I can tell him you stopped by, and I mentioned I was going over to take some pictures of the house, and you wanted to come."

"Get Adam all excited." Heather chuckled. "He'll figure, if Madeline doesn't buy it, Chris might."

"By the way, when I saw Mel at the museum yesterday, she told me some interesting things about Cordelia," Danielle said.

Heather glanced to the backseat where Danielle sat. "Who's Cordelia?"

"The ghost we're going to see," Danielle reminded her before recounting the conversation she had with Mel.

WHEN THEY ARRIVED at Cordelia's house, Adam was waiting for them. He had already opened up the house, which included pulling back the blinds to let in the sunlight and opening the windows to let in the fresh air.

"Why don't you and Heather take your pictures? I need to talk to Adam about something," Chris suggested. "I'll look at the house when we're done."

Danielle and Heather flashed Chris a smile, leaving Adam standing on the front porch with him.

"Your boss is slick," Danielle whispered to Heather as they walked through the living room.

Heather chuckled before asking, "So where do you think we're going to find Cordelia?"

"When I saw her, she was sitting in the parlor. That's where her portrait's hanging."

"What is with these ghosts and portraits?" Heather asked. "I don't have a portrait, so when I die, am I going to be considered a loser in the ghost world?"

Danielle chuckled. "Not sure, but I've noticed, when they've had a portrait done of them, they do seem drawn to it."

"Ego?"

"It's probably because they no longer see their reflection in the mirror. If they have something tangible, something of the living world that looks like them, it might be comforting."

Danielle led Heather to the parlor. Its door still closed. She stopped in front of the door and looked at Heather. "This is where I saw her. Let's see if she's still here." Danielle reached for the doorknob, turned it, and pushed open the door. She and Heather walked into the room.

"Hello. You're back. Who's your friend?"

Heather and Danielle looked at the elderly woman sitting in the wingback chair. Heather smiled at the woman and asked, "Are you Cordelia?"

Cordelia's eyes widened, as if surprised Heather had actually answered her. "Are you a witch?"

Heather suppressed her urge to laugh. "Umm, no. Why do you ask?"

"No offense intended. But how you're dressed, you look a little like what I'd expect a modern witch to dress like."

"A modern witch?" Heather asked.

Cordelia grinned. "In my day, we had to be more discreet."

Heather frowned. "We?"

Instead of answering Heather's question, Cordelia smiled and asked her own. "Who are you? And why are you here?"

"I'm Danielle Marlow, and this is my friend Heather Donovan."

"You can both see me?" the ghost asked in a quiet voice as she stared intently at the two women.

"Yes, we can. But you knew I could see you the other day, didn't you?" Danielle asked.

Cordelia leaned back in the chair, her hands now folded on her lap. "I suspected you could. I don't get many visitors, but the ones I do, well, none of them could see me. Or else they were ignoring me."

"Cordelia, we're here trying to unravel a mystery and possibly prevent a murder. We were hoping you might help."

Cordelia smiled. "I did love reading a good mystery when I was alive. There were a few mysteries I enjoyed watching on television, but only the British ones. I didn't care for the American ones. So tell me, whose life are you trying to save?"

"Your niece Bonnie," Danielle told her.

Cordelia frowned. "Heavens, why on earth would anyone want to kill Bonnie? I can think of one who has the motive, but she's not a murderer, so you don't have to worry about her."

"Who has a motive?" Danielle asked.

"Her cousin, Rylee, of course. After all, from what I've pieced together from the occasional visits I've gotten from the living world—none of whom could see or hear me—it appears that little brat Bonnie has forged my will and managed to steal Rylee's inheritance."

"Are you saying you didn't leave your estate to Bonnie?" Danielle asked.

"Of course not. Why would I do that? I'm not daft. Rylee was always such a dear girl, and while I paid her to take care of me, I always knew she was not charging enough. She could have made far more working as a traveling nurse, and not have to put up with my stubborn ways. I can be quite stubborn. As for Bonnie, I was generous with her over the years, and unlike Rylee, she never hesitated to accept what I offered. A new car when she turned sixteen. I paid for her wedding, even though I couldn't understand what she saw in that man. I don't know how Bonnie changed my will."

"According to the paralegal who handled your estate, you asked her to come see you the weekend Bonnie was staying with you. When the paralegal arrived, you visited with her privately and made the changes. Bonnie claims she had no idea you changed your will, and the paralegal collaborated that."

"That's absurd. Yes, she did come see me that weekend, but she's the one who called me. I didn't call her. She said there were some papers I needed to sign that had been overlooked. It's true, I met with her privately in this room. Bonnie was in the living room. I read over the papers I signed. None were about changes to a will. And then she left. Someone needs to talk to the paralegal. If she said I changed the will, she is lying."

"We will talk to her, I promise," Danielle said.

"And you don't need to worry about anyone murdering Bonnie. Like I said, Rylee would never kill her cousin."

"Actually, it's her brother-in-law, Adrian, who someone believes intends to kill her."

"Adrian? I remember Bonnie used to have a crush on Adrian before she married Wesley. Of course, Adrian was not interested. But I can't imagine why he'd want to kill her."

THIRTY-FOUR

When Danielle returned to Marlow House with Chris and Heather, they entered the side yard from the front gate, and they found Walt, Lily and Ian out on the patio off the kitchen, enjoying the sunny and mild July afternoon. Lily relaxed on a chaise lounge, sipping a strawberry smoothie Ian had made her, while Walt and Ian sat nearby, each with a glass of iced tea in hand.

"This looks relaxing," Danielle said as she approached the patio, Heather and Chris at her side. Sadie and Hunny, who had been napping by Walt's feet, jumped to greet the new arrivals, their tails wagging. Hunny greeted Chris, who knelt down and gave his happy pup a proper hug and greeting.

Heather glanced around. "Where are the babies? Connor?"

Walt frowned at Heather. "Babies? What babies?"

"Connor who?" Ian asked.

Danielle rolled her eyes and looked back at Walt. He chuckled before saying, "They're inside with Marie."

"She has all of them?" Danielle asked as she sat down next to Walt.

"They were sleeping, and Connor's playing with the Lincoln Logs," Ian said. "Max is in there too."

Heather and Chris each took a seat.

"Marie will send Max out if she needs our help," Lily said before breaking into a giggle and taking a sip of her smoothie.

"I'm glad to see the ghost and cat have it all under control," Danielle said before joining Lily in a giggle.

"So, did you guys find out anything interesting? Did you talk to Cordelia's ghost?" Ian asked.

"Found out lots of interesting things," Heather said.

"And was it Cordelia's ghost?" Walt asked.

"Yes, it was," Danielle said before recounting her and Heather's conversation with the ghost.

"So I was right. Rylee never abused her aunt," Lily said when Danielle finished her telling.

"Here we are, planning to expose Adrian's infidelity to possibly save Bonnie's life. But now it seems Bonnie is not such an innocent after all," Ian said.

"It's entirely possible Wesley is behind the fraudulent will. After all, he's the one who suggested the paralegal. He would have benefited from having a wealthy wife. And from what I've seen of Bonnie, she isn't the brightest bulb in the chandelier," Danielle said.

"I wish we could just ask Wesley," Heather grumbled. "I don't know what he thinks he's gaining by refusing to be transparent."

"He's already pretty transparent," Chris teased. "Some people can see right through him."

Heather rolled her eyes at Chris. "Funny. But the thing is, he has nothing to lose by opening up to us. In fact, it could help him. And those secrets he's keeping close to the vest, the Universe already knows, so he is not fooling anyone."

"I suspect Bonnie isn't the only dim bulb in that chandelier. I have a feeling Bonnie and Wesley were made for each other," Chris said.

"It really sucks for Rylee," Lily said. "Not only to have her inheritance stolen from her, but her reputation tarnished. While she obviously still has her nursing license, there are rumors of elder abuse out there."

"So, do we still have Marie try to take those pictures? Do we bother breaking them up?" Heather asked.

"Like I said, we don't know if Bonnie's involved with the fraud. Yes, she benefits, but I'd feel horrible if we found out Wesley was right, and then she gets killed, and then later we find out Wesley was behind the fraud and she knew nothing about it," Danielle said.

"How would we ever find out?" Lily asked.

"If she was killed and her ghost stuck around, then her ghost would probably tell us," Danielle reminded her.

Lily let out a sigh. "True."

"Okay, so we're going forward with ratting out the cheating boyfriend, and we're also going to look into this fraud thing?" Lily asked.

"I promised Cordelia we'd try to find out more about the paralegal. She is obviously the key to all this," Danielle said.

"How do you expect to do that?" Ian asked.

"The paralegal was obviously paid off by someone to change the will," Chris said. "And we've already established that someone is Bonnie or Wesley, or both of them."

"I would assume if the paralegal was bribed to forge a new will, they'd have to pay her a lot of money. And if it was Bonnie or Wesley, did they have that kind of money, or did they have to wait until the estate went through probate before they could pay off the paralegal?" Ian said.

"I would assume they paid her something after it completed probate. From what Cordelia said about them, they didn't have the means to pay someone a significant enough sum of money to break the law like that. Maybe they managed to give her a little something, but I would assume the bulk of a bribe was paid after it finished probate," Danielle said.

"Which means," Chris began, "if there was a bribe, we'd need to see if a large amount of money was deposited into her bank account—an amount that correlates with what came out of the estate funds—or Bonnie's or Wesley's bank account—after probate closed."

"And how are you going to find that out?" Heather asked. "Doesn't it take a warrant to access that type of information?"

"First things first." Danielle grabbed the purse she had set by her feet moments earlier. She opened it and removed her cellphone. "Let's find the paralegal. Cordelia gave me her name. Whatever they paid her to forge the will, I bet it was a substantial bit of money, which I have to assume it was; then I doubt she's still a paralegal. She's probably off somewhere, enjoying the good life on ill-gotten gains." Cellphone in hand, Danielle started searching online.

"What are you doing?" Lily asked.

"Looking for our paralegal. I'm plugging in her name, along with Astoria, Oregon, and paralegal."

"I thought you just said she probably wasn't a paralegal anymore," Heather said.

"It's a place to start," Ian said.

They were all silent for a few moments while Danielle searched for the information. After a few moments, she dropped her cellphone on her lap and looked around.

"Well?" Heather asked.

"I was right about one thing. She's no longer a paralegal."

"What's she doing?" Lily asked. "Is she still in Astoria?"

"She is. About six feet under. I just found her obituary."

"She's dead?" Walt and Chris chorused.

Danielle nodded. She picked up her cellphone and silently reread the obituary. "She died on New Year's Eve."

"What did she die of?" Heather asked.

"Obituaries typically don't mention the cause of death," Chris said.

"Actually, this one did. It mentioned that she had emergency heart surgery, and the last three years was a gift. So I'm assuming that means she had heart surgery three years before she died, lived three years longer than they thought she would, and then died. Probably a heart attack or something. But that's just my guess." Danielle shrugged.

Hunny and Sadie started barking and ran to the front gate. They all stopped talking and looked to see what had caught the dogs' attention. The gate opened, and Marlow House's next-door neighbor, Olivia Davis, came walking through the gate, carrying a large package wrapped in pink and bows. She greeted the pups, gently pushing them aside as she closed the gate behind her, and walked toward the group on the patio as Hunny and Sadie followed along, their tails wagging.

"Olivia!" Danielle greeted. "You're not working today?"

"Closed for the holiday." She exchanged greetings with the group and then walked to Lily and handed her the package. "I just wanted to bring this over. I understand our new neighbor came early!"

They exchanged hugs and thanks, Lily opened the gift, and she promised to introduce Olivia to Emily Ann as soon as she woke up. Olivia sat down on a patio chair, and Walt offered her, along with Heather and Chris, some iced tea.

Ten minutes later, Walt returned with glasses of iced tea and a plate of cookies. While Walt was in the kitchen, Danielle and the others filled Olivia in on what had been going on regarding Clay's and Wesley's ghosts. While not a medium herself, Olivia, who had once dabbled in astral projection and had been mistaken as a ghost by the local mediums when she first moved to town, had learned their secrets because of it. She had moved to Frederickport the first of the year and had taken on the job as head librarian at the local library, which took most of her time.

"I know Bonnie," Olivia told them after they finished with the update. She held a glass of iced tea in one hand and a cookie in the other. "She was one of the first people I met when I moved to town. In fact, I believe I was with her when she learned of her husband's death."

"How so?" Walt asked.

"Bonnie belongs to a book club at the library. I had stopped by to say hello to the members when Bonnie's cellphone rang. It was her husband. Honestly, had it been me, I would have taken my phone and excused myself and gone out into the hall to talk in private. But Bonnie can be...how can I say this...a little immature?"

"Immature how?" Lily asked.

Olivia took a bite of her cookie, and as she chewed, she seemed to consider how best to answer Lily's question. After swallowing her bite, she said, "Well, she talked a little loud, so naturally we could all hear the gist of the conversation. Her husband was on a business trip and had just arrived at his hotel and wanted Bonnie to know he had just checked in. There was a lot of," Olivia paused and rolled her eyes before continuing, "I love you, no, I love you more, going on. While we couldn't hear Wesley's side of the conversation, it was obvious he was saying it, too. And when she got off the phone, she let us all know how she hated when her husband took business trips because she always missed sleeping with him. Frankly, I didn't need to hear that."

"Why do you think it was the last time she spoke to him?" Danielle asked.

"Later that day, a member of the book club came back to the library to pick up something she had forgotten, and while there, asked me if I had heard about Bonnie's husband. He had apparently died of a heart attack while on his business trip. And Bonnie was a basket case. I guess she doesn't have any family, so a couple of women from the group went over to the house to be with her."

"Actually, she does have family. Rylee," Lily reminded them.

"Hi!" a new voice called out from the front gate. Both Hunny and Sadie raced over to greet the new arrival. Ian's sister, Kelly, had just stepped into the yard and now walked in their direction. Seeing Kelly, Lily quickly said under her breath, "No more ghost talk."

"Hi, guys," Kelly greeted once she reached the patio. As the others returned her greetings, she glanced around. "Where are the babies?"

"Sleeping," Lily said.

Kelly looked around again. "Where's Connor?" She sat down in a chair.

Lily and Ian exchanged quick glances and then looked at Kelly. "Umm, he's taking a nap too."

They chatted for a few minutes, with both Walt and Ian eyeing the kitchen door, each thinking the same thing. They were looking for a way to go into the house without Kelly following them. But then Kelly stood abruptly.

"You leaving already?" Lily asked.

"No, I'm going to use the bathroom. That's okay, isn't it?"

THIRTY-FIVE

In the living room of Marlow House, the ghost of Marie Nichols stood over the portable cribs, watching the sleeping infants, while Danielle's cat, Max, sat next to Connor by the fireplace, batting at the Lincoln Logs.

Marie came from a generation where girls were taught their purpose in life was to marry and have children. Unfortunately, her marriage had not turned out as she had once dreamed. Simply put, her husband had been a putz.

Like many women, she had fertility issues, and she could only have one child, who unfortunately didn't fall far from the tree, who was his father. While her son was as much of a disappointment as her husband, her grandsons brought her tremendous joy, especially her eldest grandson, Adam. While others might have considered Adam a scoundrel, she saw his softer, caring side, and because of that, she had longed for him to have children she might someday spoil.

Marie had since come to accept the fact Adam and his wife chose not to have children. Danielle and Lily had helped her accept this reality. Before her death, she had become close to both women, and saw them as surrogate granddaughters, and she loved their children as she had loved Adam when he was a baby.

A faint cry came from Emily Ann's crib. Marie was at the infant's side before the cries could wake the sleeping twins. She carried Emily Ann to the sofa and started changing her diaper when Connor showed up by her side.

"Baby," Connor said, reaching out to his sister.

Marie smiled at Connor. "You want to hold the baby?"

Connor nodded to Marie, his grin wide.

Marie finished diapering the infant and then told Connor to climb up on the nearby recliner. Connor did as he was told and looked anxiously at Marie, who carried the now swaddled baby to him. Gently, Marie placed the baby in Connor's arms, careful to not let her fall.

Connor looked down curiously at the infant in his arms as Marie hovered protectively at his side.

"Connor!" The unexpected shout woke the twins, who began to cry.

Marie looked up at the open doorway. There stood Kelly, looking at Connor, who appeared to be alone in the room with the three infants—with one in his arms.

Without thought, Marie slammed closed the living room doors and locked them and, in doing so, pushed Kelly from the room and into the hallway. Marie didn't know why she had shoved Kelly from the room, it was a reflex, just like the time when she had been in the fifth grade and Ronny Butler grabbed the ribbon from one of her braids and she turned around and punched him in the nose. She didn't break Ronny's nose, but he was a bleeder.

The cries from the twins intensified. Connor looked confused, and Marie could hear Kelly frantically jiggling the doorknobs, trying to get back into the room. But then Marie spied the eerily realistic baby doll sitting abandoned on the fireplace hearth. Pushing the limits of her powers, Marie brought the baby doll to Connor, and before he knew what happened, Emily Ann floated from his lap, back to her crib, while the doll replaced the real baby. Instead of being upset over the switch,

Connor laughed, and in the next moment, Marie released hold of the living room doors while opening one of the living room windows. The doors flew open, this time because Kelly had pushed them.

Walt and Ian stood behind Kelly, having just arrived. What Marie didn't know, they had followed Kelly into the house, hoping she would go directly to the bathroom so they could get to the living room before she looked in on the babies. Ian's plan had been to whisk his son into the downstairs bedroom so his sister would assume that was where her nephew had been napping, as opposed to being left alone with three newborns.

Connor looked up at the new arrivals, giggled, and then, to his aunt's horror, picked up the baby in his lap by its arm and flung it across the room.

THEY ALL SAT in the living room, with Danielle on the sofa and Walt by her side while she nursed the twins; Lily sat in the rocker with Emily Ann; Kelly and Ian sat side by side in the recliners, and in the corner Chris and Heather sat on the floor with Connor, who happily used two Lincoln logs as drumsticks, and the baby doll as the drum. Olivia had returned to her house before all the drama and had said she'd come back later to meet the new baby.

All the adults sat quietly, listening to Kelly. "So sorry for shouting and waking the babies. I feel so foolish. It looked like Connor was holding Emily Ann on his lap. I thought he had somehow picked her up from her crib and carried her to the chair, and all I could think was that he might drop her."

"We put Connor in the downstairs bedroom for a nap," Ian lied. "He must have come in here and found his doll."

"And then the doors slammed shut on me. Freaked me out, and then I couldn't get back in." Kelly shook her head. "How did that happen?"

"Tell her you left the window open, and the wind must have blown the doors shut," Marie coached from the corner.

"We left the front window open," Walt lied. "The wind must have blown the doors shut. Sometimes the doors stick."

Kelly looked up. "I'm so sorry for screaming and waking the babies."

"I'm sorry you had such a scare," Danielle said.

"That stupid doll looks creepily like a real baby," Lily said.

"I know I wasn't standing that close to Connor, but I swear, it really looked like Emily Ann, not a doll," Kelly muttered.

"MY POOR SISTER," Ian said after both Kelly and Marie left Marlow House.

"Do you really think that doll is stupid and creepy?" Heather asked Lily.

Lily grinned at Heather. "No. But I know my son, and when Kelly was telling us what happened, I figured she had actually walked in on Connor holding Emily Ann while Marie supervised, and Marie was trying to do damage control."

"Yeah, it was bad enough Kelly thought he came in here with the babies. Can you imagine what she would tell my mother if she knew Connor was really holding Emily Ann and no one else was in here with him?" Ian groaned.

"What did you mean when you said you know your son?" Heather asked Lily.

"I've introduced baby dolls to Connor before. He's never been interested. He's certainly never wanted to hold one on his lap and rock it before. I told Mom, when she said she wanted to get him a realistic baby doll before the baby was born, it was a waste of money. But that's just Connor. When I was in college, I used to teach preschool. A lot of little boys loved baby dolls, but some of them were like Connor, would rather use them as a bat. Same for some of the little girls. Not all little girls like dolls."

Ian let out a sigh and said, "Next time we need to tell my sister the plumbing is backed up and she can't use the bathroom."

They all laughed, and then Walt said, "Not to change the

subject, but if Marie is still willing to take those pictures tomorrow, we need to get that camera over to the florist shop tonight."

"I got the cellphone lined up; did you get the camera?" Chris asked.

Ian nodded. "I did. I even picked up a protective case."

"When it gets dark, we can go over there," Walt said.

"We also need to wait until Marie returns. I want to show her how to use the camera before we take it over there," Ian said.

MARIE ENDED up going over to the florist shop with Ian and Walt on Friday night. They parked in front of the building, and since there was no one on the street, the men stayed in the car while Marie hid the camera on the roof. She was tempted to leave it near the back door, but was afraid someone might walk by and find it before she returned to take the pictures.

The next day, she returned to the building about thirty minutes before Adrian was to arrive. She sat on the roof, keeping an eye out for his car, and when she spied it driving down the street, she took the camera and dropped to the rear of the building. At the back door, she set the small digital camera, still in its case, on the ground a few inches from the door and then covered it with pine needles. She hoped no one would see it.

Adrian parked down the street and walked the rest of the way to the shop. When he was about five feet from the rear door, a gust of wind blew down the alley and took with it the pine needles covering the camera. Marie wasn't too concerned Adrian would notice since the camera case blended in with the ground cover. Yet what Marie hadn't counted on was the afternoon sun hitting the metal handle of the case, making it glisten. Adrian was just a few feet from the door when he noticed something sparkly on the ground. He stopped and looked down.

Marie shook her head. "No, no, no!"

Adrian bent down and picked up the camera. Standing back up, he turned the case back and forth and then opened it and pulled out the small camera. "Dang, this looks brand new." He shoved the camera back in the case and then walked through the back door. Marie followed him inside.

"Look what I found by your back door," Adrian told widow Pierson. "It's a camera."

She grabbed hold of the camera case, taking it from Adrian. After looking at it a moment, she set it on the counter behind her, turned back to Adrian, and wrapped her arms around his neck. "Some kid must have dropped it. But I'm more interested in you than that camera."

MARIE WASN'T CUT out to be a peeping tom, so instead of watching the lovers, she focused her attention on the camera. It didn't take long for the couple to forget about Adrian's find and get down to business. Careful not to make a sound, Marie slipped the camera from its case. She figured if one of them looked over to the counter, they would see the case and assume the camera was still there. Of course, at this point neither Adrian nor his girlfriend cared two hoots about what was on the counter.

Marie turned to the couple, and if she could blush, she would. Instead, she closed her eyes and moved closer to the back door. Marie opened her eyes for a moment and aimed the camera at the couple and then closed her eyes again, snapping one picture after another. She had no idea if she captured a decent photo of the couple, or if there was enough light in the room, but at this point, she didn't care. She just wanted to get out of the flower shop.

When she felt she had snapped enough pictures, she eased open the back door and made a hasty exit with the camera while the couple never noticed anything unusual. Marie did wonder what they would think when they cooled off and found an empty camera case sitting on the counter.

THIRTY-SIX

Walt and Danielle sat at the kitchen table on Saturday evening, each having a slice of chocolate cake, when Ian walked into the room.

"Those were some wild pictures Marie took," Ian told them as he grabbed a cup from an overhead counter and then filled it with cold water.

Concerned the camera might get wet before they could remove the images, since it no longer had a cover, Marie hadn't returned it to the roof. Instead, she'd flown it to Marlow House, like a witch without a broom, in broad daylight, moving fast enough that if anyone noticed something overhead, they would assume it was a bird.

"Where is our photographer?" Danielle asked. "Did she ever come back?"

"Since I can't see Marie, I have no idea." Ian laughed. "But Connor hasn't acted like she's here."

"Oh dear. You said the photos were wild. How wild?" Danielle asked.

"It's pretty obvious Marie wasn't paying a great deal of attention

THE GHOST WHO SOUGHT REDEMPTION

to what she was taking pictures of. There are a lot of shots of the back room of the florist shop, with a random elbow or some body part in the picture's corner. In some shots, you could see they were getting down to business, but there was no way to tell who they were."

"So we didn't get anything?" Danielle asked.

"Fortunately, there was one good picture. It's a little dark, but I don't imagine there was a lot of light in the storage room. Despite that, you can clearly tell it's Adrian getting friendly with a woman. I did a little photoshop to blur out the background so Bonnie won't know it was taken in the flower shop. I also blurred the woman's face. Like I said before, I don't feel comfortable sending these types of photos out where you can clearly identify the woman or where she works."

"How are we going to do this?" Danielle asked.

"Chris got her phone number," Ian said. "So once we have the phone, I can send her a text message with a picture. I'll write something like, *Sorry to have to tell you this, but your fiancé is cheating on you. He is only after your money. You are better off without him.*"

"How did Chris get her number?" Walt asked.

"From Adam."

"When are you planning to send it?" Danielle asked.

"Chris is picking up the phone tomorrow morning. After he drops it off, I can send the message then."

ADRIAN PICKED up Bonnie on Sunday morning to take her to brunch at Pearl Cove. On the way over to the restaurant, she told him, "I have a surprise for you."

With his hands firmly on the steering wheel, he glanced over at Bonnie as they drove down the road. "Surprise? What kind of surprise?"

"Yesterday, the reason I was in Portland, well, I lied."

"What do you mean you lied?"

"About why I was going." She grinned at Adrian.

Again, glancing over to her, he furrowed his brows. "So why did you go?"

"I met with a lawyer, and I finally updated my will, adding you as my sole beneficiary."

"Seriously?" Adrian smiled.

"I found this guy in Portland, and he works every other Saturday. So I made an appointment with him last month."

"You never told me." Adrian grinned.

"I wanted to surprise you. Consider it a belated engagement present. But I have a favor to ask you."

Adrian pulled into the parking lot of Pearl Cove. "What kind of favor?"

"After breakfast, will you go with me to Aunt Cordelia's house? Adam Nichols emailed me a list of repairs I need to do on the house before we list it. And I was hoping you'd help me go through it so we can decide which ones we want to do, and then I can send it back to him and get the house listed."

"No problem, babe. Whatever you want."

"I love you, Adrian."

"I love you too, babe."

AFTER BRUNCH, Bonnie sat comfortably in the passenger seat of Adrian's car, looking out the side window as they drove to her aunt's house. When Adrian pulled up in front of the property a few minutes later, he parked, turned off the ignition, and sat in his seat a minute, hands still on the steering wheel, making no attempt to unbuckle his seat belt as he looked out of the car at the two-story house.

"It's weird I've never been in this house," Adrian said.

Bonnie shrugged and then started to unbuckle her seatbelt. "I haven't been in it since she died. Never saw the point. I never liked the house. Too dated." While Bonnie had not been back in the house, she had hired someone to check on the property, which Adrian already knew.

BONNIE STARTED on the first floor of the house, walking through each room, while Adrian stayed by her side, a pen in one hand while he carried the clipboard with the list of items Adam had recommended for repair or replacement in his other hand. When they finished on the first floor, they headed to the second floor and walked through each room. Before going back downstairs, they stopped at the top of the staircase while Adrian set the clipboard on the floor by the top step so he could inspect the railing, which Adam claimed was loose.

While Adrian examined the railing, Bonnie stood quietly about four feet behind him, waiting for him to finish, when her phone buzzed, signifying an incoming text message. Thinking it might be Adam telling her something he had forgotten, since she had mentioned they would be going over to the property after brunch, she pulled her phone from her back pocket and opened the message.

When Bonnie looked at her cellphone's screen, she found herself looking at a picture of Adrian in an embrace with a woman who appeared to be missing some of her clothing. She knew it wasn't an old picture, because the shirt Adrian wore was one she had bought him last week as a gift.

She froze in shock, staring at the image. But it was the message attached to the picture that served as a slap to her face, waking her from her momentary paralysis. Adrian, his back still to Bonnie, had just said something, but she could not process his words. Still talking, he turned to her, a smile on his face, and he knelt to pick up the clipboard he had set on the floor at the top of the stairs.

His smile felt like a million pins in her heart, and without thought, she let out a guttural scream and charged at Adrian, her hands extended. She shoved him off the top of the staircase.

He let out a scream and tried to grab hold of the railing, but his feet flew out from under him, and he tumbled to the first floor while screaming all the way. After he landed with a dramatic thud, his screaming stopped, and all was silent. Eerily silent.

CORDELIA STOOD on the first floor, looking up at her niece, who stood silently at the top of the staircase, looking down at the man she had just shoved down the stairs. "What have you done, child? I thought you loved him."

Cordelia heard a groan. She looked down at Adrian. Was he still alive? But then a second man stepped out of Adrian, whose body remained limp and lifeless on the floor. It took Cordelia a moment to realize what she was actually seeing. The second man was Adrian's spirit. Bonnie had killed her fiancé.

"What the hell?" The second Adrian stumbled to his feet and then, as if regaining his balance, stood up straight and looked up the staircase, where Bonnie remained standing on the top step, still looking down the stairs. "Why did you push me?"

When Bonnie failed to answer his question, he shouted it again, this time louder.

"She can't hear you," Cordelia said in a calm, low voice.

Surprised someone else was in the house, Adrian turned abruptly and looked at Cordelia. "Who are you?"

"You're dead, you know."

He frowned in response.

Cordelia laughed. "I guess you didn't know. But you are. My niece pushed you. Why did she do that? What did you do to her? Bonnie has always been quick to anger, unforgiving. Even vindictive."

Adrian said nothing; instead he turned and stared down at his lifeless body.

Upstairs, Bonnie remained frozen on the top step, looking down at the carnage she had created. Minutes passed. Finally, she reached out to the rail with her right hand and slowly descended the staircase, taking one slow step at a time while her right hand remained holding the handrail. When she reached the first-floor landing, she knelt down by the body.

From Cordelia's perspective, both Adrian and Bonnie knelt by the body, the tops of their heads practically touching. After a moment Bonnie reached out and pressed her finger along his neckline, testing for a pulse. As she did this, Adrian's spirit looked up at her and asked, "Why?"

Bonnie could not hear the question. She sat on the bottom step, took out her phone, and called 911. Moments later someone answered the call, and Bonnie began a hysterical sobbing plea to the operator, a stark contrast to her calm demeanor before pressing "send" for the 911 call.

WORD OF ADRIAN'S death reached Marlow House before the first responders arrived on the scene. It began with the 911 call. Bryan was talking to Heather on the phone when the call first came in that something had happened at Cordelia's house, and Bryan had to cut the call with Heather short. Heather then called Danielle, who told Marie, who then went to the house, but not before letting Eva know, who was talking to Wesley, which was why Marie, Eva, and Wesley all showed up at Cordelia's house before the responders arrived, and there was time for Marie to pop back to Marlow House to tell the mediums Adrian was dead before she returned to the scene of the crime.

ALBEIT FIRST STUNNED at being killed by Bonnie, the silent shock quickly turned into rage when Wesley arrived and greeted his brother with, "I had to stop you from marrying her. It's for the best."

After a brief greeting between Cordelia, Eva, and Marie, the three ghosts stood silently and listened to the exchange between the brothers, while in the background, the first responders filed into the house, and Bonnie began her telling of what had happened, telling Brian Henderson how Adrian had been helping her go through the house—with the clipboard with his handwriting as evidence—and how he had stumbled when checking the top railing, and had tragically fallen to his death.

But that was not the conversation Cordelia, Eva, and Marie found more interesting. Instead, they listened to what the brothers had to say.

"What do you mean it's for the best? What did you do?" Adrian demanded.

"I had to find some way to break you up. I couldn't let you marry her and then kill her."

"Why not? You were going to kill her. Or should I say, you wanted me to do it for you."

"But karma got to me first, didn't it? I was wrong. And so were you."

"Wait a minute, you were planning to kill your wife?" Marie demanded.

The brothers turned to the three ghosts. Adrian frowned at Marie. "Who are you?"

Marie waved her hand dismissively at Adrian while saying, "That's not important." She looked at Wesley and repeated her question. "You tried to kill her?"

When Wesley refused to answer the question, Adrian blurted, "He hired me to kill her. I was supposed to do it when he was in California on that business trip. We were going to split the money. But then he had that heart attack, and there was no point in killing her. I wasn't going to inherit any money. Not unless I married her."

THIRTY-SEVEN

It was a solemn Sunday evening at Marlow House. Marie and Eva had only briefly stopped by to tell the mediums what they had learned about the brothers, before going down to the cemetery, where the brothers had gone with Cordelia.

The chief, Brian, Lily and Ian, along with the mediums, save Evan, who had stayed home with his brother, sat around Marlow House's living room, discussing the day's unexpected events. Upstairs, Connor had already been put to bed, as had the babies. Danielle and Lily had activated all the baby monitors, and Sadie and Max stayed upstairs, watching over the little ones.

"I feel like a killer," Ian bemoaned. "Texting that picture was my idea."

"You're not a killer," Lily insisted. "From what Marie told us, you probably saved Bonnie's life."

"I never considered she'd react so violently," Ian said. "I actually suspected she might overlook or forgive his transgression."

"Regardless of her motives, or Adrian's, that was no accident, but we can't prove it," the chief said. "The coroner is convinced the manner of fall, considering how he landed, is consistent with how Bonnie described his death. An accident."

"Even with that text message she received moments before his death?" Lily asked.

Ian groaned. "Thanks, babe."

Lily smiled sheepishly at her husband and looked at the chief, waiting for his answer.

"From what the ghosts observed," Danielle answered for the chief, "Adrian told Marie that after Bonnie called 911, she started doing something with her phone, which could have been deleting that text message before the police showed up."

"And at this point, we don't have grounds to go through her phone anyway. There is nothing to suggest foul play aside from what the spirit world tells us," Brian said.

"Does it really matter, guys?" Heather asked.

The chief looked at Heather as if he disagreed.

Heather smiled at the chief. "Come on, Chief, the guy was planning to kill her. Think of all the work she saved you, not to mention saving her own life."

"I sorta agree with Heather," Danielle said. "Maybe this was the Universe's plan all the time."

"I don't know about the Universe's plan, but remember, Mrs. Pierson might still come forward, and we might have to take a closer look, which I imagine could get uncomfortable for some of the people in this room," the chief said. "Including myself."

"What can she do?" Heather asked.

"She could confess her relationship with Adrian," Chris said. "Which will get people to question if Adrian really tripped and fell or was pushed."

The chief nodded. "Exactly."

"I doubt she'll do that," Walt said. "I suspect if anything, she might be a little nervous of running into Bonnie. For one thing, if she was part of this, she's not going to the police. And if she thought Bonnie killed Adrian, she might worry Bonnie will come after her next. Women scorned don't just go after their lover, they often go after the other woman. Mrs. Pierson has no idea how much Bonnie might know about their affair."

"So does that mean the house is still a crime scene or not?" Chris asked.

"We released the property." The chief let out a deep sigh and added, "To be honest, if I didn't know Adrian intended to kill Bonnie, I would have found some reason to keep this case open and prove Bonnie had a motive."

ACROSS TOWN, in the garage apartment, Eric and Zack pulled out the sofa bed, preparing to turn in for the night, when their mother walked into the living room from her bedroom.

"Did you boys brush your teeth?"

"Yes, Mom," they chorused. She had been more attentive ever since their arrest.

"Remember, boys, I've an appointment for an oil change tomorrow, so I might be a few minutes late picking you up at the park." Tomorrow the boys were helping with a pet adoption event at one of the local parks, as part of their community service.

Zack turned to his mother. "Eric and I were talking about that. We can ride our bikes to the park; no reason to take us. That way we can go a little early, help them set up."

Debbie smiled at her sons. "That's a good idea. If you arrive early, that will show Chief MacDonald you're both trying."

Truth was, the boys weren't leaving early because they wanted to help set up for the event, but because Cordelia's house was on the way to the park, and they intended to break in and return what they had taken.

AS THEY HAD DONE the last time they visited the property, the boys hid their bikes in the bushes. They had no problem getting inside the house and had no idea it had been the scene of a murder just the day before. Once inside, they headed straight to the kitchen and opened the pantry. Before returning his can, Zack tugged on the hem of his T-shirt and used it to wipe off the can.

Eric frowned at his brother. "What are you doing?"

"We need to get rid of our fingerprints."

Eric quickly followed his brother's example and wiped off his can. After returning both cans, they closed the pantry door and started for the front door. But just as they reached the hallway, they heard what sounded like someone trying to unlock the doorknob. Panicked and worried they would be caught in the house and get in more trouble from the police chief, they turned and ran from the living room, looking for someplace to hide. The first room they came to was the parlor.

BONNIE ENTERED THE HOUSE, shut the door behind her, and tossed the keys on the entry table. Her main reason for coming today was to remove her aunt's portrait from the property. She had no intention of keeping the hideous thing, and while she intended to sell the house furnished, she didn't imagine the sellers would want it, and she feared that if she left it, Rylee would approach the buyers and offer to purchase the portrait. They would probably give it to her. Bonnie didn't want Rylee to have the portrait. It was going in the landfill.

When Bonnie entered the parlor, she didn't notice the two young boys hiding under the desk. She walked straight to the portrait. Before taking it down, she stared at her aunt's face. It seemed to look back at her.

"I guess this is the end, Auntie." Bonnie stood rigidly straight, her hands clasped behind her back as she stared up into Cordelia's face. "I had always assumed you would leave your estate to Rylee and me. I had no problems sharing it with my cousin. But oh, when I discovered you had left it to Rylee, nothing to me…" Hands still clasped behind her back, she looked away from the painting and began pacing the room, back and forth, as she talked to her aunt.

Had she made the speech the day before, her aunt would have actually heard. But Cordelia's spirit had left the house after Adrian's murder and had not returned. She continued to talk.

"I really should thank dear Wesley for finding that paralegal. If you hadn't used her, I would never have known. She came to me, you know." Bonnie paused a moment and glanced back to the portrait for a moment. "She told me it would be so easy to change the will; no one would have to know. All I would have to do, share with her."

Bonnie resumed her pacing and then chuckled before saying, "Of course, she ended up being a little too greedy and, well, it wasn't difficult to get rid of her. Maybe you'll run into her in hell?" Bonnie laughed and then returned to the painting, looking up at it.

"So, dear Auntie, time for you to come down. Off to the landfill for you!" Bonnie started to reach up to the painting when a distinct sound made her freeze. A sneeze.

She turned toward the sound, knelt down, and peered under the desk. There, huddled far against the back wall, were two little boys. One held a cellphone in his hand. She knew instantly they had heard everything she had just said, and panic overwhelmed her. Frantically looking around, she spied her late uncle's knife in the stand atop the desk. Without hesitation, she grabbed the knife and then knelt down again, jabbing it toward the boys.

"Come out right now before I show you how sharp this is."

Hesitantly, the boys crawled out from under the desk while Bonnie continued to point the knife at them. A moment later, they stood by the desk, their faces pale and eyes wide in fear. She snatched the cellphone out of the one boy's hand and hastily shoved it in her pocket while still holding the knife.

"Do you have another phone?"

They shook their heads, but she didn't believe them, so she hastily frisked each one while still holding the knife. Once satisfied they didn't have another phone, she pointed the knife's tip to the floor. "Sit down!" They immediately complied.

She paced back and forth in front of the desk, the fingers of her left hand frantically combing through her hair while her other hand gripped the knife.

The boys watched her and eyed the door for escape, yet she stood between them and the door. They looked to the window and the ominous bars, making the room feel even more like a prison.

She stopped pacing and then looked down at the boys before bolting toward the door. For a moment, the boys thought she was running away from them, and when gone, they could leave, but after she charged out of the room, she slammed the door closed behind her.

WHILE THE GHOST of Bonnie's aunt had vacated the premises, another ghost had replaced her, Clay Bowman. He had arrived with his sons, knowing what they intended to do today, and wanted to keep an eye on them.

Clay followed Bonnie from the parlor and watched as she threw the knife on the floor and then proceeded to shove the oak hall tree in front of the door, blocking it. The parlor door opened in, so it wouldn't prevent the boys from opening the door, but the piece of furniture was wide enough and tall enough to cover the doorway. Clay didn't understand how this woman was capable of moving such a heavy piece of furniture, yet he imagined the oak floors helped, making it easier to slide, and he suspected she was currently running on adrenaline. Then she said something that chilled him to the bone—if he still had bones.

"I'm going to have to burn this damn place down," Bonnie said aloud. "Along with those little busybodies. That's what insurance is for."

Clay watched in horror as she dragged more furniture in front of the hall tree, moving as if she were in the midst of some manic episode. She was obviously attempting to fill the space from the hall tree to the opposite wall, so even if the boys gave the hall tree a good shove, it would have no place to go, and they would remain trapped in the room.

Clay needed to find help, and he needed to find it now. He could go to a medium and have them call the police, but even that would take time, and there was no guarantee the police could save his sons.

One spirit could get here instantly, yet they were as useless as him—all except Marie Nichols. He would try the cemetery first.

THIRTY-EIGHT

Clay couldn't believe his luck; he found Marie immediately. She was alone at the entrance of the cemetery.

"Oh! What are you doing?" Marie started when Clay appeared out of nowhere, standing just a few feet in front of her.

"I need your help."

Marie waved him away. "I was just going to Marlow House. Whatever your problem is, it can wait." She turned away as if preparing to leave.

He lunged toward her, trying to grab hold of her wrist, but his hand moved through hers.

She turned back toward him and frowned. "Are you daft, Clay? We're ghosts. You can't rough me up to get your way."

"My sons' lives are in danger!"

Marie paused a moment. "What do you mean?"

"Just come with me, please. I'll explain."

MARIE AND CLAY stood together in the hallway near the parlor of

Cordelia's house, looking at the odd assortment of furniture stacked in the hallway in front of the parlor door.

"Are you saying she moved all that herself?" Marie asked.

"Yes. We need to get the boys out of there."

A crashing sound came from another part of the house. The next moment, Marie and Clay stood in the kitchen and watched as Bonnie hit the top of her gas range in frustration. She then tried turning on all the burners, with no luck. The two ghosts watched as Bonnie went from pounding on the stove to turning the controls for the burners. At one point, she opened her oven and stuck her head inside for a moment before pulling it out.

"Damn! The gas isn't on." Bonnie paused a moment before saying, "Matches, there has to be matches upstairs in Cordelia's bedroom." Bonnie ran from the kitchen and headed upstairs.

"Let's get the boys out of here," Clay begged.

The next moment, the two were back in the hallway near the parlor entrance.

"Go check on your boys. I'll move this," Marie told Clay. Clay disappeared.

Now alone in the hallway, Marie focused her energy on the pile of furniture. Instead of moving it piece by piece, she pushed the entire row away from her and away from the parlor door. Once the space was empty, she used her energy to open the parlor door, and then she moved into the room, where she found the two boys cowering in the corner.

"Do something," Clay begged. "They're just standing there. Make them move."

"I don't want to shove them. They look terrified enough."

"She's going to come back downstairs!"

Marie glanced around the room and saw the desk. She went to it, opened the top drawer, and found a pen and pad of paper. She lifted the pen and paper; it floated toward the boys. Eric saw it first and grabbed hold of his brother's arm before pointing at the floating objects.

The pad of paper fell on the floor by the boys' feet, and the pen began to write: *Run! Get out of this house NOW!*

The boys didn't need more instruction. They raced through the door, down the hall, through the kitchen, and out the front door.

Marie turned to Clay and said, "I'm going to see what that crazy lady is doing. Go with your sons. Make sure they're okay."

MARIE FOUND Bonnie upstairs in what looked like had been Cordelia's bedroom, considering the decor. She couldn't imagine someone young like Rylee had used the room. Bonnie apparently had not yet found the matches she had come looking for, considering the way she was opening one dresser drawer after another before dumping its contents on the floor. Marie spied an ashtray on the dresser and suspected that was why Bonnie thought she might find matches in her aunt's room, because her aunt had been a smoker.

Bonnie went from the dresser to the lone side table next to the bed. After opening the end table drawer and looking inside, Bonnie let out a squeal and pulled out not matches, but a cigarette lighter. With lighter in hand, she rushed to the window and flicked the lighter several times until a flame formed. Bonnie smiled, an expression Marie could only describe as deranged.

Marie watched as Bonnie lifted the lighter's flame to the edge of the drape.

"Oh, no, you're not going to light that on fire," Marie said right as the flame jumped onto the drape and doubled and then tripled in size.

Bonnie stood at the window and watched as the flame moved up the drapery, while making no attempt to move.

"No, you don't!" Marie shouted before grabbing a pillow; she smacked the flames repeatedly until the fire was out.

Bonnie screamed at the inexplicable assault on the flames and ran from the room, still clutching the lighter. Marie followed her out of the bedroom and down the hallway to the staircase. When Bonnie reached the stairs, she stopped briefly to look behind her, as if intuitively knowing something followed her. She turned back to

THE GHOST WHO SOUGHT REDEMPTION

the stairs, stumbled, lost her balance, and, as Adrian had done the previous day, tumbled down the stairs to the hardwood floor below.

"This doesn't look good," Marie muttered. She stood on the second floor, looking down at the body sprawled at the foot of the staircase. Marie let out a sigh. "I suppose I'll have to get Danielle to call the chief to send an ambulance over. I'm sure something is broken."

But the next moment, Marie realized there was no need for an ambulance. Bonnie's spirit stepped from her body. From afar, feeling a bit like a voyeur, Marie watched as the younger woman realized she was no longer alive. Bonnie looked down at her former self and then looked at her hands, hands that she did not yet understand were nothing but an illusion. Marie was about to make her presence known when Bonnie disappeared.

"Oh, where did you go?" Marie moved from the second floor to the first and stood by the corpse. Bonnie's body had landed on her side, looking like someone sleeping in the fetal position. Marie then noticed something on the floor, by the pocket of Bonnie's sweater. Had it fallen out of Bonnie's pocket? Marie wondered. She leaned down and picked it up. It was a cellphone, and she almost put it back, believing it belonged to Bonnie. But then she noticed the name written across the cellphone's case, *Debbie Bowman*.

"Oh my. We can't leave that here. Edward wouldn't appreciate that complication."

AFTER RUNNING out of the house and jumping on their bikes, Eric and Zack didn't want to go home. Their mother wasn't there, they would be alone, and they were afraid the crazy woman might follow them. They decided the best place to go was the park, where they would be surrounded by people, and then they could decide what to do next. While they hadn't arrived in time to help set up, as they had told their mother they were going to do, they arrived by the time the chief had told them to be there.

Had the organizer of the event known the Bowman twins before today, she wouldn't recognize this version: two skittish, timid young boys who looked as if they might start crying at any moment. She wondered if she had misunderstood the chief when he told her he was sending two boys over to help who were doing community service, which typically meant they had gotten into some sort of trouble. But when she heard their names, she began connecting the dots. *Ahh, Clay Bowman's sons.* Two troubled youngsters who recently lost their father under such tragic circumstances. She couldn't imagine what they were going through.

They kept dogs offered for adoption in a large pen, and she had intended to have the boys help hand out and collect the adoption applications, but she decided the boys needed something different.

"Are you boys afraid of dogs?" she asked the twins. They each shook their head no.

"Well, the dogs we have today are all very sweet; none are aggressive. What I want you boys to do is to stay in the pen with the dogs, play with them, give them some love, and make everyone here want to take a dog home today. Can you do that?" By their reactions, it was clear both boys liked that assignment.

EDDY AND EVAN MACDONALD had heard about the pet adoption event. While their dad said they couldn't get a dog, the boys still liked to look. They rode their bikes from home and then hopped off when they reached the park. After locking their bikes in the bike rack, they continued on to the event while chatting with each other about dogs.

"Are you saying when you die, you can talk to dogs?" Eddy asked.

"Well, Marie and Eva can." Evan silently added, *So can Walt*, but he and his dad hadn't yet told Eddy about Walt. They figured his brother had enough to take in right now. "Cats too."

"That is so fire." Eddy shook his head at the thought.

When they reached the event area, they spied the pen with the dogs and puppies, along with two boys sitting in the pen and playing with the dogs.

Upon seeing Eric and Zack, the MacDonald brothers stopped. "Are those the Bowman twins?" Eddy asked.

"Yeah, Dad said they were going to be here doing community service. Their dad is with them."

EVERYTHING SEEMED RUSHED after Clay had showed up at the cemetery to find Marie. He had told her his sons had been on the way to the park when they stopped at the house, yet he never got around to explaining why they had stopped at the house, or why Bonnie had locked them in the parlor and wanted to burn the house down with the boys inside. Marie thought those were important missing details, especially considering she had left Bonnie's dead body at the bottom of the staircase.

Marie decided to try looking for them first at the park; she wanted to get their cellphone back to them. She knew Heather had talked about today's adoption event, so perhaps she might be there to help her communicate with the twins. Marie not only wanted to return the phone, but she also needed to find out what had gone on at that house.

Just as she had done when taking the camera home from the florist, Marie flew to the park like a witch without a broom, not wanting the living to notice the cellphone. When she arrived at the park, she looked down and didn't see Heather, yet she saw the twins in the dog pen. She also saw Clay, who seemed to be having a conversation with several of the dogs who were up for adoption.

She glanced around the park one more time and then spied someone who could help. Evan MacDonald.

EVAN STOOD WITH HIS BROTHER, talking about the Bowman twins, not yet approaching the pen, when he felt something being placed in his right hand. He looked down and, to his surprise, saw a cellphone. He almost dropped it, but Marie grabbed hold of his hand, not only preventing the phone from falling to the ground, but it made him aware of her presence.

"Marie?" Now clutching the cellphone, Evan frowned at the ghost and then the phone in his hand.

"Is Marie here?" Eddy asked.

"Yeah. And she just handed me this." Evan showed Eddy the phone.

Eddy picked up the phone from Evan's hand and turned it over and saw the name written on one side. "This says Debbie Bowman. Isn't that the twins' mom?"

"Evan, you need to get this phone back to the boys, and I need you to talk to them for me. It's very important."

Evan repeated what Marie said to his brother.

"Sounds interesting. Let's do it," Eddy said.

"IS THAT THE CHIEF'S SONS?" Eric asked his brother.

"Yeah, it is. I wonder what they want."

The MacDonald boys stood on the other side of the pen, motioning for Eric and Zack to come over to them. The twins glanced at each other and then turned toward Eddy and Evan and walked toward them.

When they reached the other boys, Eric asked, "Hey. What did you want?"

Evan pulled something from his pocket and handed it to Eric through the fence separating them.

Eric took what Evan handed them and looked down at it, confused. It was their cellphone.

THIRTY-NINE

"Where did you get this?" Eric asked. He and his brother exchanged nervous glances.

"Marie gave it to me."

The twins stared dumbly at Evan.

As Evan tried talking to the Bowman brothers, both Clay and Marie kept telling Evan what they wanted him to tell the boys.

"Marie is the ghost who wrote that note at the house you were at."

The twins continued to stare at Evan, making no reply.

"Your dad is here, too. They both tell me you need to let me call my dad, and you tell him everything that happened today. It's important."

"We're going to get in trouble," Zack said.

"Your dad says it's important."

"A woman tried to kill us. She had this big old knife. She might still try," Eric said.

"Holy crap," Eddy muttered, his eyes wide as he listened.

Evan turned momentarily to look at Marie. "What?...Seriously?" Evan turned back to the twins. "Marie says she's not a threat anymore. She fell down the stairs. She's dead."

CHIEF MACDONALD SAT in his police car at the park with the Bowman twins sitting in the back seat with Eddy, while Evan sat in the front passenger seat. MacDonald understood Clay and Marie were somewhere in the car with them.

The chief sat sideways in the seat so he could see both Evan and the boys in the back seat. The Bowman twins had just recounted all that had happened to them that day, emphasizing that the only reason they had gone to the house was their desire to set things right. When describing their time hiding under the desk, all Zack said was, "The woman started talking to the painting, and then Eric sneezed."

Evan then told Marie's version of the story, ending with the part where the woman fell down the stairs and died.

MacDonald jerked upright. "Are you saying there's a dead woman in the house right now?"

Evan shrugged. "I guess, unless someone's already found her."

"Shouldn't you have started with that part?" MacDonald snapped.

"Well, it's not like you can do anything now," Evan argued. "She's already dead. And Marie said her spirit didn't even stick around."

"I've got to call Brian." The chief reached for his phone.

"Tell him to wait," Clay said.

"Wait a second, Dad," Evan said.

MacDonald looked at his son. "What?"

"I need to tell your father what the woman said to the portrait before Eric sneezed."

"MARIE'S GOING to follow you both home. I don't like the idea of you riding your bikes home, not after all you've been through. Your dad will be with you too, but he can't help you like Marie can."

Eric and Zack nodded at the chief.

"And while I don't believe a child should ever keep something from a parent—"

"You don't want us to tell our mom?" Eric finished for him.

"It would be best if you pretend nothing happened. Your father was with you all morning and is convinced no one saw you go into the house or leave. If someone had seen you, then I would be more concerned."

"We won't tell anyone," Zack vowed.

"And Marie, thank you for having the foresight to pick up their cellphone. I don't know what kind of mess we would be in if they found it with the body," the chief said.

Marie chuckled. "Edward, I never thought I would hear you condone tampering with evidence." She looked at Evan and said, "Don't tell him I said that. Just tell him I said you're welcome."

"WHY DOES the chief want us to go over there?" Joe asked Brian as they drove to Cordelia's house.

"The chief isn't convinced Adrian just fell. He wants us to take another look at the scene."

"I'm assuming he already talked to Bonnie?"

"He tried to call her, but she's not answering," Brian lied. "Since he already told her we might need to go back over, I don't see why there would be a problem."

Before coming over, they had stopped at Adam's office and picked up a key. But when they pulled up to Cordelia's, they saw Bonnie's car already parked in front of the house.

"Looks like Bonnie is here," Joe said when he parked.

When they got to the front door, they found it slightly ajar. Instead of ringing the bell, Brian pushed it open. "Hello, Bonnie? It's Brian Henderson, from the Frederickport Police Department." When there was no response, Brian called out again. There was still no answer. They walked in. The first thing Joe noticed was the ring of keys sitting on the entry table. He pointed to the keys, and they walked into the living room, all the while calling out Bonnie's name.

ABOUT FORTY MINUTES after Brian and Joe arrived at the house, Bonnie returned. When she first arrived, it felt like a repeat of yesterday, with police and other first responders swarming the property. She watched as the coroner looked over her body, as he had done with Adrian.

Two police officers stood a few feet from the corpse. One looked up at the staircase and then back to the other officer and said, "Those are some dangerous stairs."

IT DIDN'T TAKE LONG for Bonnie to realize she should never have followed her body back to the morgue. While she should have known she might run into Adrian, she didn't expect to run into her husband's spirit. The man had been gone for over six months. Was this hell? she wondered. Doomed to spend eternity with the two men she had murdered?

They weren't alone, there was a woman with them, and by the manner of the woman's dress, she had been dead a long time. She actually looked a little like the actress whose portrait hung in the local museum.

"Bonnie?" both Adrian and Wesley gasped.

"Yes, it's me."

"You're really dead?" Adrian said. "What happened?"

"What do you think happened? I died. And this must be hell, because you two idiots are here."

"Actually, I brought them here because I knew you were coming," Eva said. In the background, the staff at the morgue did their jobs while the spirits paid no attention to them.

"Who are you?" Bonnie asked.

"I'm Eva Thorndike, and I thought you might have something to say to your husband before you all move on."

"What do I have to say to him?" Bonnie snapped. Eva didn't answer as she and Bonnie locked gazes. They were both silent for a few minutes until Bonnie finally said, "What do you want me to say to him? That I murdered him?" Bonnie turned to Wesley. "Wesley, I murdered you." Bonnie looked back to Eva. "Was that what I was supposed to say?"

Wesley stared with disbelief at his wife. "You murdered me? Why?"

"Because I was in love with your stupid brother." She flashed Adrian a glare and then looked back at her husband. "Idiot that I was."

"That's not possible. You were in Frederickport. I was in California."

"I put something in your medicine, you fool. In one of the capsules. I knew you had only taken four capsules, just enough for your trip. I didn't know what day you would take it, so you could have died on the last day. But once you did, if the police investigated your death, they wouldn't find anything wrong with your medicine. But look at you, taking the death capsule on the first day." Bonnie laughed.

"I can't believe that," Wesley gasped.

"Wesley," Eva said, "why don't you tell her what you had planned for her while you were gone?"

Wesley flashed Eva an uneasy look.

"What do you mean planned for me?" Bonnie asked.

Wesley refused to talk.

Finally, Adrian blurted, "I was going to kill you for him. We had it all planned out."

Had Wesley, Adrian, and Bonnie known how to harness energy, the inside of the morgue would have been destroyed within the next fifteen minutes. Mayhem ensued, which included verbal abuse from all parties, punches that had nowhere to land, and lots of screaming.

Eva stood back and watched the three as they unsuccessfully tried grabbing, punching, and kicking each other. And it wasn't just the two brothers against Bonnie. The brothers went after each other with the same gusto they attacked Bonnie, and Bonnie showed equal loathing for each brother.

Growing bored with the chaos, Eva looked up and said, "Can't you take them now? I think they're ready."

The next moment the illusion of the three spirits gradually rose upwards, none noticing their increasing distance from the floor, while they continued to fight amongst each other, shouting curses and taking ineffective swings with fists until they disappeared, and the only sounds Eva heard were those made by the employees at the morgue.

WHEN THE TWINS RETURNED HOME, they were both unusually quiet and had little to say about working at the pet adoption event. Debbie attributed it to the boys being overly tired. But when dinner rolled around, and they both claimed they weren't hungry, she felt their foreheads and found them both burning up. She immediately brought out the thermometer and soon discovered they both had a 104 temperature. Panicked, she loaded both boys in her car and took them to urgent care. At urgent care, they sent the boys to the hospital. And two hours later, they checked Eric and Zack into a hospital room, each hooked up to IVs. Both boys were delirious.

Clay stood with Eva in the hospital room, while his wife sat in a nearby chair, occasionally dozing. The boys had finally fallen asleep. "I don't understand. They were fine this afternoon."

Eva smiled at Clay. "Things happen for a reason. But they're going to be alright. Trust me."

"When I was alive, I never understood how much I had. I kept wanting more, while ignoring these incredible things I had in my life. My wife, my sons. I made so many mistakes, have so many regrets."

"I believe your sons are going to be okay. They're on the right track now, and your wife is much better now, too. She understands she needs to be the best person she can be because she's all they have."

"Only because I was such a bad husband and father."

"In the morning you'll see their improvement, and perhaps you'll be ready to move on."

MORNING CAME, and just as Eva had predicted, the Bowman twins no longer had a temperature, and both wanted to go home. While waiting for the hospital to complete the discharge papers, they had a visitor, Chief MacDonald. He had heard about them being admitted to the hospital. Debbie left him alone to talk to her sons while she went to the nurses' station to ask a question about a follow-up visit.

"I understand you were pretty sick," the chief told the boys.

"I had so many weird dreams last night," Eric told him.

"Me too," Zack said.

"Really? What kind of dreams?"

"Crazy stuff, like our dad's ghost was hanging around. And then it saved us from this wacky lady who locked us up in a room with bars on the window," Zack said.

Eric laughed and said, "Dad was in my dream, too. But it was really goofy. We found these soup cans with money in them, and Dad told us we had to take them back."

"Mom says it's probably the medication they gave us last night," Eric said.

"Umm, tell me, boys, before your mom comes back, just between you and me, what was your day like yesterday?"

Eric shrugged. "We did our community service at the pet adoption. Which was really cool. We got to play with all the dogs. Thanks for letting us do that."

"Yeah, that was fun," Zack said.

"Before you arrived at the park, where were you boys?"

Again, Eric shrugged. "We were at home and rode our bikes to the park. Are you thinking we stopped somewhere and caught something that made us sick? Because we didn't really go anywhere, just home and the park."

FORTY

Police Chief MacDonald called before going over to Marlow House on Tuesday afternoon. When he arrived, he entered through the front gate. Sadie, who had been playing ball with Connor in the backyard, greeted him. On the patio located off the kitchen sat Walt, Danielle, Lily, and Ian, who all waved hello to MacDonald after he entered the yard. Also on the patio sat Eva and Marie.

"Where are the babies?" the chief asked when he stepped onto the patio.

"Napping in the living room." Danielle pointed to the baby monitor sitting on the patio table.

"Not in their bedrooms?" MacDonald sat down on an empty chair.

"Those stairs can be a killer," Lily said.

"They certainly have been the last few days," the chief agreed.

"Oh, I didn't mean that. I wasn't even thinking about what happened over at that house. I just meant running up and down stairs. Checking on the babies can be exhausting."

The chief flashed Lily a smile.

"You want some coffee?" Danielle asked.

"No, thanks. I'm coffee'd out. Like I mentioned on the phone, I wanted to give you an update on the Bowman twins."

"Before you go on, Eva and Marie are here." Danielle pointed to where the two ghosts sat. "Eva was telling us how Clay has moved on. He won't be dropping in on Heather anymore."

MacDonald arched his brows. "Really? That is interesting, especially considering his sons' current condition."

"Are they still in the hospital?" Lily asked.

"They should be home by now. I saw them at the hospital right before they were discharged, and they both seem perfectly fine. They look healthy, anxious to get out of there, in a good mood."

"What was wrong with them?" Ian asked.

"According to Debbie, it's a bit of a mystery. They ran high fevers, but they broke last night. At the same time."

Danielle frowned. "That's odd. Their fevers broke at the same time?"

"What's really odd, they've no memory of any, uh, shall we say ghostly encounters they've experienced. And they remember nothing about being over at Cordelia's house yesterday."

"They have amnesia?" Lily asked.

"Selective amnesia," MacDonald said. "Of course, they aren't aware of this, nor are the doctors."

Danielle frowned. "Interesting."

The chief recounted his conversation with the twins at the hospital. After the telling, he added, "Despite forgetting everything, they have remained the better versions of themselves. They weren't the same boys I talked to after their arrest. No attitude. They seemed like normal nine-year-old boys and were not showing the effects of the trauma I would expect after being locked in a room by a woman holding them at knifepoint."

"From what I've read, selective amnesia can be the result of trauma," Ian said.

"What about the fever?" Lily asked. "Is the amnesia the result of the trauma or the fever?"

"And will those memories return?" Danielle asked.

"They won't return," Eva said.

Walt and Danielle looked at Eva.

Danielle tilted her head slightly as she studied Eva. "What do you know about this?"

Eva smiled at Danielle. "There is a reason many adults believe certain memories are nothing more than a dream, as opposed to actual events they lived. Adults like Lily believe that the friend they had when they were a small child was nothing more than an imaginary friend."

"Are you suggesting this supposed amnesia is planned by the Universe?" Danielle asked.

"I'm just saying there is a reason the Universe tends to keep a barrier between your world and mine," Eva explained. "But sometimes, those who need it, such as the Bowman brothers, get a glimpse under the veil to help them on their way. And when their lesson's learned, the veil closes, because seeing too much can also be a hindrance."

DURING THE NEXT WEEK, when investigating Bonnie's death, the police searched through her cellphone and computer and discovered emails between Bonnie and the paralegal discussing their plans to change the aunt's will, which had initially left everything to Rylee. There were emails between the two detailing how they intended to prepare a false document claiming elder abuse, to discourage Rylee from contesting the will.

They also found a copy of Bonnie's newly amended will, along with information on the attorney she had used in Portland. It turned out that while Bonnie had changed the will to leave everything to Adrian, she had left Rylee as the beneficiary should Adrian predecease Bonnie. According to the attorney, Bonnie couldn't decide whom she would want to leave her estate to if Adrian died before her, so she told the attorney to leave Rylee on it until she discussed it with Adrian.

On Friday, Chief MacDonald called Rylee into the office to discuss her cousin's estate. After telling her what he could about what they had discovered, Rylee said, "Yes, her attorney has already contacted me. I was shocked to learn I was in her will." She sat in a chair facing the chief, who sat behind his desk. "Actually, I assumed you wanted me to come in for another reason."

"Another reason?"

Rylee glanced down sheepishly at her hands folded in her lap, then looked back to the chief. "A couple of weeks ago, I sorta…well…I broke into my aunt's house. After you said you wanted to see me, I figured a neighbor saw me, and they must have said something after hearing about Bonnie's death."

MacDonald leaned back in his chair. "You broke in? Why?"

"I had a folder with some family papers. Mostly things from my parents, like their birth certificates, wedding license, Dad's discharge from the military. Family history stuff that I planned to put in a scrapbook. I recently started looking for it, and when I couldn't find it, I remembered Aunt Cordelia had asked to see it, and I couldn't remember if I had ever gotten it back."

"So you went over to her house to look for it?"

"There was no way I could ask Bonnie to let me go through Aunt Cordelia's things. Ever since our aunt died, Bonnie has been horrible. Since the house was still vacant, and I had a key, I decided to go over and look for the file. Unfortunately, the key didn't work, and I ended up climbing through a window."

"Did you find your papers?"

Rylee nodded.

"Considering Bonnie was still alive after you took those papers, I don't see how entering the house had anything to do with her death. Plus, even if Bonnie had named someone else as beneficiary instead of you, it's possible the court might have determined the house belonged to you, considering what we found on Bonnie's computer."

"So I was breaking into my own house?"

The chief smiled in reply.

"For me, this thing with my aunt and cousin, it wasn't just about an inheritance or even my professional reputation. When I spoke to the paralegal on the phone, and she told me my aunt had signed a statement claiming I had abused her, I was stunned."

"Did you suspect the paralegal was working with your cousin?"

Rylee shook her head. "Not exactly. Initially, I assumed Bonnie had someway manipulated Aunt Cordelia and convinced the paralegal into believing my aunt wanted to make those changes. But the will was signed and notarized, and while I didn't believe it at first, I had to accept it must be legit. As for that statement of abuse, I felt guilt and questioned myself."

The chief frowned. "I don't understand. You thought maybe you had abused her?"

"Oh, no. But if she made such a statement, then I missed all the signs of her failing mental state. I always thought my aunt was so sharp until the end. She was old, but her mind was young. But if she really said I had abused her, then that meant she had been having some sort of delusions, hallucinations, imagining things happening. That's not uncommon with someone suffering from dementia or Alzheimer's. Why didn't I see it?"

"Because there was nothing to see."

Rylee let out a sigh. "I know that now. Bonnie told me she didn't want a family scandal, that Aunt Cordelia would have hated that, so if I didn't contest the will, I could keep my nursing license."

"With your cousin basically blackmailing you, I'm surprised you came back to Frederickport."

Rylee shrugged. "You know, this might sound crazy, but after all that happened, I left town and decided I would never come back. As it was, some rumors had already come out about me abusing my aunt. After all, why else would she leave everything to Bonnie? But then I had a reoccurring dream. My father, he kept telling me to come back to Frederickport, that it would be alright. I kept having that dream. So I came back. I bet that sounds crazy to you."

MacDonald smiled softly and then said, "No, it doesn't."

THE NEXT TWO weeks flew by. Heather was no longer worried about running into Clay while visiting the bathroom in the middle of the night. The residents of Marlow House were relieved the only ghosts popping in were Eva and Marie.

The judge overseeing Eric and Zack's breaking and entering charges considered the age of the boys, along with their recent family trauma and the chief's recommendation, and after talking to the hobby shop, the case was dropped. Debbie agreed to get family counseling after they moved, which turned out to be in early August. While packing up to move, Debbie found the crumpled pieces of typing paper she had shown to Chief MacDonald in one of her dresser drawers. But sprawled across the pages were illegible childish scribbles, not the cursive handwriting she remembered.

Did I really show this to my sister and Chief MacDonald, claiming a ghost wrote it? she asked herself. Embarrassed to have shown the pages to her sister and the police chief, she attributed the episode to her drinking after Clay's death.

Over on Beach Drive, during the weeks leading up to August, John Bartley and his crew completed the work on Ian and Lily's house, and by the second week in August, Lily and her family were back in their home.

While setting up the nursery and Connor's bedroom, June mentioned how it might be a good idea to put a lock on the nursery so Connor couldn't let himself in whenever he wanted. Ian and Lily didn't respond, but both understood Kelly must have finally told her mother about finding Connor alone with all the babies.

On the third week in August, Lily's parents arrived.

THE MILLERS' arrival proved chaotic, not a surprise to anyone who knew the family. Both Lily's parents entered the house with an armful of packages for their grandchildren. Lily's mother, Tammy, couldn't wait to see Connor and meet her new granddaughter, yet she was also excited to have a tour of the new remodel.

They had been there for about an hour before Lily's father brought in the suitcases from their car. Ian helped his father-in-law carry the suitcases up the stairs to the new guest room, secretly wishing Walt were there to use his telekinetic powers. Connor, Lily and her mother followed them up the stairs, with Tammy holding Connor's hand while Lily carried Emily Ann.

"I'm sorry the guestroom is upstairs," Lily apologized to her mother as they followed the men up to the second floor, with both Lily and her mother holding onto the handrail with their free hand.

"Oh, don't be silly. We were upstairs when we stayed with Danielle. And while I'm grateful for the times Danielle opened her home to us—she's a wonderful host—I'm excited to stay with my little girl." Tammy flashed her daughter a smile. "And you need to have the children's rooms on the first floor with your bedroom. Smart to put the office and guest room upstairs. But you be careful walking up the stairs with Emily Ann."

Lily glanced at the baby in her arms. "I'm being careful. I had a lot of practice with babies and stairs when we stayed with Dani."

Tammy laughed. "I imagine! Can't wait to meet the twins."

"I'm so excited you're staying with us, Mom."

Thirty minutes later, they were all back downstairs, with Ian pouring Gene a glass of scotch while the two men discussed the recent home remodel, and Connor played on the floor with the new toys his grandparents had brought him.

Lily sat in the nursery, breastfeeding Emily Ann, while her mother sat on the second rocking chair in the room, visiting with her daughter. When the baby finished nursing and fell asleep, Lily laid her down in the crib, and the two women went out to the living room, where Ian and Gene were now sitting on the recliners.

Just as they reached the living room, the doorbell rang. Lily raced to the front door, leaving her mother standing in the living room. She didn't want the doorbell to wake the baby, and fortunately, Sadie knew better than to bark.

Once at the front entry, Lily opened the door and found herself looking at her sister-in-law, who wore a silly grin.

THE GHOST WHO SOUGHT REDEMPTION

"Kelly, why did you ring the doorbell? The baby is sleeping. Remember, Ian said to just text us and we'll open the door."

Kelly's grin only widened. She said nothing, but a moment later stepped to one side, revealing a person standing behind her.

"Laura!" Lily squealed. "You're back from Europe!"

"I had to meet my new niece," Laura said before the two sisters embraced in a hug.

"I CAN'T BELIEVE you didn't tell me she was coming," Lily told her mother after they were all sitting in the living room ten minutes later.

"Laura wanted it to be a secret. We were going to drive to Portland and pick her up, but Laura and Kelly thought it would be more fun this way."

"I have so much to tell you!" Laura told Lily.

The doorbell rang again. Ian started to get up to answer it, but Lily instantly jumped up and told him she would get it and then added, "You know, if people keep ringing our doorbell, Emily Ann is going to wake up."

"That's okay with me. I want to meet her!" Laura called after Lily, who raced to the door again.

When Lily opened the front door, she found herself looking at an attractive woman holding the hand of a little boy. If she were to guess, the woman was in her early or mid-twenties, and the child was around six. Yet she had no idea who either of them was, as she had never seen them before.

"Can I help you with something?" Lily asked.

The woman looked embarrassed. She glanced around and then looked back at Lily. "I'm looking for Chris Johnson's house. I was told he lived along this section of Beach Drive. They said his house was one of the newer ones and faced the ocean."

"Umm, we just remodeled our house, so I guess it looks newer than some of the other houses in the neighborhood. And you are?"

"So, this is Chris Johnson's house?"

"No."

"Can you tell me which house is his?"

"And you are?" Lily repeated the question.

The woman stared at Lily for a moment and, instead of answering, turned from the door, still holding the child's hand, and said, "Come on, Christopher; this is the wrong house."

Return to Marlow House in
The Ghost and Wednesday's Child
Haunting Danielle, Book 36

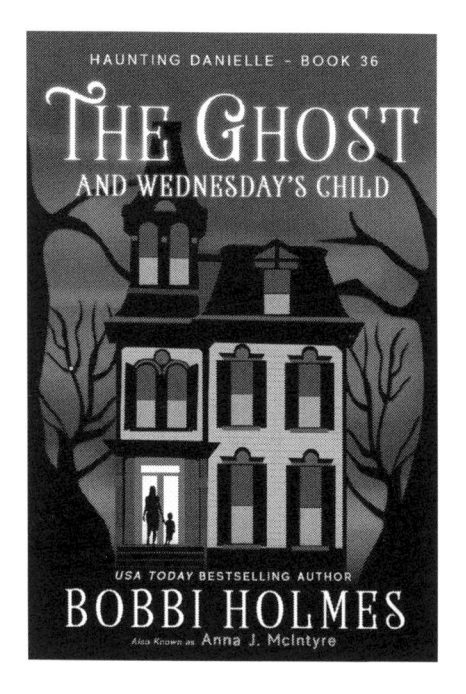

Lily and Ian have finally returned home with Connor, Sadie, and the newest addition to their family.

Across the street, Walt and Danielle are settling into parenthood, and down the street Heather is no longer worried about a certain annoying ghost surprising her in the middle of the night.

But the calm on Beach Drive doesn't last long. It isn't just the arrival of Lily's parents, or the surprise visit from Lily's sister, Laura, who has been in Europe. It's the woman who shows up on Lily's doorstep, young boy in hand named Christopher, looking for directions to Chris Johnson's house.

BOOKS BY ANNA J. MCINTYRE

COULSON FAMILY SAGA

Coulson's Wife

Coulson's Crucible

Coulson's Lessons

Coulson's Secret

Coulson's Reckoning

Now available in Audiobook Format

UNLOCKED HEARTS

Sundered Hearts

After Sundown

While Snowbound

Sugar Rush

NON-FICTION BY
BOBBI ANN JOHNSON HOLMES

Havasu Palms, A Hostile Takeover
Where the Road Ends, Recipes & Remembrances
Motherhood, a book of poetry
The Story of the Christmas Village